Praise for the
Farmer's Daughter Mysteries

"With witty and personable writing, Cochran's new series is off to a great start!"   —RT Book Reviews (starred review)

Praise for the
Cranberry Cove Mysteries

"A fun whodunit with quirky characters and a satisfying mystery. This new series is as sweet and sharp as the heroine's cranberry salsa."
—Sofie Kelly, *New York Times* bestselling author of the Magical Cats Mysteries

"Cozy fans and foodies, rejoice—there's a place just for you, and it's called Cranberry Cove."
—Ellery Adams, *New York Times* bestselling author of the
Books by the Bay Mysteries,
the Charmed Pie Shoppe Mysteries,
and the Book Retreat Mysteries

"I can't wait for Monica's next tasty adventure—and I'm not just saying that because I covet her cranberry relish recipe."
—Victoria Abbott, national bestselling author of the Book Collector Mysteries

"First-class mystery fun."   —*Suspense Magazine*

BOUGHT THE FARM

PEG COCHRAN

BERKLEY PRIME CRIME
New York

BERKLEY PRIME CRIME
Published by Berkley
An imprint of Penguin Random House LLC
375 Hudson Street, New York, New York 10014

ISBN 9780425282045

First Edition: June 2018

Printed in the United States of America
1   3   5   7   9   10   8   6   4   2

Cover art © Betsy Ross Koller
Cover design by Emily Osborne
Book design by Laura K. Corless

ACKNOWLEDGMENTS

I want to thank my editor, Sarah Blumenstock, for all her help in making this book the best it could be. I'd also like to thank my writing buddies Janet Bolin, Allison Brook, Janet Cantrell, Laurie Cass, Krista Davis, and Daryl Wood Gerber for all their help in cooking up diabolical plot twists, clever clues, and misleading red herrings!

Dear Reader,

Spring is one of my favorite times at Love Blossom Farm. The flowers in my front garden are thriving, and the pink of the begonias with the purple and white of the petunias creates a beautiful kaleidoscope of color that never fails to cheer me up.

The earth is giving off a rich, fertile fragrance and the vibrant greens of grass and leaves provide the perfect backdrop for Mother Nature's riot of color.

Shelby's dogs wove in and out between her legs as she clomped across the muddy and rutted field that was drying rapidly in the warm rays of the sun. For days on end, every time she had pulled aside the curtains in the morning, the windows had been streaming with rain and the skies dark with swiftly moving clouds. *Dear Reader, hardly auspi-*

cious weather for a wedding, don't you agree? Everyone had been praying the storm would pass on, and it looked as if their prayers had finally been answered.

This wasn't the first wedding to be held at Love Blossom Farm—she and William "Wild Bill" McDonald had stood under the twisted branches of the old apple tree in the backyard and made their vows. She remembered the day so clearly—how could it have been so many years ago already?

She hadn't wanted a long gown—the wedding had been too informal for an elaborate organza or tulle creation. She'd found a pretty white eyelet tea-length dress with a fitted bodice and a full skirt. She'd worn it with an elbow-length veil and carried a basket of wildflowers.

She shook her head. No use thinking about the past—Bill was gone now and it was time for her to move on. Today was meant to be a joyous day—the day her best friend, Dr. Kelly Thacker, tied the knot with Dr. Seth Gregson.

Shelby headed toward the old red barn in the distance. It was faded from all the years of bright sun and strong wind and was listing slightly. It had taken a lot of work, but it had been transformed into the perfect spot for Kelly and Seth's reception. Kelly had had her heart set on a real country wedding, and Seth had paid to bring in electric generators and for a rough wood floor to be laid.

There was a rustling sound in a nearby clump of tall grass, and Jenkins, Shelby's West Highland white terrier, dove into its midst in pursuit of whatever small creature was trying to make its home there.

Shelby was relieved when Jenkins backed out of the long, waving grass, his mouth empty. She knew it was in his nature to go after mice, chipmunks, and the like, but she hated seeing anything so small and helpless killed.

Bitsy, a giant lumbering mastiff, had no interest in hunting and was lying in the sun, her pink tongue lolling out of her mouth and her eyes closed in the blissful warmth.

"Hey, Mom," Shelby's nine-year-old son, Billy Jr., called from the distance. "I've found a frog. Can I keep it? Please?"

Shelby smiled as she walked toward Billy. So far this spring, he'd brought home a turtle, which had promptly escaped; a wounded sparrow, which they had nursed back to health; a garter snake, which Shelby had made him take right back outside again; and a very frightened baby rabbit.

"Look how big he is." Billy held out his hands as Shelby reached him.

"He is very handsome. But don't you think we should let him go?"

A stubborn look came over Billy's face—one Shelby knew well. This was when he looked most like his late father.

"I really think we should let him go."

"But I've already named him. I'm going to call him Bob."

"That's nice, Billy, but where would we keep him? It's not fair to lock him up inside. He would be miserable. He belongs outside."

Billy opened his mouth, but before he could argue any further, Bob the frog squirmed out of his grasp and hopped briskly away.

"Awwww," Billy cried, looking after him.

"Come on," Shelby said. "You need to take a bath and get dressed for the wedding. You have an important job to do—you're the ring bearer."

Billy looked as if he was about to protest, but then he saw Shelby's face—she could put on a pretty decent stubborn expression herself—and gave in and started to run toward the house.

Shelby was about to follow when she heard a slobbering sound—the kind of noise Bitsy made when she was drinking out of her water bowl. She turned around to see Bitsy lapping up rainwater from an old rusted trough that was left over from when Shelby's parents used to raise dairy cows.

Shelby and Bill had taken over the farm when her parents decided to retire and tour the country in their second-hand RV. The cattle had been too much work for her after Bill died, so she'd leased most of the pasture to Jake Taylor, a dairy farmer who looked more like a movie star than a farmer.

Shelby now grew herbs and a variety of lettuces and heirloom tomatoes and other vegetables. She kept a kitchen garden that supplied her family with fresh produce in the summer and canned in the winter.

Bitsy had finished drinking, and after shaking vigorously and splattering drops of water thither and yon, she caught up with Jenkins and the two of them ran ahead of Shelby toward the farmhouse. Shelby gave a last look at the old trough—maybe she would clean it up and use it as a planter. When you lived on a farm, your motto was "Waste not, want not."

Shelby had her hands on the door handle when a dusty and dented green van pulled into the driveway. The doors opened and a number of people spilled out, putting Shelby in mind of one of those clown cars in the circus. She supposed this must be the band Kelly had arranged to play at the reception.

One woman and three men stood next to the van, looking around and talking quietly. An equally dusty Taurus came down the drive and pulled up in back of the van. The man that got out was older than the others, with thinning hair at the crown of his head. He was the only one of the five not wearing ripped and faded jeans, but rather a pair of neat khakis and a blue-and-white-striped oxford shirt with the sleeves rolled up his thick forearms.

Shelby recognized Travis Cooper, the band's front man, right away. He'd grown up in Lovett and made a name for himself by taking first place on the television show *America Can Sing*. He had long since left Lovett behind. He'd already been on a tour of the country, scored a record deal, and had more than one song playing on the radio. Peter, the band's guitarist, was Kelly's cousin, and he had convinced Travis to play at Kelly and Seth's wedding. Kelly had been thrilled when they said yes. She hadn't told Seth about it—only that she'd booked a band for the reception—and she was looking forward to surprising him.

Shelby wasn't sure which of the other men was Kelly's cousin—probably the one with hair the same reddish hue as Kelly's.

Shelby heard the door to the mudroom slam and turned around to see Bert, a longtime family friend and a second mother to Shelby, walking toward her, wiping her hands on her red-and-white-checked apron. Although Kelly's wedding was being catered, Bert was helping put together a few of Shelby's signature side dishes that Shelby had promised to make.

She stopped alongside Shelby, her eyes trained on Travis.

"That is a good-looking specimen of a man if I've ever seen one. Although sadly way too young for me. Just who is that long, tall drink of water?"

Shelby looked at Travis. Bert was right. It wasn't just his voice that had attracted his legions of fans. He was tall and slim with blond hair that flopped over his forehead and that he was continually pushing back. He was wearing a pair of well-worn jeans that were tight in all the right places and a snug T-shirt that made it obvious he spent plenty of time in the gym working out. No wonder women were attracted to him and threw love notes onto the stage at his concerts.

Shelby caught Bert looking at her with a peculiar expression on her face.

"What?" Shelby said.

"Nothing." Bert shook her head. "But don't you think he's attractive?"

"Yes," Shelby agreed. "But . . ."

Shelby already had enough men in her life. She'd been casually dating Matt Hudson, who owned the Lovett General Store, and then there was her neighbor Jake Taylor, who had made it more than plain that he was ready to ask her out anytime she gave the sign.

And then there was Frank. Frank was her brother-in-law, and he had made it very clear that he was in love with Shelby. Shelby thought she might be in love with him, too, but she wasn't sure whether that was because of who he was as a person or it was because he looked so much like her late husband.

"Who are all these people?" Bert said, shading her eyes with her hand as she looked at the group gathered in the driveway.

"The cute one with the blond hair is Travis Cooper." Shelby nodded in Travis's direction. He was leaning against the van, chugging from a bottle of designer water.

"Should I know who he is?" Bert said. "I can't keep up with everything that's going on these days." She sighed. "My grandkids call me an old coot."

"I don't know much more than you do," Shelby said. "Only that Travis is a local boy who came in first on that television show *America Can Sing*. And those must be his musicians. I think that girl sings with him sometimes." Shelby pointed to a slender girl in ripped jeans, a purple tank top, and enormous dangling earrings that looked like dream catchers. "Kelly wants to surprise Seth."

"Oh, good heavens," Bert exclaimed. "That's Debbie Coster's boy. I knew he looked familiar. What was his name? Robert—that's it. But they used to call him Butch." Bert snorted. "Travis Cooper, indeed."

"I guess he's reinvented himself. He's quite an up-and-coming star now."

Shelby watched as a young man with dark hair buzzed short and the tattoo of a guitar peeking out of the right sleeve of his T-shirt muscled a huge amplifier out of the van while Travis stood and watched.

The fellow looked around helplessly. "Where are we setting up, Travis?"

Shelby thought it was time she introduced herself.

"I'm Shelby McDonald." She held out her hand.

She waited for the usual joke about the fact that her last name was McDonald and she was a farmer, but no one said anything and she gave a sigh of relief.

"Cody Baldwin," the young man said in return. "I'd shake your hand, but . . ."

"You're fine," Shelby said. She pointed past the house. "The reception is back there in the barn." Shelby pointed to a far-off blur of red.

Cody stared into the distance with a look of dismay on his face. He shifted the amplifier in his arms, resting the edge on his hip.

"You can pull the van closer. That should make it easier to unload."

Cody smiled. "A lot easier."

He shot a dirty look over his shoulder at Travis, who continued to lean languidly against the van.

"There's a dirt path," Shelby said, pointing beyond the driveway. "You can see it's been worn into the ground. If you follow that, it will take you out to the barn, where you can set up."

Shelby glanced toward the house, hoping Billy had started to get ready. They had only one full bathroom and had to take turns.

"I can come and show you if you want," Shelby said when she saw the confused look on Cody's face.

"If you don't mind," Cody said.

Cody maneuvered the amplifier back into the van, and Travis, Cody, the girl, and the other man piled in. The older fellow got into his own car and started the engine. Shelby pointed toward the path, then followed behind the van as it jounced over the rutted ground toward the barn.

Cody, who was driving, stopped in front of the open barn doors.

"You can pull the van around back," Shelby said. "That way it will be out of sight of the guests when they arrive."

The double barn doors were folded back, and each was adorned with a wreath of baby's breath and ivy, wound with a pale pink ribbon tied in a bow. Shelby couldn't believe how the interior of the barn had been transformed. It was no longer a dusty, creaking structure with bags of feed stacked in the corner and rusty farm implements leaning against the wall, but the perfect spot for a cozy country wedding.

Kelly hadn't wanted anything too fancy. She and Shelby had pored over wedding magazines and Pinterest boards online, looking for ideas. Barn weddings were all the rage, it seemed, but most were very elaborate with chandeliers hung from the rafters, long white tablecloths, massive flower arrangements, and silver candelabras.

Instead, simple strings of white lights were looped from the rafters, and long wood trestle tables were set with white runners down their middles. Bouquets of colorful flowers had been set in mason jars, surrounded by squat white candles in antique birdcages that Kelly had scrounged from barn sales. An old-fashioned bright red-and-yellow popcorn machine stood in one corner and a cotton candy machine in the other.

Shelby was expecting the caterers to arrive any minute. They would be setting up industrial-sized grills outside the barn for barbecuing the chicken and ribs. Kelly had ordered gallons of potato salad, homemade coleslaw, and plenty of corn bread with honey to go along with the main course. Bert would help Shelby make several huge green salads with lettuce from Shelby's garden. And then, of course, there would be wedding cake and an ice cream sundae bar complete with whipped cream, hot fudge sauce, sprinkles, and maraschino cherries.

The musicians were busy dragging their equipment out of the van and into the barn, where a stage had been set up along one wall. Cody seemed to be doing most of the work and he didn't look too happy about it.

He called to Travis as he wrestled one of the large amplifiers out of the van. "Hey, give me a hand, would you?"

Travis was deep in an animated conversation with the girl in the purple top, who fussed with the ends of her hair, examining them up close and then putting several strands in her mouth.

Travis finally turned to Cody. "Can't you see I'm busy, man? Ask Brian." He pointed toward the van, where the other man was fiddling with a tangle of black cords.

Cody muttered something under his breath and then struggled toward the open barn doors with the amplifier.

Shelby turned and was about to walk back toward the house when someone tapped her on the shoulder. It was the girl in the purple tank top.

"I'm Paislee Fields," she said, holding out her hand.

Up close, Shelby could see there was a faint smattering of freckles across the bridge of her nose and the tiniest chip in one of her front teeth, which overlapped slightly.

Shelby took her hand. "Shelby McDonald."

"I hate to bother you, but"—Paislee twisted a lock of hair around her finger—"is there a bathroom somewhere nearby?"

Shelby laughed. "Sure. Follow me. We've set up some portable toilets for the wedding."

Shelby led Paislee around to the other end of the barn.

"Where are you from?" Shelby said as they walked.

"From the other side of the state," Paislee said. "Near Ann Arbor. My mother teaches economics at the University of Michigan."

"So you're a Wolverines fan?"

Paislee shrugged. "Not really. I didn't go to college. My mother wasn't too happy about it." She nibbled the cuticle of her left thumb. "I've always wanted to sing and be involved with music. I've never wanted anything else. College would have been a waste, don't you think?"

"Perhaps," Shelby said, searching for the most noncommittal rejoinder she could think of.

"Here you go." Shelby pointed to two white portable toilets. A black silhouette of a woman's head was on one and a man's on the other.

"Thanks," Paislee said. She started to walk away, then

turned back to Shelby. "I hope everything is going to go okay," she said.

The way she said it gave Shelby a frisson of unease. "Why wouldn't things go okay?"

Paislee shrugged. "I don't know. When Travis left here, he left behind some people who weren't too happy with him."

2

Dear Reader,

I love making my own salad dressing, although the kids always seem to want a bottle of the same stuff they see at their friends' houses. The dressing can be as simple as some good olive oil mixed with some red wine vinegar, or you can add a handful of chopped fresh herbs for variety. You can substitute balsamic vinegar for the red wine or use another acid like lemon or lime juice.

An Asian-flavored dressing is easy to make if you use peanut oil, rice wine vinegar, ginger, and a dash of sesame oil. I sometimes make buttermilk ranch dressing and add a good handful of chopped cilantro to give it a Mexican flavor.

With an infinite variety of dressings and numerous ingredients to choose from, a salad need never be boring!

"What do you mean she's not here?" Shelby said, feeling her mouth go dry. She stood with her back pressed against the kitchen table, her hands reaching behind her to grasp the edge.

Bert glanced up from the lettuce she was cleaning. "Just what I said. I mean she's not here."

Shelby looked at the clock hanging above the sink. "Kelly should have been here more than twenty minutes ago. She's supposed to get ready here. I have her dress and veil all laid out on the bed in my room." Her grip on the table tightened.

"Do you suppose she's gotten cold feet?" Bert removed the lettuce she'd plunged into a bath of cold water and transferred it by handfuls to a cotton dish towel.

Shelby shook her head. "No, I'm sure she hasn't. She and Seth have been planning to marry for ages now. It's not some spur-of-the-moment thing. They're mature adults—not a couple of kids."

She and Wild Bill had been a couple of kids, Shelby thought. But things had worked out okay. Sometimes she wondered if they would have continued that way if Bill hadn't died in that motorcycle accident.

"They could have had a fight." Bert wrapped the lettuce in the towel and set it aside. "It happens."

Shelby frowned. "I suppose so. But it's not like them. Kelly might be a bit hot-tempered, but Seth has always been as cool as a cucumber." She pulled out a kitchen chair and plopped into it. "I suppose he has to be in his job. Besides, they wouldn't let some silly misunderstanding come between them."

Seth was the county's family doctor and he dealt with everything from stitching up cuts to delivering babies.

Bert began scrubbing some bright red radishes Shelby had picked earlier. "Then perhaps Kelly is stuck somewhere. That ancient truck of hers might have broken down. I don't know how she's kept it going as long as she has."

"Or, heaven forbid, she's had an accident." Shelby began imagining all sorts of horrible scenarios. "I tried calling her on her cell phone, but she didn't answer." She drummed her fingers on the kitchen table.

"Let's not go thinking the worst," Bert said as she began to peel strips of skin off the radishes, leaving them striped red and white like peppermint candies.

"I hope Billy's ready at least." Shelby got up from the table and joined Bert at the sink. She picked up her favorite knife—the one with the carbon steel blade that was sharper than the others—and began to slice the radishes into one of the large wooden salad bowls Bert had lined up along the counter.

"I heard the water running and a lot of splashing a bit ago, so I assume he's had his bath at least."

Shelby snorted. "Just because he filled the tub doesn't mean he actually got in it."

She thought of the time Billy had nearly overflowed the tub with water but, instead of taking a bath, had spent almost an hour sailing his boats around and around in it. He'd still had dirt on his face and on the back of his neck when it came time to put on his pajamas.

"I don't suppose there was much hot water left, seeing as how Amelia spent a good thirty minutes in the shower."

"At least I know she'll be ready on time," Shelby said. Her thirteen-year-old daughter had transitioned from never wanting to bathe to using the entire linen closet full of clean towels every time she took a shower.

Shelby let out a puff of air that sent the bits of hair curling around her face flying. "I might as well get ready myself, then, so I can help Kelly when she gets here," she said. "*If* she gets here," she mumbled under her breath.

"There's still time," Bert said. "I wouldn't fret too much if I were you."

||||||||||||||||||||||||

Shelby took a quick shower, jumping out just as the water began to turn cold. Judging by the ring around the tub, Billy had actually gotten in, and even if he hadn't scrubbed himself with a washcloth, at least most of the dirt had floated off him.

As Shelby toweled dry and donned the pretty pink sundress she'd driven forty-five minutes to the nearest mall to purchase, she kept an ear out for the sound of the mudroom door opening and slamming shut. So far, the only noises she'd heard were Bert's banging pots and pans around in the kitchen and the steady hum of activity outside.

By the time Shelby had finished applying a light bit of makeup and fashioned her hair into some semblance of a casual updo, she was really beginning to worry. She slipped into a pair of flat sandals—it would have been impossible to traverse the farm grounds in high heels—and went downstairs.

"Any news?" she said as soon as she walked into the kitchen.

Bert was sitting at the kitchen table with a glass of water at her elbow.

"Are you okay?" Shelby frowned. "You look a bit pale."

Bert shook her head. "Don't go fussing at me. I'm fine. A bit of indigestion is all. Those sausages I had for breakfast aren't sitting too well." She sighed. "I guess Dr. Gregson is right. I'd best start watching my diet now that I'm getting a bit on in years."

Shelby hid a smile. Bert had been saying that for ages, and as far as Shelby could tell, she was still eating everything and anything she pleased. How she managed to keep from gaining weight, Shelby didn't know.

Shelby tied an apron over her dress and began mixing the ingredients for the various salad dressings she planned to serve—a simple but elegant vinaigrette, of course, ranch made with fresh buttermilk from Jake Taylor's cows, and a poppy seed dressing from a recipe that had been passed down from Shelby's great-grandmother.

"Do you think I should call Seth?" She turned her head to look at Bert.

"I wouldn't worry him. Not yet at least. Kelly will probably show up any minute now and you'll have left the poor man fearing that he's going to be stood up."

Shelby let out a sigh. She wanted to do . . . something.

She was about to reach for her cell phone again when the screen door to the mudroom banged open and Kelly charged into the kitchen. She was wearing her usual uniform of ripped and stained jeans and a faded T-shirt with *Lovett County Fair* on the front, and she had her mass of red curls coiled on top of her head and stuck through with a pencil.

Shelby's nose automatically wrinkled at the scent of manure that clung to Kelly from head to toe.

Kelly was the local veterinarian, who dealt with all the farmers' animals as well as holding a weekly clinic to take care of people's cats, dogs, birds, and other small creatures they chose to keep as pets.

"Where were you? We were getting so worried. There's only twenty minutes until the ceremony starts."

"Oh, pooh," Kelly said, helping herself to a glass of lemonade from the pitcher in the refrigerator. "I've gotten ready in less time than that before. Most days as a matter of fact."

"Maybe," Shelby said, "but most days you weren't getting married."

Bert looked over her shoulder. "Shelby thought you were standing your poor bridegroom up."

"No," Kelly wailed. "I would never do that. It was Mr. Mingledorf's cow again. It was suffering from gassy bloat, and I had to introduce a stomach tube. . . ."

Kelly must have noticed the look on Shelby's face, because she quickly came to a halt. "TMI, huh?"

"Definitely too much information."

"Has the band arrived? Have you met my cousin Peter yet?" Kelly took a gulp of her drink. "He's the one with the red hair. He plays guitar."

"Not yet," Shelby said, making shooing motions at Kelly, slowly moving her toward the stairs to the second floor. "The band is here, but there wasn't time to talk.

"You need to get in the shower and get dressed," Shelby said as they headed upstairs. "Amelia said she would help do your hair. She's quite good at it."

"I don't need to do anything fancy with my hair."

"You'll need to dry it at least. You can't walk down the aisle with it wet and dripping down your back."

Shelby waited until the bathroom door clicked closed behind Kelly and she heard the water running before heading back downstairs to check on things.

Bert was still sitting at the kitchen table, flipping through a week-old newspaper. She insisted she was fine, but Shelby couldn't get rid of the niggling doubt in the back of her mind. Bert's color had come back a bit, but she was still a little too pale for Shelby's taste.

⁞⁞⁞⁞⁞⁞⁞⁞⁞⁞⁞⁞⁞⁞⁞⁞⁞⁞⁞⁞⁞⁞⁞⁞⁞

Outside on the lawn, folding chairs had been set up in a semicircle around the old apple tree, and tall metal pails filled with flowers lined the aisle down the middle. Shelby straightened a couple of the chairs and then stood back to admire the scene. Everything was in order—now if only Kelly would hurry and get ready.

Inside the barn, the musicians had all their equipment set up and Travis was testing the sound system, which emitted the usual discordant screeching noises when he tapped the microphone. He dispatched Cody to fiddle with a bunch of dials until everything was adjusted to his satisfaction.

The caterers were firing up industrial-sized grills where they would barbecue chicken and ribs for the guests.

Shelby sighed in relief. Everything seemed to be in order. She was about to walk back across the field to the house when she saw a figure in the distance waving a white handkerchief at her. It looked like Seth's mother, Nancy. Shelby wondered if she was waving the handkerchief in surrender, and she snickered to herself. Nancy had been against the whole wedding-at-the-farm idea from the start, campaigning for a black-tie dinner and dancing at a fancy hotel instead, but Kelly and Seth had prevailed.

Nancy was always impeccably dressed and coiffed, making Shelby feel like the proverbial country bumpkin. As Shelby got closer, she could see Nancy was wearing a long turquoise chiffon dress more suitable for a ballroom than a barn. It was trailing along the ground, and the hem was already dirty.

She appeared to be teetering, and when Shelby looked down, she could see that Nancy was picking her way across the field in strappy high-heeled sandals dyed to match her dress.

"This is ridiculous," Nancy said as soon as she reached Shelby. "What are my friends going to think when they see my son getting married in the middle of a cow pasture?"

"Actually, I don't have any cows," Shelby said.

"But the smell!" She grabbed Shelby's arm. "Where is that coming from, then?"

Shelby sniffed. There was the faintest odor of manure in the air. To her, it was hardly noticeable. "There's a dairy farm next door. With cows. The smell drifts over when the wind is blowing in this direction."

"Can't you do something about it?" Nancy stumbled and clutched at Shelby's arm. "There's got to be some way to get rid of the odor."

Dear Reader, the smell is really not that bad. Besides, I don't think we can bring in a truckful of potpourri to hide it.

"I don't know what on earth made Seth agree to this ridiculous notion of a barn wedding." Nancy said *barn* as if it left a bad taste in her mouth. "I'd found a lovely venue—a beautiful room with arched windows looking out over a lake. The manager said the chef does an exquisite filet mignon with a mushroom demi-glace and a gratin dauphinoise. And, of course, buckwheat crepes with caviar to start."

That certainly sounded appetizing, Shelby thought, her mouth beginning to water. Although perhaps it was because the caterers had started the grills and the scents of barbecued chicken and ribs were drifting across the field.

Shelby linked her arm through Nancy's. A diversion might be the best tactic. "Wait till you see the barn," she said in what she hoped was an enticing tone. "It looks absolutely lovely."

Nancy sniffed and gave Shelby a doubtful look but let herself be led over to the apple tree where the ceremony would be held. A white trellis, covered with pink and white flowers and strands of ivy, created a soft backdrop for the ceremony.

Guests were beginning to arrive—the women in pretty pastel sundresses, the men in blazers and striped ties.

"I've put a seat back here for you," Shelby said, resting her hand on the back of a folding chair set slightly apart from the others. "You can sit here until the wedding party is assembled and Kelly is ready to walk down the aisle. The usher will then seat you, and that will be the signal for the procession to start."

Nancy made a big show of brushing off the chair before finally taking a seat. Shelby noticed that the heels of her fancy shoes were stained with mud—she wasn't going to be too happy about that when she discovered it.

Nancy sat down, carefully arranging and rearranging the drapes of her elaborate gown, her face settling into its usual disgruntled lines and stern expression.

Shelby put a hand on Nancy's shoulder. "Will you be okay?"

"Yes," Nancy said through pursed lips. "I suppose so."

Shelby hurried back toward the house, nodding at the wedding guests crossing the field to where the ceremony was going to be held. She hoped Kelly was getting ready. She half feared she'd find her seated at the kitchen table, wrapped in a towel with dripping hair and chatting with Bert.

"Is she ready?" Shelby said to Bert as soon as she burst through the door into the kitchen. "The ceremony is supposed to start in ten minutes."

Bert pointed to the ceiling. "They're still upstairs. I heard the shower going, so she's done that at least."

Shelby ran up the stairs so fast she had to stop at the top for a moment to catch her breath. She heard voices coming from the master bedroom and hurried down the hall.

The sight of Kelly nearly made her gasp. Barely half an hour ago she had been wearing clothes that looked like she'd picked them out of a ragbag, her hair had been more snarled than Little Orphan Annie's before she was adopted, and she'd smelled like a cow pasture. Her swift transformation was amazing.

Kelly was wearing a tea-length dress with a lace overlay, a sweetheart neckline, and wide-set lace straps. Amelia had tamed Kelly's unruly red curls into a French braid tied at the end with a pink satin ribbon that matched the ribbon around her waist. A ring of pink roses encircled her head.

Shelby stood in the doorway, transfixed. "You look gorgeous," she said, tears springing to her eyes. "Wait till Seth sees you."

Kelly laughed. "He won't recognize me."

Shelby walked over to her friend. "You sure do clean up real good, as Bert would say."

Kelly stuck out a foot. "What do you think?" She gave an impish grin.

"I think those are going to give Mrs. Gregson a heart attack." Shelby laughed.

"I'm pretty sure you're right."

Instead of strappy sandals like Nancy's or plain ones like Shelby's, Kelly was wearing her pair of well-worn and much-loved cowboy boots.

||||||||||||||||||||||

Bitsy and Jenkins were waiting by the back door when Shelby got downstairs. They'd had a bath and been brushed, and were wearing pink bow ties around their necks. Seth was bringing Kelly's golden retriever, Dolly, who'd had a day at the spa as well.

"The florist dropped off the bouquets," Bert said, pointing to a large white box sitting on the kitchen table.

Bert had changed into what she would probably have referred to as her *Sunday best*—a navy blue dress with a short matching jacket, low-heeled pumps, and a strand of pearls around her neck. For a moment Shelby was taken aback—she was so used to seeing Bert in jeans and T-shirts or sweatshirts that the change was almost as unnerving as Kelly's had been.

Kelly lifted the lid of the florist's box. "Oh," she breathed as she took out a nosegay made up of a variety of multicolored flowers and finished with trailing pink ribbons.

She held it up to her nose and took a deep breath. Shelby had given the florist a selection of fresh herbs with which to stud the bouquet—rosemary for remembrance, thyme for strength, and sage for wisdom.

Shelby took out smaller bouquets for her and Amelia and a sprig of lily of the valley for Billy.

Kelly put her bouquet down suddenly and when Shelby looked at her, she saw that Kelly was trembling.

"Are you okay?" Shelby put a hand on Kelly's arm. It was cold to the touch.

"A case of nerves, I guess." Kelly pulled out a kitchen chair and sank into it. "Suddenly it all seems so real. I think I feel a bit dizzy."

"You're right. It's only nerves. I remember feeling the same way on my wedding day."

"You need a shot of Dutch courage," Bert said, getting up from her chair. She turned to Shelby. "Is the whiskey still in the pantry?"

Shelby nodded. "It should be."

Bert disappeared into the pantry briefly and emerged with a slightly dusty bottle of Jack Daniel's. She grabbed a juice glass from the cupboard next to the sink and poured a small measure of whiskey into it.

"Here you go." She handed Kelly the glass. "Down the hatch."

Kelly closed her eyes, held her nose, and tossed off the Jack Daniel's in one gulp. She coughed and sputtered as she put the glass down on the table.

Bert thumped her on the back. "Get her some water," she said to Shelby.

Shelby hurried to comply. She handed the glass to Kelly. "Feeling better?"

"Much. But I'll tell you—I'm glad I only have to get married once."

Shelby glanced at the clock. "Where is Billy?" she said, feeling slightly panicked, realizing she hadn't seen him since he'd gone to get ready. She hoped he wasn't getting dirty all over again.

"He's in the living room watching television. He wanted to go outside and play. Can you believe it? But I told him 'over my dead body,'" Bert said, taking a seat at the kitchen table.

"Billy?" Shelby turned toward the living room and called. "Time to get ready."

Shelby had to stifle the urge to grab Billy and give him a big hug when he strode into the kitchen. He'd never looked more adorable with his cowlick momentarily tamed and his face scrubbed clean. He was wearing khaki pants, a pale pink shirt that they'd argued over—*But pink is for girls,* Billy had protested—a pink-and-blue-striped tie, and a navy blazer.

Billy squirmed as Shelby fastened the sprig of lily of the valley to his lapel. She hoped he would be able to contain his exuberant energy long enough to get through the ceremony.

"Okay." Shelby clapped her hands. "Time to go."

Bert got up from the chair with a grunt.

"Amelia, you'll go first, then me, and then Billy. And finally, once we're down the aisle, Kelly will follow."

Shelby managed to get everyone out the door. She felt like a sheepdog herding its flock.

Kelly grabbed Shelby's arm suddenly. Her hands were still cold, but warmer than they'd been earlier. She threw her arms around her friend.

"I can't thank you enough for doing this for me."

Shelby gave Kelly a squeeze. "Ready?" She looked at her friend.

"Yes." Kelly took a deep breath and squared her shoulders. She smiled. "I'm ready."

<hr />

Shelby gave Billy last-minute instructions as they waited in the shade of an oak tree for the string quartet to begin Pachelbel's Canon, which Kelly had chosen for the processional.

"Walk slowly," Shelby whispered to Billy, putting her hands on his shoulders. "And no detours. Go straight to the front and stand where we showed you at the rehearsal."

Billy squirmed. "You already told me that."

"I know, but I don't want you to forget it." Shelby was tempted to ruffle his hair, but she didn't want to mess it up.

The last notes of "Clair de Lune" faded away and after a short pause, the quartet began the processional.

Amelia started to walk down the aisle, and Shelby felt

her heart contract a bit at the sight. She looked so beautiful and much too grown-up. How had her little baby with her halo of blond curls morphed into this lovely young lady so quickly? Before she knew it, Amelia would be walking down the aisle toward her own groom. Shelby wished she could make time stand still—just for a little while.

As matron of honor, Shelby was next. She gave Kelly's hand one last squeeze, tucked an errant strand of hair behind her ear, and then started walking. The expectant faces of the audience turned toward Shelby as she made her way down the makeshift aisle. She felt a grin spreading across her face when she caught Seth's eye. He was waiting at the altar looking hopeful, happy, and nervous all at the same time.

Billy came next. Shelby managed a quick glance behind her and he was walking slowly like he'd been told, with an almost comically somber expression on his face.

Then the audience rose to their feet and all heads turned toward the bride.

Seth beamed when he saw Kelly walking toward him. Mark Davis, an old friend from college, was standing next to him, and Dolly was stretched out at his feet. The men were wearing outfits similar to Billy's—navy blazers, pink shirts, and striped ties—and Dolly had a pink ribbon tied in a bow around her neck instead of her usual collar.

Shelby watched as Kelly took her place next to Seth and smiled up at him, the perfect picture of a happy bride.

Reverend Daniel Mather from St. Andrews was performing the ceremony. He stood, holding his well-worn prayer book, in front of Kelly and Seth. He opened his prayer book, thumbed through the pages till he found the section he wanted, then cleared his throat, and the ceremony began.

Shelby crossed her fingers until Billy produced the ring—a simple gold band—at the right moment, and the proceedings continued on without a hitch.

Shelby held her breath when Daniel came to the *speak now or forever hold your peace* part, for fear Mrs. Gregson would say something, but she was mercifully quiet. And when Daniel pronounced Seth and Kelly man and wife and said, "You may now kiss the bride," Dolly threw back her head and let out an exuberant howl with Jenkins and Bitsy quickly following suit.

The whole gathering, including the bride and groom, began to laugh and the good cheer carried them all the way to the barn for the start of the reception.

Shelby waited until all the guests had made their way across the field before she followed after them. Delicious smells drifted from the grills set up outside the barn, making Shelby's stomach grumble. She'd been too busy and too excited to eat anything for lunch. Shelby dodged a waitress, clad in jeans, a checked shirt, and cowboy boots, as she hustled plates of barbecued chicken and ribs into the barn.

Shelby examined the tantalizing array of food, which was set out on a long table covered with a red-and-white-checked tablecloth. Everything seemed to be in order. Her salads sat alongside potato salad, coleslaw, and a bowl of cowboy caviar—a mixture of beans, black-eyed peas, corn, onions, and garlic dressed with olive oil, vinegar, and a dash of hot sauce.

The wedding cake stood in the corner atop a thick slab cut from a tree trunk. Shelby saw Billy eyeing it longingly. She hustled toward him as he scooped a bit of icing off the bottom with his finger. "We'll have cake later," Shelby said, as she put her hands on Billy's shoulders, turned him away from the table, and gave him a gentle push.

Amelia was standing by the makeshift stage, watching Travis tune his guitar. *Dear Reader, if she gave her math class that sort of undivided attention and concentration, she'd be getting all As.*

Amelia had clearly developed an instantaneous crush on Travis, and judging by the looks from some of the other women guests, she wasn't alone. Shelby even caught Bert looking in Travis's direction a little longer than was strictly necessary.

Shelby mingled with the guests, nodding and smiling and stopping to chat here and there. The bride and groom were still outside having their picture taken, and guests milled around, nibbling the hors d'oeuvres that were being passed, enjoying one another's company.

Isabel Stone was dressed almost as inappropriately as Nancy Gregson, Shelby noticed, in a long floral-print chiffon dress and stiletto-heeled white sandals. She had one arm linked through Daniel Mather's and was feeding him a bite of something off her plate. No one had thought their relationship would last longer than a day, but now, months later, they seemed to be happily settling in as a couple.

The band suddenly grabbed their instruments and began to pick out a few bars of "Here Comes the Bride." The guests smiled and turned toward the open doors of the barn. A few of them applauded as Kelly and Seth walked in—both of them beaming. Shelby was, too—it was wonderful to see her friend so happy.

Guests began drifting toward the laden food tables to fill their plates, and a waiter bustled over to Kelly and Seth with two bubbling flutes of champagne.

Shelby joined Nancy at the buffet, where she was standing, her plate in her hand, a puzzled expression on her face.

"It all looks so good, doesn't it?" Shelby said.

Bert came up behind them. "It's a real down-home country meal—that's for sure."

Nancy turned to Bert. "Oh. Is that what you call it?"

Bert seemed oblivious to Nancy's sarcastic tone and slapped her on the back as if they were old friends. "Go on. Fill your plate. Everything will be delicious. I guarantee it."

Nancy looked doubtful but reluctantly added a few bites of food to her plate.

The band was waiting for the meal to start before beginning to play in earnest. Travis was talking intently to a young man Shelby didn't recognize. He was a little taller than Travis with the same dirty blond hair and lanky build. Travis motioned toward the door of the barn and they both disappeared outside. Cody was seated on one of the amps, slumped forward with his head in his hands, and Paislee was conferring with the older man, who Shelby had discovered was their manager and the band's drummer—Brian Ross. Kelly's cousin was sitting on the edge of the stage, thumbing through messages on his phone.

Amelia had taken a seat at a table as near to the stage as she could get, staring at the spot where Travis had been standing as if she could conjure him up with her gaze alone.

Slowly the rest of the guests took their seats, and only a few were still standing in the buffet line when Travis walked back in and the band gathered up their instruments.

They launched into one of Travis's biggest hits—"Don't Leave Me Now"—and in moments the party was in full swing.

Shelby stood at the edge of the crowd, her hands relaxed at her sides. Everything was coming together beautifully. She felt the tension in her shoulders ease and gave a deep sigh of satisfaction.

Kelly and Seth were at the buffet table filling their plates when Seth turned around to look at the band. He stood staring for several seconds, surprise and anger on his face. Then he shoved his plate into Kelly's hands and stalked through the open door of the barn. Kelly gazed after him, her expression crestfallen, obviously on the verge of tears.

Shelby felt her stomach knot and her hands tighten into fists.

Bert sidled up to Shelby. She pointed to Kelly and raised an eyebrow. "Trouble in paradise already?"

3

Dear Reader,

If you're like most of us, you've probably suffered from heartburn or indigestion at one time or another—especially after a party, when you may have eaten more than usual. No need to head to the drugstore—there are a number of home remedies you can try first. You probably won't believe it, but a spoon of raw, unfiltered apple cider vinegar will often do the trick. As will the old tried-and-true baking soda in water.

Some people swear by gingerroot tea and others find the herb chamomile very soothing. And of course, mint is well-known for being able to settle a sensitive tummy.

Shelby hastened over toward Kelly. "Is everything okay?" She grabbed her friend's hands.

Kelly gave a wobbly smile. "It's nothing. A silly misunderstanding."

"Is there anything I can do . . . ?"

Kelly shook her head.

Before Shelby could say anything else, a woman wearing a bright orange dress and too much perfume walked up to Kelly.

"I must congratulate the bride," she said, kissing Kelly on the cheek.

Shelby hesitated for a moment, her hands knotted in the skirt of her dress, but the woman continued to chatter. With a last glance at Kelly, she began to make her way to the buffet table.

"Excuse me. I've got a fresh bowl of salad here, if you'd like some."

Shelby glanced over her shoulder to see Jessie positioning a large wooden salad bowl next to the platter of chicken. Shelby had recently hired Jessie to work for her during the spring and summer, when there were so many things that needed to be done around the farm. Bert was a huge help, but she was getting older, and despite her protestations to the contrary, she couldn't do as much as she used to. Besides, Shelby wasn't about to let her. If Bert didn't know her limitations, Shelby did.

Jessie wasn't a local girl—she'd moved to Lovett when she married her husband. She had long dark hair pulled back in a ponytail and was pretty in a quiet sort of way. She was shy, too, although she was slowly warming up to Shelby. Shelby thought she had an air of fragility about her—like someone who had been injured emotionally and was still carrying the scars.

When Shelby had asked her if she would be willing to

help at the wedding, she'd jumped at the chance to earn some extra cash.

Shelby was scanning the tables for an empty seat when she saw someone waving at her. It was Matt Hudson. Matt owned the Lovett General Store and had moved to Lovett from New York City to flee the trauma of 9/11. He was boyishly attractive with light brown hair that tended to flop onto his forehead no matter how many times he pushed it back and crinkles around his green eyes that suggested he was quick to smile. He and Shelby had gone out a few times and had developed an easy relationship. Shelby didn't consider it a serious romance—at least not yet—but she suspected that Matt did and it made her nervous. She wasn't quite ready for that.

Shelby carried her plate over to Matt's table and slid into the empty seat opposite him.

"You've done a splendid job," he said, looking around the barn.

Shelby laughed. "It wasn't my doing. Mrs. Gregson was so concerned about everything being just right—even if it was taking place in a barn, as she kept reminding us—that she hired a wedding planner to work with Kelly to oversee the decor. Most of the ideas were Kelly's, but with her veterinary practice being as busy as it is, she was more than happy to let someone else perform the actual execution."

Matt glanced toward the stage and smiled. "Amelia seems quite taken with the band's front man."

Shelby followed Matt's gaze. "She's at the right age for it. I remember having quite a crush on Jon Bon Jovi myself."

Matt gave a half smile and glanced down at his plate. "For me it was Madonna."

"It seems such a long time ago now," Shelby said.

Matt sighed. "A lot has certainly happened since then."

The band began a slow song and numerous couples got up to dance. Shelby glanced toward the dance floor and saw Jake Taylor steering a friend of Kelly's around the floor. She was everything Shelby wasn't—tall, willowy, and blond. Shelby felt a surprising pang of jealousy. Jake had hinted many times that he was interested in asking her out. *Dear Reader, I have no right to feel jealous, since I have never given Jake any encouragement and it's no wonder he's moved on.*

She certainly found Jake attractive—he was lean and muscular with dark hair and blue eyes—and she wasn't the only one. And he was wonderful with her kids, especially Billy, giving him rides to school when he'd missed the bus and letting him tag along as Jake performed chores around the farm. But deep down she knew he wasn't right for her. The only thing they really had in common was living next door to each other.

Shelby turned back to Matt and smiled. Travis was singing now—a duet with Paislee—both of them leaning in toward the same microphone, their heads almost touching, their voices blending as one. It was an intimate scene, and Shelby could tell from the way they were looking at each other that the intimacy probably went beyond merely singing together.

She heard a gasp in back of her and turned to glance over her shoulder. Jessie was right behind her and had both hands over her mouth. She looked as if she was about to cry. Before Shelby could ask her what was wrong, Jessie ran from the barn, nearly colliding with one of the waitstaff who was coming in with a platter of freshly barbecued chicken.

Shelby felt responsible for Jessie, and she excused her-

self from Matt and pushed back her chair. She followed
Jessie as she ran toward the house. Shelby heard the screen
door to the mudroom slam shut as Jessie bolted inside.

Shelby went through the mudroom and into the kitchen.
Jessie wasn't there, but Bert was. She was slumped over the
kitchen table, a grimace on her face, which was alarmingly
pale. Shelby rushed over to her, Jessie momentarily forgotten.

"Bert, are you okay? What's wrong? Is it your heart?"

Bert shook her head. "My heart's perfectly fine. I'm
afraid it's my gallbladder. Dr. Gregson told me I needed to
have it out, but you know how I hate hospitals. Never could
stand them. The smell gives me the willies."

"But you're in pain. You need help. I'll get Dr. Gregson."

Shelby was seized by a panic that turned her palms cold
and clammy. She couldn't let anything happen to Bert. She
didn't know what she'd do without her. It wasn't only her
help around the farm—Shelby could always hire someone
for that—it was Bert's support she counted on. No matter
what the situation, Bert always had an answer and a shoulder for Shelby to cry on. Because Shelby's parents were traips-
ing around Oregon in their RV, Bert had become like a
mother to Shelby.

"It's his wedding day. You can't bother him," Bert said.
"Besides, I've had these attacks before, and they always go
away. I need to give it some time."

Shelby squeezed Bert's shoulder. "I'm going to get Seth."
She held up a finger as Bert started to protest again. "It's
either that or I'm taking you to the emergency room."

"All right," Bert mumbled. "Anything's better than the
ER."

A new wave of pain must have hit her, because she

slumped over the table again, her eyes closed, her mouth twisted into a grimace.

Shelby ran outside and headed back toward the barn. The band was taking a break, and Travis was outside leaning against a tree, his arms folded across his chest. Jessie was standing in front of him, her shoulders tense. She must have run into the house and right back out again.

Shelby had almost forgotten about Jessie in her panic over Bert, but she didn't have time to talk to the girl now— she had to find Seth.

Seth and Kelly were seated together at one of the tables, their heads close together. Kelly was feeding Seth a bite of her salad. *Dear Reader, it looks as if all is right in the world of the newlyweds again.*

As Shelby approached them, she saw Kelly take the edge of her napkin and wipe a smudge of barbecue sauce off Seth's chin. They had eyes only for each other, and they both jumped when Shelby tapped them on the shoulder.

"I'm so sorry, Seth, but it's Bert. She's in terrible pain. She says it's her gallbladder."

"I'll be right there," Seth said, wiping his mouth and pushing back his chair. He tossed his napkin on the table. "She's in the house?"

"In the kitchen."

Seth leaned over and kissed Kelly, then followed Shelby out of the barn and across the field to the farmhouse.

"I feel terrible, taking you away from your own wedding," Shelby said as they walked. "I didn't know what else to do."

Seth squeezed Shelby's shoulder. "You did the right thing."

Shelby wanted to ask him why he had stomped out of the

barn so abruptly earlier, but she didn't want to sound as if she was prying.

"The wedding has been lovely so far," Shelby said tentatively, hoping Seth would respond to the bait.

"It has. And Kelly and I can't thank you enough. Everything is perfect—just the way we'd envisioned it." Seth laughed. "Even if my mother was having dreams of ball gowns and men in black tie and a sit-down four-course dinner lit by thousands of candles."

"So everything is fine?" Shelby said.

"Yes, of course." Seth glanced at Shelby. "You must have seen that little scene earlier."

"Well . . ."

"It was childish of me to react the way I did. Kelly had no idea."

"No idea . . ."

"That I knew Travis Cooper. Although that wasn't his name at the time."

"I didn't know that either."

"It's not something I talk about very much. Travis and I were at Michigan State together, and we were in the same fraternity. One night he had the bright idea that it would be funny to pull a prank on me. He monkeyed with my car, and in the morning it wouldn't start.

"Unfortunately, I had a very important exam to take in the science building all the way on the other side of the campus. I had to walk and by the time I got there, the exam was already in progress and the professor wouldn't let me into the room."

"That's awful."

"What made it worse was that the professor wouldn't let me make up the test and I got a failing grade for it. That affected my final grade for the class and ultimately my grade point average. And when you're planning on applying to medical school, that becomes very important."

"So there's no love lost between you and Travis."

"You've got that right," Seth said as he held the door to the mudroom open for Shelby. "I'm afraid I acted childishly." He hung his head. "Fortunately, I have a very forgiving wife, and she's agreed to accept my apology.

"What do we have here?" Seth said in a jovial voice when they entered the kitchen.

Bert was still in a chair by the kitchen table, but Shelby thought she looked slightly better—her color had improved and she was no longer grimacing.

"I told Shelby not to bother you," Bert said. "It was only a gallbladder attack. Nothing to get all worked up over."

Seth put on a stern face. "Those attacks aren't going to stop, you know, until we take out your gallbladder."

"I know. I know," Bert said with a scowl. "You've told me often enough."

"Does that mean you're going to call my office and get a referral for a gastroenterologist? Dr. Hampton is excellent. You'll like him."

"Fine," Bert said, using one of Shelby's teenage daughter's favorite words.

4

Dear Reader,

I love wedding traditions. Don't you? At one time, the bride's gown was considered good luck and guests would try to snatch a piece of it. In order to protect the newly married girl from this savage practice, the tradition of throwing the garter came about to appease the crowd.

The bridal veil was originally meant to hide the bride from evil spirits. The diamond engagement ring is a more recent tradition created when the advertising slogan "A Diamond Is Forever" was coined by copywriter Frances Gerety.

As for the wedding cake, it's rife with traditions. The bride and groom serving each other symbolizes their commitment to provide for each other.

Shelby didn't want to leave Bert, but Bert insisted she was going to be okay. She promised to get comfortable on the sofa and put her feet up. Shelby saw Bert glance at some dishes piled up next to the sink and had a sneaking suspicion that Bert wouldn't spend very long on the couch.

The band was still on the stage when Shelby walked into the barn, although they'd paused momentarily for a break. Travis was bending down to pick up the bottle of water at his feet, and Brian had come out from behind the drums to jump off the stage and head out the door.

Travis took a long, deep drink from the bottle, then put it down and picked up his microphone. He whispered something to Cody, who nodded.

Brian was walking back into the barn as Cody began strumming the opening chords to a song with Travis humming along. Brian got a strange look on his face. *Alarm?* Shelby thought. He glared at Travis as he brushed past him to take up his place behind the drums. His expression remained strained throughout the song, which sounded hauntingly familiar to Shelby. She supposed she must have heard it on the radio at some point.

Paislee joined Travis and once again, their heads bent together over the microphone. Cody glared at the pair as he fingered his guitar. Was he jealous that Travis and Paislee were singing together or simply that Travis was the one standing up front while he played in the background? Shelby couldn't tell for sure.

The final notes of the tune faded into silence, and Paislee stepped away from the microphone.

Travis grinned at the crowd. He took the microphone from the stand and walked toward the edge of the stage, waiting until he had the crowd's attention. He looked over his shoulder at Brian.

"Can I get a drumroll, please?"

Brian obliged and the crowd looked around expectantly.

"It's that time, folks," Travis said, kicking the microphone cord in back of him and walking up and down the stage.

A murmur of expectation went through the guests.

"It's time for the bride and groom to cut each other a piece of cake. Put your hands together for Mr. and Mrs. Seth Gregson."

The crowd burst into applause as Kelly and Seth, with sheepish grins on their faces, approached the table where the cake was displayed.

Seth picked up the silver-and-crystal cake knife, and Kelly put her hand over his. He held the knife poised over the cake for a moment before slicing through the multiple layers and carving out the first piece. One of the waitresses rushed forward with a small plate and two forks. Seth slid the piece of cake onto the plate and then licked the buttercream frosting off his fingers.

Seth picked up the first fork, scooped up a bite of cake, and held it toward Kelly. Kelly then did the same for him. Seth turned toward the crowd and gave a thumbs-up and everyone burst into applause.

Several waitresses scurried forward to deal with the business of serving the rest of the cake.

The band played another full set of their unique blend of country and rock, and then the party started to break up. People slowly drifted out of the barn and the band began to pack up their gear. Travis had already disappeared outside while Cody broke down the equipment. He was about to pick up one of the amplifiers when he changed his mind and dug a pack of Marlboros and a lighter out of his shirt pocket. He walked outside and a moment later, Shelby caught a whiff of cigarette smoke as it drifted through the open doors of the barn.

The rest of the band had vanished. Shelby thought she'd heard Paislee say something about going to the Dixie Bar and Grill for some cold beers.

Kelly, Seth, and Matt had insisted on staying behind to help clean up, and there was no way Shelby could talk them out of it. Seth and Matt had draped their blazers over the back of a chair, had rolled up their sleeves, and were folding up the chairs and stacking them against the wall. Kelly had kicked off her cowboy boots and was walking around the barn barefoot, plucking dirty glasses off the tables, while Shelby pulled the linens off the cleared tables and bundled them up.

Shelby looked around for Jessie, but she was nowhere to be seen. Shelby was slightly miffed—she'd been counting on Jessie for help cleaning up. If she had other plans, she should have said so.

Seth had turned off the fans they'd rented for the occasion, and the barn was heating up. Shelby felt a trickle of sweat make its way down her back, and she dabbed at her forehead with a slightly used napkin. She felt like she was stifling and she stepped outside briefly, hoping there would be a breeze to cool her off.

She heard raised voices coming from behind the barn and became curious. She walked around back to see Travis talking to Jessie. They both looked angry. Jessie's fists were balled at her sides, and her face was red. She looked like she was about to cry. Travis looked more annoyed than angry, Shelby decided. He was making the sort of face a person makes while waving away a pesky bug—a persistent gnat or mosquito.

Jessie suddenly turned on her heel and stalked off. Shelby

quickly slipped around to the other side of the barn and watched as Jessie stalked across the field. A man was coming from the opposite direction—Shelby couldn't see who it was until he got closer. Then she realized it was the man who had been talking to Travis earlier before the band began to play.

He grabbed Jessie's arm, but she shook his hand off and folded her arms across her chest. Obviously she knew him. And equally obvious was the fact that she wasn't very happy to see him.

Shelby continued to watch, curious, as they headed toward the farmhouse, their strides out of step with each other.

Shelby took a deep breath of fresh air and went back into the barn. The caterers had taken away their grills and Kelly was sitting in a folding chair, rubbing her feet.

The bowls for Shelby's salad were gone—she suspected Bert had come out to help and taken them back to the house. So much for Bert getting some rest, Shelby thought, rolling her eyes. *Dear Reader, I'm pretty sure that the expression "stubborn as a mule" was coined with Bert in mind.*

Cody hadn't come back inside, Shelby noticed. There were still a few pieces of equipment that needed to be loaded into the van. She hoped they would hurry. Suddenly she was very tired and the thought of sipping a tall glass of iced tea while sitting in one of the rocking chairs on the front porch seemed like the best thing in the world.

Matt rolled down his sleeves, grabbed his jacket, and slung it over one shoulder. He quickly folded up the last remaining chair and added it to the stack against the wall.

"I'm afraid I have to take off," he said, walking toward Shelby. "Will you be all right?" He gestured toward the barn. "Everything is ready to be picked up by the rental company."

"Thanks, Matt. You've been a huge help." Shelby stood on tiptoe and kissed him on the cheek.

He grinned. "My pleasure, ma'am. I'll call you. I think it's time we went back to Lucia's for dinner. Don't you?"

Shelby nodded. "I'd like that."

She and Matt had gone on their first date to Lucia's—a lovely restaurant in nearby Allenvale.

She waved as Matt headed toward the open door of the barn.

Kelly was sitting on a bale of hay, pulling her cowboy boots back on.

"Where's Seth?" Shelby sat down next to her.

"He said he'd wait for me outside. He wasn't getting very good reception on his cell in here." Kelly made a face. "His mother called to wish him bon voyage even though we're only going as far as Niagara Falls. She was acting as if we were going to the moon. She said she'd meant to do it before she left but had forgotten. Frankly, I think she couldn't wait to get out of here."

Shelby laughed. "I hope you have a grand time on your honeymoon even if you are only going across the border. You deserve it."

Kelly smiled. "We will. Neither of us could take much time away from our practices at the moment, so we only have a few days. But we're planning a two-week trip out west next year. I've always wanted to see the Grand Canyon."

Shelby realized she rarely left the farm except to go to the farmers' market, the store, and church, and she hadn't traveled more than an hour outside Lovett in years. Now that her blog was taking off and she was being asked to advertise cookware and other kitchen products, perhaps she could plan a trip somewhere that would be fun for Billy and

Amelia—although their interests were so different that it was hard to imagine any place other than Disney World that would appeal to both of them. And it would be years before she could afford a trip to Florida. Shelby suspected she'd be buying a new roof for the farmhouse long before she bought airplane tickets to the Sunshine State.

Sometimes she wondered if life wasn't passing her by. Shelby gave herself a shake. She loved life on Love Blossom Farm and wouldn't trade it for anything.

Kelly gave Shelby a hug and when she let go and stood back, Shelby could see she had tears in her eyes.

"I can't thank you enough," Kelly said, swiping at the tears glistening on her face. "You've given me my dream wedding, and I'll never forget it."

"I'm so glad everything turned out as well as it did."

Kelly nodded. "Except for the whole Travis thing. But Seth quickly realized I had no idea about him and Travis." Kelly shrugged. "At the time, I thought it would be a great surprise." She laughed. "Well, it was a surprise, just not the way I anticipated."

"The band did a great job, and everyone enjoyed them."

"Yes. Like they say—all's well that ends well." Kelly gave Shelby another quick hug. "I'm going to find Seth so we can get going. Thanks again." As Kelly walked away, she called over her shoulder. "Love you!"

"Love you, too." Shelby waved as Kelly disappeared through the barn door.

The sudden silence was almost palpable. Shelby plopped down on the bale of hay and stretched her legs out. Fatigue washed over her, leaving her feeling limp. She ran a hand along the back of her neck, which was damp with perspiration.

Cody still hadn't returned for the rest of the band's equipment. Shelby was wondering if she could leave him to it and head back to the house when he reappeared.

"I was about to go looking for you," Shelby said.

Cody must not have noticed her sitting there, because he jumped.

"Sorry. You startled me. I guess I was in my own world."

He scratched at a red spot on his left arm. Shelby thought he seemed nervous about something, but then again maybe he was simply as tired as she was.

"I'll get the rest of this stuff out of here." He gestured toward the tangle of cords and microphone stands still on the makeshift stage.

"Thanks."

Shelby hesitated but decided she'd stay until Cody had finished. If he was going to meet up with the rest of the band, he might need directions to the Dixie.

"You still out here?"

Shelby turned at the sound of Bert's voice.

"I'm waiting for Cody to load up the rest of his equipment. How about you? Shouldn't you be going home and getting some rest?"

Bert waved a hand at Shelby. "I'm fine. Don't go coddling me like I'm some kind of invalid. My gallbladder is a little dicky, that's all."

Shelby smiled to herself. Coddling Bert would be about as difficult as coddling a porcupine.

The stage was now empty—Cody had gone out to the van with the last load of equipment. He stuck his head through the open barn door. He was holding a lit cigarette behind his back.

"Do you know where Travis has gotten to? I called and Brian said he's not at the Dixie with them, and I don't see him outside." He frowned and glanced at his watch. "We've got to get on the road. We've got a gig tonight in South Bend, and we'll need time to set up."

Shelby and Bert walked outside with him.

"He didn't say anything to me." Shelby turned to Bert. "Did he go back to the house maybe?"

Bert shook her head. "Not while I was there. Unless he's sitting on the front porch."

"That's where I'd be if I were him," Shelby said. She turned to Cody. "Why don't you drive the van around to the front of the house, and we'll see if he's there?"

"Okay." Cody opened the door of the van and slid into the driver's seat.

The engine coughed, sputtered, knocked a few times, and finally started up.

"It looks like Travis needs to spend some of that money he's making on a new van," Bert said.

They watched as Cody pulled away, the ancient vehicle bumping over the rough ground until he reached the driveway.

Shelby started walking after the van, when Bert grabbed her arm.

Bert pointed into the distance and laughed. "Looks like your scarecrow has had a few too many."

Shelby turned and looked in the direction Bert was pointing, where a figure hung from a post, its chin resting on its chest, its shoulders slumped, and its legs buckled. A brimmed khaki hat had been plopped on its head.

Shelby gasped. "Bert, that isn't a scarecrow. I don't have one."

5

Dear Reader,

Did you know that scarecrows have been used by farmers for almost three thousand years? The Egyptians, Greeks, Romans, and Japanese all used them in ancient times. Farmers erect them in fields to scare away crows, blackbirds, sparrows, and other pest birds that might eat the farmers' newly cast seed. While scarecrows might work for a while, the birds usually get accustomed to their presence and are soon back to wreak havoc again.

Bert started toward the figure in the distance, but Shelby grabbed her by the arm and stopped her. "You stay here. I'll go see what it is. Maybe it's some kind of prank?"

"I'm coming with you," Bert said. "You don't have to

treat me with kid gloves. My gallbladder is past its prime, not my heart."

Shelby knew better than to argue. Besides, she really didn't want to approach—whatever it was—alone. Her stomach was churning and her palms were sweaty. Maybe she ought to call the police. But if it turned out to be nothing more than a joke, she would have wasted their time and looked like a ninny besides.

The sick feeling in the pit of Shelby's stomach intensified as she got closer. She looked over at Bert, who had turned awfully white despite the fact that she was perspiring in the heat.

Shelby was several yards away from the body when she knew this was no joke or childish prank. The figure tied to the pole was human and looked an awful lot like Travis Cooper, although with its chin slumped on its chest, Shelby couldn't see its face clearly. The faded and ripped jeans and white T-shirt appeared to be the same clothes Travis had been wearing, although at any given moment you could probably find a couple dozen men in Lovett wearing the exact same thing.

A single pesky fly settled on the man's cheek and Shelby half expected to see an arm reach up and brush it away.

But it was fairly obvious that Travis—if this was Travis—was beyond being bothered by a fly or much of anything else.

Shelby stopped a few yards away and put out a hand to stop Bert from going any closer.

"We need to get the police," Bert said.

"We ought to check for a pulse first," Shelby said, swallowing hard against the bile rising in her throat. She reached for Travis's arm and gently felt his wrist. She shook her head. "No sense in calling an ambulance. You're right. It's the police we need." Shelby took a step backward and felt her knees buckle momentarily. A buzzing sound filled her head and her vision became hazy. She had to quell the urge to start running until she couldn't run anymore. "We'll have to go back to the house. I don't have my cell phone with me."

"You go. Billy is outside playing. I wouldn't want him to come near this."

Dear Reader, you know how odd things go through your mind in times of stress? That's what happened to me as I ran back to the house. Things like, did Billy change out of his good clothes before going out to play? I suppose it's our mind's way of cushioning us against a reality we're not ready to accept.

Shelby felt like she was moving in slow motion as she made her way back to the house. Each step she took felt deliberate as if she had to think about it—right foot, left foot, right foot. Finally she reached the door to the mudroom and dashed through it, letting it slam shut in back of her—something she was always trying to get the children not to do. Her cell phone was on the kitchen table. She grabbed it, took a deep breath to steady her hands, and dialed 911.

The dispatcher answered immediately and assured her that a squad car would be on the way.

Shelby slipped the phone into her pocket and went back outside to wait for the police.

Her brother-in-law, Frank, was a detective on the Lovett police force. Things had been a bit awkward between them since the fall, when Frank had made it plain that he was in love with Shelby. But in spite of that, when his dusty pickup truck pulled into the driveway ahead of the squad car, Shelby felt an overwhelming sense of relief. She knew she was now in good hands.

Shelby was again struck by Frank's resemblance to Bill—although Frank's brown hair was shot through with gray strands and thinning on top, and Bill had gone to his grave with a full head of dark hair—as he walked up the driveway toward her. It had nearly made her fall in love with him in return, but she realized that wasn't fair to him. He deserved to have someone who loved him for himself and not because he evoked poignant memories of another man.

Frank pulled off his baseball cap and ran a hand through his hair as he walked toward Shelby. He was wearing his usual uniform—jeans as faded as Travis's had been and a shirt with the sleeves rolled up.

"Shelby." He grabbed her by the shoulders as he scrutinized her face. "Are you okay?"

"Yes," Shelby said, although her voice shook slightly.

Dear Reader, I wanted to say, "I'm fine now that you're here," but that would have given Frank the wrong idea.

"Tell me what happened," Frank said. "All I got from dispatch was that there was a dead body."

"I'm afraid I wasn't terribly coherent." Shelby shook her head. "You'd think after finding those other two bodies . . ."

"It's something you never really get used to." Frank put a hand over Shelby's. "And you wouldn't want to. No one should be that jaded."

Shelby noticed the two patrol officers were keeping a respectful distance, static occasionally squawking from the radios on their hips.

"We thought it was a scarecrow at first, but I don't have a scarecrow." Shelby knew she was rambling, but she couldn't help it.

Frank looked confused. "A scarecrow?"

"Yes. The body . . . Travis's body . . . has been strung up to look like a scarecrow."

Frank drew his brows together, creasing the skin between them. "Who is Travis?"

"Travis Cooper. He's the front man for the band Kelly hired to play at her wedding."

Frank blew out his breath. "Okay." He hesitated. "You're sure he's dead?"

Shelby nodded her head.

"You'd better take me to where you found the body."

"Bert's standing guard," Shelby said as they picked their way across the field and past a verdant patch where early lettuces in tidy rows were unfurling their pale green leaves.

"You want us to come, Detective?" one of the patrolmen, whose hair was curling up around the edges of his hat, said.

"Yes." Frank waved a hand toward them. "It sounds like we're going to need to secure the scene."

They continued to walk until Travis's figure came into view. Frank gave a loud whistle. "This certainly is one for the books," he said.

"Thanks, Bert, for standing guard," Shelby said when they reached Travis's body. The bodice of Bert's dress was splotched with damp patches and the hair around her face was limp.

"Why don't you go back to the house and get a cold drink?" Shelby said. "You must be roasting out here. You'll find some pitchers of iced tea and lemonade in the refrigerator."

Bert looked reluctant to leave, but Frank waved a hand at her. "I'll catch up with you inside," he said as she started to walk back toward the farmhouse.

Frank began to examine the body. He circled the post twice, his brows furrowed. "There's no blood or obvious signs of trauma," he said as if he was talking to himself. He took off his hat and scratched his head. "No sign of a bullet wound either as far as I can see." He sighed. "I suppose the autopsy will tell us how he died. One thing I think we can be sure of—he didn't die from natural causes."

He turned to the patrolmen. "One of you had better get the medical examiner out here." He looked at Shelby. "He's going to love this one—a real puzzle."

Frank squatted down and examined Travis's body again as if the slightly different angle might reveal something new. He sighed and straightened up. His knees gave a loud crack.

"Tell me about Travis. He was here with his band for the wedding? So not local, I take it."

"Actually he is local. According to Bert, he grew up in Lovett but changed his name when he decided to go on-stage."

Frank gave a bark of laughter. "Leave it to Bert. She would know."

"She said he's Debbie Coster's boy. The name rings a bell, but that's about all."

"First name?"

"It was—let me think—Robert. But apparently everyone called him Butch."

Frank sat back on his haunches. "That does ring a bell, now that you mention it." He scratched the side of his nose. "He was on that show, wasn't he?"

"Yes. *America Can Sing*."

"Doreen at the station is always talking about that program. I don't have much time for television watching myself."

By now the patrolmen had finished wrestling with the crime tape and had strung it up around the scene. Frank lifted it up and ducked underneath.

"So the killer could be anybody," Frank groaned. "A member of the band, a guest at the wedding, or someone here in Lovett." His eyes narrowed. "Speaking of the band—are they still here?"

"Cody—he's one of the guitar players—is over by the house." Shelby gestured in that direction. "He was looking for Travis. I'll have to go and tell him about—"

"Let me talk to him first. I want to get his reaction to the news. Does he have any reason to hate Travis that you know of?"

Shelby shrugged. "I don't know. I don't really know anything about him. Travis did seem to expect him to do all the work, and frankly, Cody didn't look too happy about it."

"Not a particularly good reason to kill someone, but then, is there ever really a good reason?" Frank kicked at a clump of weeds with the toe of his boot. "What about the rest of the band? How many are there?"

"There's Brian—he's the manager and the band's drummer. And Paislee, who plays the tambourine and sings duets with Travis. Cody—who I've told you about. Then there's Peter. He plays the guitar. He's Kelly's cousin."

Frank grunted. "You said Travis is a local boy." Frank rubbed the spot between his eyebrows. "So the murderer could be someone from his past just as easily as someone in the band. Someone who's maybe harbored a grudge and saw this as their opportunity to get revenge."

Frank toed the clump of weeds again. "So that means it could have been a guest at the wedding who might have been surprised to see Travis back in town. And wasn't too pleased about it."

Shelby's mind immediately flew to Seth and his reaction when he saw Travis. She pushed the thought away quickly.

"You've remembered something?" Frank said.

"No, why?" Shelby put on her best poker face, which even under the best of circumstances wasn't particularly good.

"The look on your face . . ."

"No. It's nothing." Shelby looked away quickly.

"So is the rest of the band around here somewhere? I hope they're not halfway to Kansas or something by now."

Shelby shook her head. "They said they were going to the Dixie to get a drink."

Frank pivoted on his heel and pointed to one of the patrolmen. "Get out to the Dixie and round up the rest of the band. There should be two men—Brian and another guitar player. And a girl named Paislee. Right?" He turned to Shelby.

She nodded.

"Do you want me to stay?" the younger patrolman asked. "And guard the scene."

"Yes. No, never mind. You go, too, in case they give Dennis any trouble. I'll wait here for the ME."

The second patrolman took off at a trot. Jenkins, who had been lolling in the sun, raised his head, and for a moment it looked as if he would take off after him, but instead he sighed and put his head back down.

"So, there was no one else at the wedding that you know of who might have known Travis?"

Shelby went still. What could she say? If she didn't tell Frank about Seth, she wouldn't be lying, but it would certainly be a sin of omission. But there was no way Seth was capable of murder. And Kelly and Seth deserved the chance to enjoy their honeymoon—brief as it would be.

"You're holding out on me," Frank said, and Shelby jumped. "Why?"

Shelby realized that if she didn't tell Frank about Seth, it would make things look worse when he found out.

"Seth—he's the bridegroom—knew Travis when they were in college together."

"I know Seth," Frank said. "He patched up my arm that time a drunk lunged at me with a broken beer bottle when I tried to bust up a fight behind the diner. I don't suppose he had anything to do with this, but I'll have to talk to him anyway."

Shelby felt guilty—guilty for telling Frank about Seth and guilty for not telling him that Seth had a very good reason to hate Travis.

"Is Seth still here?"

"No. He and Kelly were going to his place to change before leaving on their honeymoon."

Frank groaned and pulled a cell phone from his pocket.

"Doreen," he said when the call was answered. "Send a car around to Dr. Seth Gregson's house and ask him and his new bride to come down to the station." Frank listened for a moment. "Yes, he just got married." Another pause. "Today."

Frank rolled his eyes as he ended the call. "When it comes to knowing what's going on in Lovett, Doreen is almost as good as Bert. But it looks like this wedding wasn't even on her radar." He laughed. "She sounded annoyed. Go figure."

Suddenly Jenkins was on his feet, his ears alert and his head tilting this way and that as if he was trying to pick up a faint signal. He'd noticed someone in the distance. Within seconds, he'd taken off at a run to check out the newcomer.

"There's the ME," Frank said.

"What have we got here?" the man said when he reached the spot where Frank and Shelby were standing. "How long has he been there like that?"

"That's what I'm hoping you'll be able to tell me," Frank said. "Not long, though—not more than an hour or two."

"I'd better get on with it, then." The ME smiled, revealing a gap between his two front teeth. He opened his bag, his hand hovering over the contents.

"I need to ask someone a few questions." Frank nodded at the ME. "I'll be back."

Shelby stared at all the bowls and utensils stacked on her kitchen counter waiting to be washed. She opened the cupboard and reached for the dish soap, then changed her mind and slammed the door shut again.

She'd been on her feet all day already. The dirty dishes would still be there in an hour. She grabbed a pitcher of iced tea from the refrigerator, poured herself a glass, and pulled out a kitchen chair. She sank into it gratefully and propped her feet on another chair. It felt heavenly to sit down.

She had almost finished her iced tea when the door to the mudroom opened and Frank stuck his head into the kitchen.

"Okay if I come in?"

"Of course." Shelby pulled her feet off the chair and wiggled into a straighter posture. She waved toward the refrigerator. "There's iced tea, if you want it. Glasses are in the cupboard next to the sink."

"Thanks."

Frank helped himself, then took a seat opposite Shelby. He pulled off his baseball cap and ran a hand through his hair.

"Was the ME able to tell you anything?"

Frank took a sip of his iced tea and swiped the back of his hand across his mouth. "Not very much, I'm afraid." He frowned. "There's no obvious evidence of any kind of foul play—no knife wounds, bullet wounds, broken bones . . . nothing. The only thing the ME found was a bruise on the back of his neck that vaguely suggested a thumbprint. But whether that has anything to do with Travis's death, he can't say."

Frank massaged his forehead with his fingertips. "We know it can't have been an accident. Not with Travis strung up on that pole like a scarecrow."

"So he couldn't tell you a thing?"

Frank shrugged. "Nothing useful. He said rigor had barely set in, so Travis hadn't been dead all that long. But we already knew that from your description of his movements." Frank drained his glass, making a slurping sound as he reached the bottom. "Hopefully he'll be able to tell us more after the autopsy."

6

Dear Reader,

Have you tried roasting vegetables? Take it from me, they are ten times better that way. Roasting brings out their sweetness and caramelizes their exterior. You can use almost any vegetable you fancy and even Brussels sprouts become a delectable side dish. It's really simple to do, too. Just be sure not to crowd your baking sheet or the veggies will steam instead of roast. You can add herbs and spices, use different types of oil, add aromatics like garlic, ginger, and shallots, and finish them off with something crunchy like crisp bacon, fried onions, or nuts and seeds. Believe me, you'll no longer have to beg your children (and maybe your hubby) to eat their vegetables when you prepare them this way.

After Frank left, Shelby changed into a pair of shorts and a T-shirt and decided to tackle the dishes. She didn't want to leave them sitting out all night. They would be harder to clean in the morning, and besides, she hated waking up to a sink full of food-encrusted plates.

Shelby slipped a large plain glass bowl into the sudsy water and began to scrub it. Suddenly she pulled it out of the water and held it up, looking at it. It wasn't her bowl—someone must have brought it in by mistake. It looked like it matched the other bowls the caterers had been using. Shelby finished washing it, dried it, and put it aside. She'd take it over to Grilling Gals next time she went into town.

Shelby had just finished putting away the last serving spoon when there was a frantic knocking on the front door.

She put down her dish towel. Maybe it was Frank with more questions?

But it was Kelly standing on her doorstep, no longer in her wedding dress but in her usual uniform of faded and well-worn jeans and a navy T-shirt with *Lovett Feed Store* in white letters on the front. The outfit looked incongruous with her unaccustomed makeup and her hair, which was still in its elegant French braid.

Kelly's eyes were red and her mascara was smeared.

"Oh, Shelby," she wailed as Shelby let her in. "It's all my fault." She put her hands over her face, and Shelby could see her shoulders shaking.

"If only I hadn't asked the band to play at our wedding," Kelly said through her fingers.

"It's not your fault Travis was murdered," Shelby exclaimed. "You can't possibly think that."

"It's not that." Kelly let her hands drop into her lap. "The police came by—Seth was putting our suitcase in the trunk

of his car, and I was checking that all the lights were off—
and asked us to come down to the station to answer some
questions."

"They're talking to everybody."

"Maybe. But I've never been asked to actually go to the
station."

"I'm sure it was simply more convenient for the police
that way. Did you talk to Frank?"

"Yes. He tried to put me at ease, but I was still so scared
my hands were shaking." Kelly pulled a tissue from her
pocket and blew her nose. "And they had Seth and me in
separate rooms, which made it worse."

Shelby reached out and squeezed Kelly's hand.

"They asked me about the hat that had been on Travis's
head. They showed me a picture." Kelly shivered. "I couldn't
see anything but the hat, but still . . . I could just imagine . . .

"And they asked if I recognized the hat." Kelly twisted
the hem of her shirt between her fingers. "It was Seth's hat.
A goofy-looking thing. He bought it on his trip to Australia
before he started medical school. He wore it whenever he
had to be out in the sun." She touched her face. "You know
how pale he is."

"He was wearing it while we were setting up, wasn't he?"
Shelby remembered the hat—khaki with a floppy brim.

"Yes. He said he left it on one of the tables and forgot
about it. Someone obviously took it."

"Did you tell the police that?"

Kelly's face reddened. "I didn't." Her voice was barely
above a whisper. She looked down at her hands. "I didn't
tell them it was Seth's hat."

By now Kelly had twisted the whole bottom half of her
T-shirt around her left fist.

"Seth must have told them it was his, though, if they asked him about it. And I don't see why they wouldn't have asked him if they asked you."

Kelly shrugged. "I suppose so." She peered up at Shelby with a pleading look on her face. "I couldn't tell them. Not after that story Seth told me about him and Travis . . . What if Seth had something to do with it? I can't help seeing the expression on his face when he first saw Travis. And how angry he was."

"Seth's a pretty rational guy. He wouldn't let something that happened so many years ago drive him to murder. And on his wedding day?"

Kelly gulped and fiddled with the frayed hem of her T-shirt.

"Come on, Kelly. You know Seth better than that. You have to know he would never do something so . . . so heinous as murder."

Kelly sniffed loudly. "You're right." She gave a tiny smile. "I do know Seth better than that. I guess I needed someone to remind me."

Shelby reached over and squeezed Kelly's hand. "The police will find out who did it. Don't worry."

iiiiiiiiiiiiiiiiiiiiiiiii

St. Andrews was buzzing with talk of the murder the next day. It didn't take long for news that dramatic to circulate among the residents of Lovett. Shelby often thought their communication system was far swifter and more accurate than any of the latest technology.

The buzzing inside the church before the Sunday service began reached a fever pitch as Shelby slipped into her accustomed pew, and didn't stop until the choir processed in and drowned out any attempts at further conversation with their strong voices.

Mrs. Willoughby, the church secretary, had organized a craft fair after the service to help raise money for the church, which badly needed a new roof and numerous other equally urgent repairs that the parish could ill afford. She was very efficient in an officious way, which often put her at odds with the rest of the congregation.

As soon as the service was over, Billy took off with two of his friends and headed toward the grassy area between the church and the rectory, where they began an impromptu game of tag. Shelby headed down the sloping hill alongside the church where booths were set up featuring crafts of every sort, from handmade belts to macramé dream catchers. The St. Andrews knitting group, of which Shelby was a somewhat reluctant member, had their own booth, where they displayed hand-knitted baby blankets and caps as well as adult-sized scarves, mittens, and gloves.

The day was overcast with such high humidity it made everything wet. Shelby's white blouse was damp in patches, and her pleated cotton skirt stuck to the backs of her legs, making her feel decidedly uncomfortable.

"At least it's not raining," Mrs. Willoughby said as she approached Shelby on the lawn. "But it would have been nice if it had been as fine as it was yesterday." She frowned. "What a shame that lovely wedding you planned was ruined by that young man getting himself killed."

Shelby didn't think Travis had exactly *gotten himself killed* as Mrs. Willoughby put it, but she decided it would probably be politic to not point that out.

"I imagine the police must have arrested the culprit by now. Was it some vagrant passing by who thought he might take advantage of the opportunity to relieve the young man of his wallet?"

Shelby had to smile. Mrs. Willoughby was quite possibly the only person she knew—or had ever known—who would use the word *vagrant. Dear Reader, the word makes me think of a dusty old volume by Charles Dickens or George Eliot.*

"I honestly don't know," Shelby said, removing a strand of hair from where it had stuck to her forehead.

Mrs. Willoughby frowned again and gave Shelby a severe look. "But surely with your brother-in-law on the force, you must have some news."

"I'm afraid not," Shelby said, attempting to inch away from Mrs. Willoughby.

Mrs. Willoughby frowned again—even more sternly this time—and fiddled with the jet beads around her neck.

"You're so good at solving mysteries." Mrs. Willoughby patted Shelby on the arm.

Shelby opened her mouth to protest, but Mrs. Willoughby sailed on undeterred. She lowered her voice. "We have another mystery here in Lovett that I hope you will look into for us."

"Oh? What's that?"

It couldn't be another murder, Shelby thought. She'd have known about that by now.

"This is just between you and me. It can't go any further." Mrs. Willoughby lowered her face so close to Shelby's that Shelby could see the wiry white hairs protruding from Mrs. Willoughby's chin. "But I happened to overhear the reverend and that woman talking—"

"Isabel Stone?"

Mrs. Willoughby's nostrils flared. "Yes. Her." She took

a deep, fluttery breath. "I couldn't hear every word they said, of course. They were in the reverend's office and the door was closed."

Dear Reader, I am quite sure Mrs. Willoughby had a glass pressed to the wall.

"But it sounded as if . . ." Mrs. Willoughby stopped. She made a noise like she was choking. "It sounded as if they are planning on getting married."

"That's wonderful," Shelby said without thinking.

Mrs. Willoughby reared back as if Shelby were a rattlesnake about to strike.

"Wonderful? How can you say that? We know nothing about that woman. Nothing. Nothing whatsoever."

"Don't you think Reverend Mather is old enough to make his own decisions?"

Mrs. Willoughby dismissed that idea with a derogatory snort. "Daniel? He fell for Prudence, his first wife, didn't he? When everyone else could see her for what she was. A troublemaker and a busybody. No wonder she got herself killed."

That wasn't exactly true, Shelby thought. Prudence had fooled plenty of people.

"Before Daniel makes another mistake, we need to know more about Isabel Stone."

"Like what?" Shelby pictured Mrs. Willoughby demanding an entire dossier on the woman from birth to the present time.

"Well, where she comes from . . . who her people are . . . things like that. We certainly don't want some snake in our midst."

"I hardly think—"

But Mrs. Willoughby was already shaking her head, setting her chins wagging. "That's what I wanted to talk to you about," she said, tapping Shelby smartly on the arm. "We need your help."

"Me?" Shelby pointed to herself. "I don't see how I can help."

"You know how to find out . . . things. You've done it before," Mrs. Willoughby said in an accusatory tone.

"Yes, but—"

"You have to help us. I'm appealing to you as a member of St. Andrews Church."

Shelby sighed. "What is it you want me to do?"

"Find out what you can about the woman. Put our minds at rest."

Shelby didn't think anything was going to put Mrs. Willoughby's mind at rest. She hadn't liked Isabel from the moment Isabel set foot in St. Andrews Church, and Shelby doubted anything was going to change her mind.

But Shelby also knew it was useless to argue. Mrs. Willoughby was known for always getting her own way and for good reason.

"Fine," Shelby said finally. "I'll see what I can find out. But I can't make any promises."

Mrs. Willoughby beamed. "Thank you, dear. We'll all feel so much better when we know the truth."

Maybe the truth was simply that Isabel was a completely normal, honorable, and likable middle-aged lady, Shelby thought.

"I'd better be going. I promised I would buy Billy a cupcake from the bakery stall."

"Let me know when you have some information," Mrs. Willoughby called after her as Shelby walked away.

Shelby passed the St. Andrews knitting group's booth and felt a pang of conscience. All the members had worked so hard to have items available for the fair, and Shelby hadn't been able to contribute a thing. Her knitting hadn't gotten any better during the course of the year, although she'd tried her best. The scarf she was knitting with the intention of offering it for sale at the fair had turned out uneven and pocked with holes where she'd dropped stitches. It certainly wasn't something anyone would pay money for unless perhaps the shopper was going for a seriously Goth look.

Several people approached Shelby as she made her way through the crowd, and she did her best to avoid conversations about Travis's murder, but of course it was the only thing people wanted to talk about.

She was heading toward a booth where they were selling handmade beaded jewelry when she spotted a face in the crowd that looked familiar although she couldn't immediately place the person.

As she got closer, she realized it was Paislee Fields, the girl who had performed with Travis at Kelly's wedding. She was wearing a flowing peasant blouse and had a stack of handmade-looking bracelets dangling from her left arm.

"You probably don't remember me," Shelby said, but Paislee interrupted her.

"I do. You're the lady from the farm, right?"

"How are you doing?" Shelby said. Paislee looked as if she hadn't slept very much the previous night.

Paislee shrugged. "Okay, I guess. It's been a shock—Travis dying like that. We hadn't known each other all that long, but still, working together so closely, we got to know each other quickly." She dabbed at her eyes with the hem of her blouse. "It didn't help that it was so noisy last night at that motel over on the highway." She pointed in back of her. "Trucks going by all night long." She shuddered. "The police won't let us leave. We had to cancel our gig in South Bend."

"I'm sorry."

Paislee shrugged again and made a face. "There's nothing to do here and the desk clerk mentioned this fair." She waved a paper bag toward Shelby. "I bought some earrings and a necklace. I like this handmade stuff." She touched the bracelets on her wrist.

The clouds had thinned and the sun peeked through in spots, steam rising from the damp ground. Shelby fanned herself with her hand. She felt the hair around her face curling in the humidity.

"Do you need a ride or . . . or anything?" Shelby said.

"No, but thanks. Cody brought me. I suppose I should get going. I'm sure he's bored waiting for me."

"He works awfully hard, I noticed."

Paislee rolled her eyes. "Travis treated him awfully bad sometimes." A faint blush colored her cheeks. "Cody has a crush on me and Travis teased him about it."

"He must have resented that."

"I don't know. Cody's a good sport. I don't think he minded."

Dear Reader, I seriously doubt that.

"What about you and Travis? Were you—"

"An item?" Paislee finished for her. "We sing together and yeah, we've been together on and off. When I first joined the group, I started going out with Cody, but then Travis started paying attention to me, and, well, he was hard to resist. Know what I mean?"

Shelby nodded. "I'm sorry. This must be so difficult for you—Travis dying the way he did."

Paislee braced her thin shoulders. "I don't know. After what Travis did . . . well, maybe he had it coming."

"What do you mean?"

Paislee's face closed down. "Nothing. I shouldn't have

said that." She looked around. "Cody must be wondering where I am."

She turned around and quickly disappeared into the crowd.

What had Paislee meant by saying Travis had it coming to him? How much did Cody resent Travis's teasing? Not to mention the fact that Travis had stolen Paislee away from Cody.

Maybe Cody minded more than he let on and had been only waiting for a chance to get even. And that chance had come yesterday.

𝗂𝗂𝗂𝗂𝗂𝗂𝗂𝗂𝗂𝗂𝗂𝗂𝗂𝗂𝗂𝗂𝗂𝗂𝗂𝗂𝗂

Billy walked in the house when they got home from the fair and before Shelby could say anything, he'd bolted through the mudroom door and outside to play. Amelia hadn't wanted to go in the first place and was up in her room. Shelby knew without even looking that she was probably lying on her bed texting her friends.

Shelby went upstairs to change. The temperature got warmer and warmer the higher she climbed. She peeled off her damp blouse and skirt and kicked off her shoes, exchanging them for a pair of shorts, a T-shirt, and her gardening clogs. She grabbed a hair elastic off the dresser and pulled her hair back into a makeshift ponytail. It felt good to get it off the back of her neck.

Shelby went into the bathroom and splashed some cold water on her face before going downstairs and outside to her herb patch. She was thinking about Mrs. Willoughby and the promise she had managed to wrangle from Shelby to pry into poor Isabel Stone's life. Isabel was simply minding her own business—which was what Mrs. Willoughby ought to be doing. If Reverend Mather wanted to date Isabel, that was his choice. He was a grown man.

Shelby picked a handful of different herbs—thyme, rosemary, and some basil. She planned to make chicken baked with lemon and herbs for dinner with a salad of red butterhead lettuce, oven-roasted carrots, and buttered potatoes. She would share the recipes on her Farmer's Daughter blog the next day.

She stood up with a slight groan and moved to another section of the garden, where she picked some of the tender leaves of red-tinged lettuce, then carried her bounty into the kitchen. She was washing the lettuce when the telephone rang.

"Hello?"

"Shelby? This is Peter. Peter Baskin. I'm Kelly Thacker's cousin. It's about the band. Kelly said I should call you." His voice rose up at the end as if he was nervous.

"Hi, Peter."

"Listen. I . . . we . . . were wondering . . ." His voice trailed off.

Shelby held the phone between her ear and her shoulder and continued dunking the leaves of lettuce in the cold water in the sink.

"It's like this, see. We've decided to keep the band together. Our manager—that's Brian—thinks it's a good idea."

"Yes." Shelby couldn't imagine what on earth this had to do with her.

"But we need a place to practice. We're bringing in a new lead singer, and we haven't worked together before. We have to iron the kinks out, if you know what I mean. Before we perform our first gig."

"Oh?"

"The police aren't letting us leave town yet and there's no way we can set up in our motel room."

Shelby still wasn't sure where this was going. With the phone still clamped to her ear, she gathered the leaves of lettuce together, removed them from their cold-water bath, and dropped them into the salad spinner.

"So we wondered," Peter said again, "if we could use your barn? Just for a few days—the police have to let us go soon." He paused. "We'll pay you."

It was the last thing Shelby had expected and for a moment she was at a loss as to what to say. What if it was one of the band members who had killed Travis? It wasn't beyond the realm of possibility. Then again, Peter was Kelly's cousin, which practically made him family. And the extra money would be a bonus. For a moment she allowed herself to dream of taking the kids to Disney World.

Then a thought occurred to her, and she giggled. Would the music put Jake's cows off giving milk? Maybe they would like the band's signature blend of country and rock.

"I guess that would be okay." Shelby began spinning the lettuce dry. "The generators are still here. The rental company isn't picking them up until next week."

"Really? You're sure?"

"Yes."

"Thanks so much. Kelly said you're the best, and she's right," Peter said.

Shelby heard Peter say something to someone in the room with him and suspected he was giving the other band members the good news.

"There's just one thing," Shelby said, fidgeting with the handle of the salad spinner. "I don't know how late you're planning on practicing, but you'll have to stop by nine o'clock. People around here go to bed early."

All she needed, Shelby thought, was complaints from her neighbors, although she doubted whether the sound would even carry that far. But she didn't want to be kept up until midnight herself listening to the band rehearse, and the kids had to be up early for school.

"That's fine. Can we come over now, then?"

"Sure. I don't see why not. If you need anything from me, just knock on the door. I'll be home."

iiiiiiiiiiiiiiiiiiiiiiiiii

Shelby heard the noise of an engine and when she looked out the window, she saw the band's dusty van, with Cody at the wheel, followed by Brian's rusted and dented Taurus coming down the drive. Shelby let the curtain fall back into place and took a seat at the kitchen table. Her chicken was all prepped and in the refrigerator ready to cook for dinner. She opened up her laptop and scrolled to the blog she had started and quickly typed in the recipe for the chicken, trying to remember exactly what proportion of herbs she'd used. Once again she swore that next time she would take notes while creating a recipe.

She added some of the pictures she'd taken as she'd prepped the meal, and once the chicken was baked, she'd get some photos of the end result with the skin glazed and golden brown from the oven.

Shelby was finishing up her blog entry when she heard faint strains of music floating in the open kitchen window. Shelby moved closer until she could hear guitar notes and drumbeats. A voice joined in, but it wasn't Paislee's—it was a male voice.

Curious, Shelby stepped out the back door. She could hear the music more clearly now and someone singing. Was that the new lead singer Peter had mentioned?

Without realizing it, Shelby began walking toward the barn. The person singing sounded eerily like Travis, but perhaps it was the fact that she was hearing him sing one of Travis's biggest hits that made it seem that way.

Shelby reached the barn and stood listening for another moment, tilting her head back to catch the rays of the sun on her face. After a moment, she went over to the open barn door and looked in. A young man was standing at the microphone—tall and willowy just like Travis had been. Was it an illusion or did all young men look the same? Shelby wondered. The thought made her suddenly feel old.

The young man looked like the same fellow Jessie had been talking to—arguing with, it looked more like—at the wedding.

The song ended and the band began playing another one—something Shelby hadn't heard them play before. Paislee joined the young man at the microphone. They were singing a love song and Paislee's beautiful voice was filled with longing and heartache. Shelby wondered if the emotion was real and she'd actually been in love with Travis, or if she was simply an accomplished performer able to call up different emotions at will.

The song gave Shelby goose bumps and she rubbed her bare arms. She found herself thinking of Bill and how much she missed him. She felt tears spring into her eyes—she'd thought she was over the worst of the loss, but perhaps the pain never went away completely.

The last notes of the song died away and for a moment everyone was still, wrapped in the spell conjured up by the music. To Shelby, it looked like a scene in a movie being put on pause.

"Okay, everybody, let's take a break," Brian called out, breaking the spell, and the band scattered like marbles flung on a bare floor.

Paislee wandered over to where Shelby was standing by the open barn door.

"That was beautiful," Shelby said. She dashed at a tear that had formed at the corner of her eye.

Paislee shrugged. She looked embarrassed. "I'm glad you liked it. It still needs a little work."

"I thought it was perfect. You sounded as if you'd spent hours practicing it already."

Paislee looked slightly uncomfortable and began fiddling with the beaded bracelets around her wrist.

"How did you find a replacement for Travis so quickly? And he sounds so much like Travis."

Paislee's discomfort intensified. She drew circles on the floor with her toe. "The singer is Jax. He's Travis's brother."

No wonder he looked and sounded so familiar, Shelby thought. He was certainly as talented as his brother.

She wondered why Travis had become a star when his brother hadn't. And had that caused problems between the two of them?

7

Dear Reader,

Did you know it's easy to store your root vegetables for the winter? First, leave them in the ground as long as possible, but do pick them before the first black frost, which occurs when the temperatures are low and the humidity is very, very low. Harvest them in the morning and let them dry throughout the day.

You shouldn't wash them after picking, and you should pick the best specimens—no nicks or bruises. They need a cool, moist, dark environment like your unheated cellar, your garage, or under the back porch. You can pack them in sand, sawdust, or dry leaves. And be sure not to crowd them.

By canning, storing, or freezing your late fall crop, you can enjoy the bounty of homegrown vegetables all winter long.

Billy shot into the house as Shelby was peeling carrots in the kitchen. His face and hands were filthy, his shirt had acquired another hole, and the knees of his jeans were caked with mud. Shelby smiled—in other words, it was business as usual.

She was glad that Billy didn't seem to have been too affected by Travis's death. His eyes had widened when he saw the police pull into the driveway, and Shelby knew he had been disappointed when Bert had shooed him inside the house.

Amelia had reacted more strongly, and Shelby suspected that the crush she'd developed on Travis had made her feel his death more keenly, even though she didn't actually know him. She was at the age when girls' emotions were easily triggered.

Shelby cut the carrots into strips. She planned to toss them with olive oil, salt, pepper, and some thyme and roast them to bring out their sweetness.

She glanced out the kitchen window. The low-hanging clouds had parted to reveal patches of bright blue sky. Shelby felt a sense of contentment wash over her—no matter what happened at Love Blossom Farm, the place would always bring her peace.

Shelby leaned across the counter and flipped on the radio—Amelia thought she was a dinosaur for having one in the first place when everyone was now playing music on their phones—and one of Travis's songs came on. She stopped for a moment to listen. He really had been very talented.

She knew he'd been on *America Can Sing*, but it wasn't a program she usually watched. Shelby washed and dried her hands and slid into a chair at the kitchen table, where her laptop was still sitting out. She jiggled the mouse and the screen sprang to life.

Shelby typed in Travis's name and numerous entries popped up. There was the usual Wikipedia paragraph along with Travis's own Web site and a link that led to *America Can Sing*'s site.

Shelby clicked on the Wikipedia site. Not for the first time, she wondered how they'd gotten along before the Internet.

The entry on Travis wasn't particularly detailed—he was born in Lovett, had a brother and a sister, and had dropped out of college before graduation to be on *America Can Sing*. Nothing really new there.

Shelby scrolled down until a line caught her eye—*Travis and his brother, Jax, began performing while in high school and were on the fast track to success when they were in an auto accident. Travis sustained minor injuries, but Jax spent several months recovering in a rehab facility while Travis went on to win the title on* America Can Sing. *The duo never did get back together even after Jax recovered, and Travis went on to pursue a solo career with his backup band.*

Shelby sat and stared at the words for a moment. Then she quickly clicked on the *America Can Sing* site.

She read through the brief biography of Travis posted there—there was no mention of Jax or his and Travis's former partnership. Shelby leaned back in her chair and stared at the screen. How must Jax have felt about that?

There was a knock on the mudroom screen door and Shelby jumped, wincing when her knee banged against the edge of the table. She pushed back her chair and went to see who it was.

"I'm sorry to bother you." Paislee hesitated outside the door. "But I wondered if I could use your bathroom."

"Of course. Come in." Shelby stepped aside to let Paislee

in. "It's down the hall." She gestured toward the kitchen door and the hallway beyond.

Paislee smiled. "Thanks."

Shelby read through a few more of the entries on Travis—a piece in a Michigan newspaper, a photograph and a one-paragraph story in *People* magazine, and an item in *Star* that had a picture of Travis with his arm around Paislee as they left a well-known restaurant in Nashville.

Shelby was so engrossed in her reading she didn't hear Paislee come into the kitchen and she was startled when she realized the girl was standing in back of her.

Paislee looked over Shelby's shoulder and tapped the screen with her finger.

"I see you're reading about Travis. It's still so hard to believe. . . ."

She began to cry and buried her face in her hands.

Shelby stood up and patted Paislee on the shoulder. "Let me get you some water."

She went to the sink, filled a glass, and handed it to Paislee.

"Thank you." She swiped at her eyes with the back of her hand. Shelby noticed her fingernails were jagged and bitten.

"Why don't you sit down?" Shelby said, resuming her seat at the table.

"Thanks." Paislee pulled out the kitchen chair opposite Shelby.

"I *have* been reading about Travis," Shelby said, fiddling with her computer mouse. "I didn't know he used to sing with his brother."

Paislee nodded. "He did until the accident at any rate. Jax gave it up after that."

"What happened?" Shelby leaned across the table toward Paislee.

"That was before I met Travis." Paislee began playing with some frayed strings that had come loose from one of her beaded bracelets. "I guess Jax took a corner a little too fast and . . ." She shrugged. "Travis wasn't too badly hurt, but Jax spent ages in the hospital."

"So Jax was driving."

"Yeah." Paislee took a sip of her water. "That's what Travis told me."

"Did Jax resent the fact that while he was struggling to recover from the accident, Travis's career was taking off? I mean, it sounds like Jax had been expecting the two of them to perform together."

Paislee shrugged again. "I don't know. I don't think so. Jax is pretty laid-back, and he and Travis have always been close."

After Paislee left, Shelby began to wonder. Wouldn't it have been normal for Jax to resent his brother's success?

But did Jax resent his brother enough to kill him?

||||||||||||||||||||||||||

Shelby was drying the last of the pots and pans when the front doorbell rang. She'd sent Billy up to take a bath and Amelia was in her room finishing up her homework. Or so she said—judging from the sound of the music drifting down the stairs, Shelby wondered how she was able to concentrate.

The song was familiar. For a moment Shelby couldn't place it, but then she realized it was Travis singing. She felt a sudden pang—a merciless killer had snuffed out a very bright light. Travis had had a great future ahead of him before someone snatched it away.

Shelby couldn't imagine being driven to murder—what on earth had Travis done to make someone hate him enough to feel justified in killing him? she wondered as she scurried to the foyer.

Frank was standing on her doorstep when she pulled open the front door. As always, the sight of him gave her pause—he looked so much like her late husband that she often thought her mind was playing tricks on her and it really was Bill standing there.

Shelby smoothed the front of her T-shirt, which had a wet splotch on it.

Frank twirled a baseball cap around and around in his hands.

"I hope I'm not disturbing you?"

Ever since Frank and Shelby had kissed—a moment Shelby half regretted and half never wanted to forget—there had been an invisible barrier between them, an awkwardness neither of them seemed to be able to get over.

"No." Shelby tucked her hair behind her ears. "Come in." She led Frank into the kitchen. "I was just finishing the dishes."

Frank took a deep breath. "It smells wonderful in here." He gave a half smile. "A lot better than my frozen microwaved dinner."

"There's plenty left—chicken with lemon and herbs, roasted carrots, and buttered potatoes. I could heat some up for you. I'm afraid the salad is all gone, though."

Frank's smile became a full grin. "You've twisted my arm." He frowned. "As long as it's not too much trouble."

Before Shelby could answer, Billy skidded into the room.

"Uncle Frank," he yelled before throwing himself into Frank's arms.

Billy's hair was damp, but the stubborn cowlick on top

of his head still stood up like a rooster's comb. He was wearing his Superman pajamas, and Shelby noticed that they'd gotten short on him since the last time she'd looked.

"Billy," Frank said, lifting his nephew into the air. "How's my favorite young man?"

Billy squealed in delight. "I took a bath and washed behind my ears and everything, just like Mom said to."

"Good for you." Frank put Billy down and patted him on the back. "I need to have a word with your mother in private, okay, champ? But how about I come over next weekend and you can practice your pitching?" He looked over at Shelby. "I hear you're almost as good as your old man was."

Billy's face turned red with pride. "That would be super, Uncle Frank."

After Billy left the room, Frank turned to Shelby and laughed. "I figured he wouldn't leave without some sort of bribe."

"You don't have to if you don't—"

"Don't be silly. I'll look forward to it."

Shelby turned away and opened the door of the refrigerator. She pulled out several foil-wrapped bundles and retrieved a plate from the cupboard.

"White or dark?" She opened one of the packages and looked at Frank, her fork poised over the chicken.

"Dark for me."

Bill had been a dark-meat fan, too, Shelby thought as she arranged the food on a plate and slipped it into the microwave.

Frank pulled out a kitchen chair and sank into it with a groan.

"Tired?" Shelby said as she pushed the appropriate buttons on the microwave.

Frank scrubbed his face with his hand. "A bit." He

looked up at Shelby. "I thought you'd want to know what we've found out."

The microwave dinged. Shelby pulled out the plate and slipped it in front of Frank. She opened a drawer and grabbed a fork and a knife and set them beside the plate.

"This looks delicious."

"Would you like some iced tea?"

Frank looked sheepish. "You wouldn't happen to have a beer, would you? It's been that kind of day."

Shelby wasn't much of a beer drinker, but she'd stashed in the refrigerator a couple of bottles that were left behind after Kelly's wedding.

"Here you go." She set a bottle in front of Frank and then took the chair opposite.

"What have you found out? Anything to do with Travis's murder?"

Frank nodded as he finished chewing his bite of chicken. He pointed at the plate with his fork. "This not only looks delicious—it is delicious," he said.

Shelby smiled. The way to a man's heart really was through a home-cooked meal.

"The ME phoned tonight. He'd finished the autopsy. And in record time, if you ask me—this new guy is really on the ball. A real eager beaver." Frank forked up a few carrot spears and took a bite.

Shelby waited while he chewed.

"He, too, was puzzled by the cause of death because nothing was particularly evident just by examining the body. It did look as if Travis had been hit on the head, but the blow certainly hadn't been enough to kill him. Stun him maybe—but not much more than that. Other than that, there was only that bruise on his neck—but that hardly would have killed him either."

"But he did find something?" Shelby said, absentmindedly twirling a lock of hair around her finger.

Frank nodded as he cut a piece of chicken. "He found pulmonary edema—in layman's terms, water in Travis's lungs." Frank pointed his fork at Shelby. "Now, the ME also said that pulmonary edema could come from natural causes—heart failure, for instance—or even from something like a drug overdose."

"Pulmonary edema? Water in the—"

"Lungs, yes."

"As in drowning?" Shelby raised her eyebrows.

"There's no definitive test for drowning, according to the ME, but that seems the most likely. His heart was perfectly fine, so no reason it would have failed, and preliminary toxicology tests showed he didn't have any drugs in his system—legal or otherwise."

"But drowning? There wasn't any water. . . ." Shelby wrinkled her forehead.

She flashed back to the scene with Travis hanging from that pole like a scarecrow. How could he have drowned in the middle of a dry field? It didn't make sense.

"Oh!" Shelby exclaimed as a thought came to her.

Frank looked up sharply. "What is it?"

"The trough. I'd almost forgotten about it. I noticed it on Saturday morning. I thought I might turn it into a planter."

Seeing the confused look on Frank's face, Shelby hurried to explain. "There's an old rusted trough out in the field—left over from back when my parents kept cows. It was filled with rainwater."

Frank stopped with his fork halfway to his mouth. "So the killer could have held Travis's head underwater. That would explain the bruise on the back of his neck." He put down his fork. "The ME hasn't had the results from all his tests yet. They'll be doing an analysis of the water found in his lungs—that should tell us something. But I think you're right—someone held Travis's head in the water in that trough until he drowned."

"And then strung him up like a scarecrow."

8

Dear Reader,

If you buy your eggs in the supermarket, most likely they are either white or pale brown. But different breeds of chickens lay different-colored eggs. For instance, your Araucanas, Ameraucanas, and Cream Legbars lay pale blue eggs. Marans lay deep brown eggs—much darker than your usual brown eggs. Welsummers also lay brown eggs—deep chocolate-colored ones with darker brown speckles—and your Penedesencas will give you a very dark brown egg.

Sometimes Shelby felt like it was always Monday morning. Not that there was any such thing as a weekend when you owned a farm. The chickens wanted to be fed no matter what day of the week it was, and there was so much other work to be done that she couldn't afford to take two whole days off during the growing season.

She'd gotten a bit behind what with Kelly's wedding. Even though the wedding planner had taken care of virtually everything, Shelby had still had plenty to do to get the farm ready for the guests.

Today she would be planting seeds for squash and cucumbers. Jessie was coming to help—with an extra pair of hands it would take much less time to work the compost into the soil.

Shelby always enjoyed looking at the nice even rows of seeds when she was done planting. She would start by placing a stake at the ends of each row and then string twine between them to act as a guide.

Cucumbers needed to be planted one inch deep and six to twelve inches apart. Zucchini, on the other hand, needed to be planted only a half inch deep. The zucchini flowers were edible, and Shelby sometimes added them to salads.

Technically zucchini are a fruit, but they are most often served in a savory preparation. Shelby even used zucchini in her lasagna—once the plants began producing fruit, it was easy to become overwhelmed with the squash and she was always looking for new ways to prepare it.

Amelia and Billy were heading into their last weeks of school before summer vacation. It seemed as if the closer they got, the longer it took to get them out of the house in the morning.

Billy had missed the school bus twice in ten days and Amelia once. Shelby hoped they'd be on time today—she had a lot of work to do.

The back door slammed shut and Bert appeared in the kitchen.

"Are we going to plant those zucchini today?" she said as she slipped off the light cardigan she was wearing. "We're late as it is. We could have had them in the ground a week or two ago without any worries about frost."

"I know," Shelby said. She had to admit she'd been thinking the same thing herself. "Jessie is coming to help, so we should be able to get it done today."

"I'm ready when you are," Bert said.

Shelby spun around. "Now, Bert."

"Don't you go *now, Bert*–ing me. You're going to need help, and here I am."

"But your gallbladder . . ."

"Isn't going to get any better or worse if I put in a day's work."

"Have you scheduled your doctor's appointment yet?" Shelby lowered her eyebrows and gave Bert a stern look.

Bert stuck out her lower lip like Billy did when he didn't want to take his medicine. Shelby had to put her hand over her mouth to stifle a laugh.

"Yes," Bert said with a sigh. "I have. He'll probably want to cut me open."

"You make it sound like he's going to take a butcher knife to you. He might be able to do the surgery laparoscopically."

"I hope so." Bert put her hands on her hips. "Well, let's get going. We're not getting anything done by standing here talking."

Shelby knew when to drop the subject. She headed toward the door to the mudroom with Bert behind her and Jenkins and Bitsy weaving in and out of Bert's legs, champing at the bit to get outside.

Once they reached the garden, Shelby pulled a roll of twine and two stakes from her basket and began laying out the rows for the seeds. She got several rows staked out, then stood up with a hand at her back.

Where was Jessie? She should have arrived by now.

"Where's that girl you hired?" Bert said almost as if she could read Shelby's mind.

"She should be here," Shelby said, scanning the distance for any sign of Jessie.

"Is that a car I hear?" Bert said.

Bert's hearing certainly hadn't gone, Shelby thought. Moments later a figure rounded the corner of the farmhouse.

"Here she is." Shelby waved to Jessie, who was slowly making her way toward them.

As Jessie approached, Shelby noticed her shoulders drooped and her mouth was set in a thin line.

"Hey," she said when she reached them.

"Good morning," Shelby said. "Nice day, isn't it?"

Jessie grunted and shrugged.

"I'm going in to get myself a cold drink," Bert said, pulling off her gardening gloves. "I'll be back in a minute."

Shelby knelt down beside her wicker basket and separated the cucumber seed packets from the zucchini seeds.

"We're going to plant the zucchini first." Her knees cracked as she stood up. She bent down and picked up her hoe.

"Fine." Jessie hung her head, her dark bangs nearly mingling with her eyelashes.

Shelby leaned on her hoe. "Is everything okay? You seem upset."

"I'm fine," Jessie said, but a tear rolled down her cheek, giving the lie to her words.

"Can I help?" Shelby said gently.

Jessie shrugged again. "I don't think so."

"Why don't you tell me what's wrong? It might make

you feel better even if there's nothing that can be done about it. But you might be surprised—there's usually a solution of some sort."

"I doubt it." Jessie sighed. "I hope you're not going to think badly of me . . . us. But the police came and questioned me and Jax this morning."

Shelby was confused. "Jax? You know him." It was more of a statement than a question, since Shelby suddenly remembered seeing the two of them arguing at the wedding.

"Yes. He's my husband. We got married a couple of years ago." Jessie gave a loud sniff. "I was still in my pajamas and hadn't even put the coffee on yet when they came knocking at the door. I couldn't imagine who could be coming to visit at that hour."

Shelby frowned. "You both must be very upset about what happened. I'm sorry—it has to be hard for you."

Jessie nodded. "What makes it worse is they—the police—seem to think me or Jax might have had something to do with Travis's murder. At least that's the way it sounded."

"The police have to question everyone. It doesn't necessarily mean you're a suspect."

Jessie looked up, her face brightening slightly. "Really? Is that true?"

"Yes, of course."

"But why did they interview us, then? I know Jax is Travis's brother and I am . . . was . . . his sister-in-law." Jessie's eyes shifted away from Shelby's momentarily.

Shelby put her hand on Jessie's arm. "They'll probably interview everyone who knew Travis. It's the only way they'll be able to find out who killed him."

"Jax would never hurt his brother," Jessie said. "Never."

And she dropped to her knees and began digging a hole for the first seeds.

||||||||||||||||||||||||

"It's getting hot out here, isn't it?" Bert said when they decided to quit for lunch. The band was practicing in the barn, and Jessie decided to take her sandwich and go listen to them play.

"It sure is." Shelby swiped a hand across the back of her neck and blew a lock of hair off her forehead. "I made some egg salad this morning, if that sounds good."

"Sounds like those Rhode Island Reds of yours are producing well. I told you they would."

"And you were right," Shelby said, putting an arm around Bert as they walked back toward the farmhouse.

Shelby stripped off her gardening gloves and dropped them on the table in the mudroom. She headed to the kitchen sink and turned on the hot tap. Shelby scrubbed her hands while Bert filled a pair of tall glasses with iced tea.

Shelby made the sandwiches, cutting them into triangles the way her mother used to do them for her when she was a little girl, and put them on plates.

"Here you go." Shelby slid a plate in front of Bert and sat down opposite, unfurling her napkin and placing it in her lap.

"We got a lot done this morning," Bert said, taking a sip of her iced tea. "That Jessie doesn't look particularly useful, but she can really work when she puts her mind to it. You just have to keep after her."

"I'm glad she helped as much as she did. She was quite upset when she arrived. I was afraid she would turn out to be useless." Shelby took a bite of her sandwich.

"Really? Why?"

"The police showed up at her door first thing in the morning, asking questions."

"You don't say?" Bert scooped up a bit of egg salad that had seeped out of her sandwich.

"Jax is taking Travis's place in the band." Shelby pointed vaguely in the direction of the barn.

"I'd forgotten that there was another Coster boy. He was always in the shadow of his older brother." Bert patted her lips with her napkin. "Why were the police questioning him? Was there something amiss between Jax and his brother?"

"I don't know. But I'm thinking there was. Jessie acted sort of . . . I don't know. Sort of like she was hiding something. But what, I don't know."

Shelby grabbed the pitcher of iced tea and refilled her glass.

"Do the police even know what killed the poor fellow?" Bert shook her head. "What a shame—he was so young. It's one thing for someone as old as I am to pass on, but you'd expect someone his age to have plenty of years left. But if someone killed him, how did they do it?"

Shelby leaned forward. "Travis drowned. Frank told me."

Shelby was pleased to see that for once she'd taken Bert by surprise and not the other way around.

"Drowned? But there's no water within miles of that field."

"That's what I said to Frank." Shelby nibbled on the last bit of crust from her sandwich. "But then I remembered that old trough that Mom and Dad abandoned out there after they stopped raising cows."

"A trough? A person wouldn't fit in there. That doesn't make any sense. Has Frank lost his marbles?"

Shelby laughed. "The murderer didn't have to put Travis's whole body in the trough—just his head."

"But where did the water come from?" Bert looked at Shelby as if she was now doubting Shelby's sanity.

"Rainwater. The trough was filled to the brim with rainwater after all the storms we'd had."

"How horrible." Bert pushed her plate away as if the sight of food suddenly sickened her.

"And the bruise they found on the back of Travis's neck makes sense—it was most likely caused by the killer forcing Travis's head into the water."

Bert shivered. "But why tie him up to that pole and make him look like a scarecrow?"

"Who knows?" Shelby shrugged. "Maybe the killer was making some kind of statement."

By three o'clock, Shelby and Jessie had finished planting the zucchini seeds. Shelby had sent Bert home because she'd started looking tired, although Bert had, of course, denied it vehemently and Shelby had had to insist she leave and go get some rest.

Shelby stood back to admire the neat rows of slightly rounded rich dark earth. In no time, the plants would be sprouting with tender shoots pushing up through the soil, and before she knew it, the ground would be covered with leafy green vines. Jessie stood next to Shelby and gave her first genuine smile of the day.

"It looks nice, doesn't it?" Jessie said. "It's satisfying to create something so neat and orderly."

"I know what you mean," Shelby said, peeling off her gardening gloves. "If only life could be arranged so easily."

She looked at her hands. Somehow they always managed to get dirty despite the thick gloves she wore. Fortunately it was easily fixed with a good scrub. And her T-shirt and shorts could go through the wash. They'd emerge clean, if not new, and of course the holes would still be there.

Jessie headed toward the driveway, her posture a little straighter than it had been when she had arrived that morning. Shelby could only imagine how she must have felt being questioned by the police and what a shock it must have been—even though it was probably just routine—especially coming on the heels of the death of her husband's brother.

Shelby followed Jessie across the field, breathing a sigh of relief when she reached the relative coolness of the mudroom.

A hair elastic was sitting out on the kitchen counter, and Shelby grabbed it. She scraped her hair back off her face and secured it. The air on the back of her neck felt good.

She was about to head upstairs to wash up and change her clothes when the door to the mudroom opened and closed.

"Hi, Mom," Billy said, flinging his backpack in the general vicinity of a kitchen chair. "I'm hungry. What do we have to eat?"

Shelby smiled. Billy was always hungry. He'd shot up a couple of inches during the school year, and it looked as if his growth spurt wasn't over yet.

The back door slammed again and Amelia strolled in, in a much more leisurely fashion.

"How was school?" Shelby said, although she already knew what the answer would be.

"Fine."

"Are you hungry?"

Amelia shrugged. "Sort of."

"There's homemade hummus in the refrigerator along with some cut-up vegetables."

Billy didn't need a second invitation. He opened the door to the refrigerator and helped himself.

"Hey, Billy," Amelia said. "I want to practice my pitching. Will you catch the ball for me? Please?"

"Sure," Billy said, and it was obvious his mouth was already full.

Amelia had discovered a passion and a talent for baseball—perhaps not so surprising given that her father had been a pitcher for the Bobcats, the Lovett High School baseball team. Shelby was thrilled she'd joined her school's team. Sports were a good influence and likely to keep teens out of trouble, according to things she'd read.

And it was nice that she was following in her father's footsteps. Billy, although he loved baseball, hadn't shown any special talent for it. But time would tell—he might develop the skills he needed with practice.

Shelby thought of her husband, "Wild Bill," and smiled. Playing baseball hadn't exactly prevented him from getting into mischief, although by today's standards, his antics and those of his friends would be considered pretty tame and come under the *boys will be boys* category.

"I'm going to go change," Amelia said as she started toward the stairs.

"You're sure you don't want anything to eat? You said you were hungry—and you love hummus."

"I'm fine. Thanks."

Shelby bit her lip. She probably worried too much, but every time she turned on the television or picked up a magazine, there were stories or articles about losing weight and the latest diet craze. Amelia was a healthy weight—she'd had a sports physical not long ago—and Shelby didn't want to see her start dieting like so many other girls her age.

||||||||||||||||||||||||||

Shelby was opening the door to the bathroom, releasing a cloud of moist humid air from her shower into the hall, when Amelia came out of her room. She'd changed into shorts and a T-shirt with *Bobcats* written on it. Her curly blond hair was pulled into a ponytail and threaded through the back of the Tigers baseball cap she was wearing. She was tossing a baseball back and forth from one hand to the other.

"Call me when dinner's ready," she said to Shelby as they passed in the hall.

"Sure."

Amelia ran down the stairs, taking them two at a time.

Dear Reader, will wonders never cease! Shelby shook her head in disbelief. Amelia and her brother were not only getting along—they were actually doing something together. Something other than playing games on the computer or watching television.

Shelby changed into a T-shirt and a pair of jeans that were clean, although a bit faded around the seams and with frayed hems.

The door to Amelia's room was open, and Shelby noticed the flickering light of her computer monitor. Shelby's parents had given it to Amelia for Christmas. Amelia had been over the moon—up until then, she'd had to borrow Shelby's laptop and that had limited the time she was able to spend on social media communicating with her friends.

The computer was open to Amelia's Facebook page. Shelby hesitated on the threshold. She was of two minds about parents snooping through their children's things—on the one hand, it could mean uncovering a problem that needed to be dealt with, but on the other hand, it was an intrusion and a betrayal of trust.

Shelby couldn't help herself. She'd only take a peek—after all, if Amelia was putting things out on Facebook, how private could they be?

Shelby felt like a thief as she crept into Amelia's room, looking over her shoulder at least half a dozen times. The monitor had gone to sleep and she had to jiggle the mouse to bring up the page on the screen again.

It wasn't Amelia's Facebook page after all but a page belonging to a girl by the name of Lorraine Spurlinger. The picture at the top of the page was small and grainy, but Shelby could see that Lorraine had an unfortunate bite that made it look as if she were biting her lower lip when she wasn't. Other than that, she was fairly nondescript—brown hair that was neither particularly light nor dark and that was neither straight nor curly.

Her face was fleshy and her eyes on the small side. Shelby felt sorry for her, but she knew from experience that girls who didn't come into their looks in their teens often blossomed later in life.

She was about to leave Amelia's room, when one of the comments on Lorraine's timeline caught her eye and she stopped to read it. Shelby's hand flew to her mouth. How awful! She knew teens could be cruel, but this went beyond normal teenage behavior.

The poor girl! The person who left the comment hadn't posted a photograph of him- or herself but one of a figure whose face was hidden by a black hood. Shelby shivered. It was creepy. And the name had to be made up—Black Knight. Even in this day and age with children being given names like Apple or Breeze or Rainbow, Black Knight was a little too far-out to be real.

Obviously other students found the remark a cause for hilarity because their replies were just as mean and spiteful as Black Knight's original comment had been.

Shelby was about to turn away from the computer when Amelia's name caught her eye. She'd written her own comment under Black Knight's, defending the hapless Lorraine and calling Black Knight out as a bully.

Shelby felt her chest swell with pride. It would have taken courage for Amelia to stand up to the other kids that way. But these bullies shouldn't be allowed to get away with harassing other students like this. Shelby wondered if the school administration was aware of this problem.

Now she was in a bind, Shelby thought as she went down to the kitchen to bundle up some herbs she'd picked earlier. She would be selling them at the general store along with some of her yogurt cheese. Did she let on to Amelia that she'd seen this girl's Facebook page? She'd have to admit to snooping, and she knew that would make Amelia angry.

Shelby hadn't come to any conclusions by the time she'd finished tying up the rosemary, thyme, and sage with blue-and-white-checked ribbons bearing tiny tags that said *Love Blossom Farm* in pretty script.

⁞⁞⁞⁞⁞⁞⁞⁞⁞⁞⁞⁞⁞⁞⁞⁞⁞⁞⁞⁞⁞⁞

As soon as she'd cleaned up the dinner dishes and turned on the dishwasher, Shelby set her laptop on the kitchen table and powered it on. Her blog needed updating—if she ignored it for too long, she would begin losing her audience.

Shelby started writing, but the words weren't coming the way she'd hoped. She twirled a piece of hair around her finger as she stared at the blinking cursor. She felt as if every word were being dragged out of her with a pair of forceps. Sometimes that happened. She'd found that the only cure was to leave it for a few minutes, do something else, and hopefully come back with a fresh perspective.

She thought about her promise to Mrs. Willoughby and realized she hadn't done anything about investigating Isabel Stone. She didn't want to face Mrs. Willoughby's disapproval when she saw her in church on Sunday.

She typed in Isabel's name and was bombarded with dozens of entries. It seemed there were more than a few people in the world with that same name. Shelby scrolled through the information until she found a link to a Facebook page she thought might belong to the Isabel Stone living in Lovett, Michigan.

There was no profile picture—or at least there wasn't a picture of a human. Instead, this particular Isabel Stone had posted a photo of a darling black-and-white tuxedo cat blinking at the camera.

The timeline dated back only a few months and there weren't a lot of entries. Shelby scrolled through them— more pictures of the tuxedo cat, a handful of funny memes, and finally a photograph that was clearly of Lovett's Isabel Stone and a slightly younger woman who looked to be her sister.

Bingo, Shelby thought. She scrolled some more and found a picture of Isabel obviously taken a number of years ago with an attractive man who appeared to be a good decade older. He was holding some sort of plaque—an award perhaps?

All very nice, but it certainly didn't tell her enough about Isabel Stone to set Mrs. Willoughby's mind at rest. If that was even possible. Mrs. Willoughby was determined to dislike Isabel even if she turned out to be as saintly as Mother Teresa.

Shelby clicked on the About section. There she learned

that Isabel had been born in a small town somewhere in Canada and had worked as an executive secretary for Glide Corporation, a company that made parts for snowmobiles. No clues as to her personal life, when she came to the States, or what brought her to Lovett.

Shelby sighed and powered off her computer.

She was afraid Mrs. Willoughby was going to be disappointed in her investigative skills.

9

Dear Reader,

If you have children, you've probably already done the experiment with them where you suspend an avocado pit in a glass of water and wait for it to sprout. But did you know that you can grow numerous vegetables from your kitchen scraps? If you put a third of a tomato into a container filled with soil, cover it with more soil, water it, and keep it in a sunny place, it will eventually sprout. You can plant lemon seeds in soil as well as seeds from strawberries and raspberries. Try it with your children—they love watching and waiting for the tiny green shoots to push their way through the soil.

Her bedroom was still dark when Shelby woke up the next morning. She flicked on the light and stretched before grabbing her usual jeans and T-shirt out of the closet. Her hair was in a tangle of curls that gave new meaning to the term *bedhead*, she thought as she yanked a comb through it before pulling on a sweatshirt and padding downstairs.

Shelby slipped out the back door and made her way to the barn to take care of the chickens. The chickens gathered around her feet as she tossed feed onto the ground. Her bucket now empty, Shelby replaced it in the barn and headed back toward the farmhouse.

The sky was lightening, but the air was still damp and cool and Shelby pulled her hands up inside the sleeves of her sweatshirt. The warmth the kitchen had retained felt good, but she knew that in a few hours she would be flinging open the windows and praying for a breeze.

Her slow cooker was sitting out on her counter. She'd filled it last night with a gallon of the milk Jake had delivered yesterday along with some yogurt starter.

She unwrapped the bath towel she'd used to keep the slow cooker warm, and lifted the lid. The milk had transformed into delicious creamy yogurt. Shelby spooned it into a fine mesh sieve that she'd suspended over a bowl to catch the whey that would slowly drain off. The resulting yogurt would be thick enough to mix with herbs and use as a spread or a dip.

Shelby went to the foot of the stairs and called up to Billy and Amelia. It was time for them to get ready for school. Before she even turned around, she heard Billy's feet hit the floor. Amelia was always a little slower to awake.

Shelby checked on the yogurt, which was draining nicely and had already produced several cups of whey. She pulled off her sweatshirt, slipped into her gardening clogs, and went out the back door.

Bitsy and Jenkins followed her out into the yard, running ahead of her and crisscrossing back and forth in front

of her. Jenkins took off at full speed after some small creature he'd spotted, while Bitsy rolled around on a particularly fragrant patch of dirt.

The air was still slightly cool and damp on Shelby's bare
arms. The scent of newly mown hay mixed with the pungent
odor of manure drifted over from Jake's pasture. She stopped
and took a deep breath. She dreamed of mornings like these
during the long winter months when they were trapped inside
with dark skies and snow piling up outside the door.

Drops of dew sparkled on the leaves in the garden as
Shelby made her way down the rows of herbs neatly planted
in straight lines. She knelt in the dirt, moist from the dew
and the morning air, and picked handfuls of thyme, rosemary, and basil.

By the time she got back to the kitchen, Billy was slumped
over the kitchen table, waiting for his breakfast, and the
water was running overhead in the bathroom.

Shelby ladled some of her homemade granola into a cereal bowl, mixed in a scoop of the yogurt draining in the
bowl on the counter, and added a handful of the blueberries
she'd frozen from last summer's crop.

Billy grunted as she slid the dish in front of him, and
immediately began to spoon up his breakfast.

While he ate, Shelby washed and dried the herbs and
began chopping them. As soon as the yogurt had drained
sufficiently, she would mix them in and then make up the
small plastic containers she used to sell the yogurt cheese
at the general store and at the farmers' market in town.

By the time Billy and Amelia left to catch the school
bus, Shelby was ready to fold the herbs into her thickened
yogurt. As soon as she'd mixed them in thoroughly, she
spooned the green-flecked cheese into her containers. Soon
she had a tidy row lined up on the kitchen counter ready to

go. She retrieved the herbs she'd tied in bundles from the container of water in the refrigerator, which she'd propped them in the night before, and added everything to the wicker basket she used to carry things.

She grabbed the dish that belonged to the caterer and added it to her bundle and checked that the dogs' water bowls were full. Shelby smiled at them—both were enjoying their first nap of the day in the sunbeam slanting across the kitchen floor.

Shelby flipped out the lights and headed out the back door.

The gas gauge on her ancient car, which she often joked was held together with rubber bands and Elmer's glue, was hovering perilously close to the empty mark. Shelby made a face. Taxes were coming due soon and Shelby's bank account was almost as empty as her gas tank. She sighed. She loved her life the way it was, and not having a lot of money was a small price to pay for waking up each day glad to be alive.

The money the band was paying her for their use of the barn was certainly going to come in handy. And her blog brought in a small stream of extra cash. Shelby was often approached about advertising various cooking products to her growing group of followers. And she was noodling the idea of putting together a cookbook. She'd been researching how to write a book proposal, and she thought she could do it.

Writing a cookbook would be a perfect winter project when work on the farm had slowed and sunny skies and warm breezy days weren't luring her outside. Shelby made a mental note to start on a proposal as soon as possible.

The drive to the Lovett General Store took only a few minutes, although Shelby got stuck behind a slow-moving tractor on one of the narrow one-lane roads. She sighed impatiently as she waited for it to turn off so she could speed up again.

A handful of cars were in the gravel parking lot behind the store. Shelby pulled into a space next to a Taurus with a dent in the front passenger door. It looked like the same car Brian, Travis's group's manager, had been driving. Shelby peered through the window and noticed a set of drumsticks next to several sheets of music scattered across the backseat.

The bell over the door tinkled when Shelby walked into the shop. Matt was hunched over the counter, with a book spread open in front of him, his eyes glued to the page.

"Hello," Shelby said when she reached him.

Matt looked up, startled. He slapped the book shut. "Sorry." He smiled. "I didn't hear you come in." He tapped the cover of the book. "I was reading."

"It must be good." Shelby peered over the counter at the cover.

Matt turned the book around so Shelby could read the title.

"Behind Enemy Lines," Shelby read. "By Damian Devine." A picture of a car exploding against a black sky was featured on the cover.

"Is it any good?"

Matt grinned sheepishly. "I'm enjoying it. Jack Morrison is a sort of super operative sent to rescue innocent American prisoners held in some of the world's worst jails." He shrugged. "It's male fantasy, I guess." Matt turned the book back around. "Probably not your cup of tea, but it's got me glued to the page."

'You're probably right about that," Shelby laughed. "It's the author's fantasy at least. He's probably short, with ears that stick out and horn-rimmed glasses."

Matt flipped the book over. "No author picture, so who knows? You could be right." He slipped the book beneath the counter. "So . . . what goodies have you brought me today?"

"A batch of fresh herbs and some yogurt cheeses." Shelby put her basket down on the counter.

"Wonderful. I'm all out of both. The herbs usually sell the day you bring them in."

Matt lifted the ribbon-tied bunches of thyme, sage, and rosemary from Shelby's basket and their pungent scent perfumed the air between them.

He put a hand on Shelby's arm. The soothing warmth of his palm against her bare skin made her sigh.

"How about dinner tomorrow night?" Matt said. "I've got an early start the next day—I have to drive down to Kalamazoo to discuss some new products for the store—but we could grab a quick bite at the diner." He made a face. "Not the most elegant place in the world, but when it comes to down-home-type cooking, you can't beat it."

The Lovett Diner was a second home to most of the locals, as well as the truckers who came through late at night, downing cups of coffee to keep themselves awake and forking up the eggs and bacon that were on the menu all day long.

The owners—a husband and wife who'd taken over the diner nearly thirty years ago—did all the cooking. They had been using as many fresh local and seasonal ingredients as possible long before the trend caught on with fancy upscale farm-to-table restaurants.

Shelby did some swift mental calculations. Bert would look after the kids—she was willing to do anything in her power to find Shelby a man—and she could whip up a macaroni-and-cheese casserole for them for their dinner.

"I'd love to."

"Would six thirty be too early for you? Like I said, I've got to hit the road first thing the next morning."

Shelby smiled. Although Matt had been in Lovett for over ten years, he hadn't completely shed his New York City ways. By six thirty, most of the locals not only had finished dinner but had washed and dried the dishes, had put them away, and were ensconced in front of the television watching the news, their feet propped up after a long hard day of work.

"That would be fine."

Shelby was getting ready to leave when Cody came around the end of an aisle, his arms laden with purchases. He smiled at Shelby as he dumped his load on the counter.

"I should have taken a cart, I guess," he said with a sheepish grin.

Shelby looked down at the counter. Cody certainly had an unusual assortment of items—bug spray, deodorant, a small bottle of laundry detergent, two cans of chicken noodle soup, a box of doughnuts, and a bottle of gardenia-scented bath oil.

Cody pointed to the bath oil. "That's for Paislee. She said she can't live without it and hers is all gone." He shrugged.

As Shelby left the general store, she wondered if Paislee had transferred her affections to Cody now that Travis was dead.

Although it was hard to picture Cody as a killer, she couldn't help but think that that certainly gave him a motive for murder.

||||||||||||||||||||||||

The caterer Grilling Gals was on the outskirts of town in a long, low, nondescript building. According to the sign out front, they shared half the space with a beauty supply company.

Shelby parked her car and got out. The sun was stronger now, and she felt perspiration forming on her upper lip and the back of her neck.

A sign with an arrow directed Shelby to an entrance on the north side of the building where the glass door had the company's logo painted on it in white—a grill with smoke rising from the top and *Grilling Gals* underneath in script.

Shelby shifted the bowl to her left hand and tried the door. It was locked. She peered through the glass—lights were on, so someone must be there. She'd raised her fist to knock when she saw the bell alongside the door. She pushed it once, then again for good measure.

Moments later, she could make out a figure coming down the hall, and moments after that, the door was opened.

"Can I help you?"

The woman standing in the doorway was shaped somewhat like a bowling pin—thin on top and wider on the bottom. She was wearing khakis and a red golf shirt with the Grilling Gals logo on the breast pocket. Her hair was light brown and the ragged ends reached her waist. Shelby recognized her from Kelly's wedding, although then she had worn her hair up in a bun and covered by a hairnet.

"I wanted to return your bowl." Shelby held out the serving dish. "Someone must have thought it was mine and left it on my kitchen counter."

The woman held the door wider. "Come on in. My name's Valerie. I'm the owner of Grilling Gals."

Shelby followed her down a dim hallway and into a small room crammed with mismatched office furniture.

Valerie put the bowl down on a desk overflowing with piles of papers. She gestured toward the mess. "I'm paying bills." She made a face.

"I know what you mean," Shelby said. "Not my favorite job either."

Dear Reader, especially not when you're trying to stretch ten dollars to cover twenty dollars' worth of expenses.

"It was nice of you to bring our bowl back. Most of the time people just keep them. We're constantly replacing our stock. We hire a lot of temps and some of them don't pay as much attention as they should."

"Everything was lovely and people are still raving about the food."

Valerie smiled. "I'm glad to hear it. I was afraid that the murder would have left people with a bad taste in their mouth. Pun intended." She smiled again. "A detective was around here just before you got here, questioning me and looking for the contact information for the staff who was at the wedding."

Shelby's ears perked up. That must be Frank Valerie was talking about.

"He asked me if I'd seen anything, but there wasn't much I could tell him."

"But there was . . . something? Something you saw?"

Valerie picked at a mosquito bite on her arm. "It was when one of the bartenders asked if I would dump the melted ice from his bucket. I went around to the back of the tent—I didn't want to create a mud puddle right where people might be walking."

She lifted her hair off her neck and shoulders with her hands and then let it fall against her back again. "I didn't see the body—the detective said he was strung up like a scarecrow. . . ."

"Yes," Shelby said. Travis's image flashed across her mind and she saw the slumped figure, the chin on the chest, the legs buckled, and the hat perched on top of the head.

"I didn't see much of anything, to tell you the truth, but the detective seemed pretty excited by what I told him."

"What was that?" Shelby felt her palms turn clammy. What had Valerie seen?

"I saw a man walking back toward the field where they found the body. He was wearing a hat. It had a sort of floppy brim." Valerie made a twirling motion around her head.

"What else was he wearing?"

Valerie looked apologetic. "To be honest with you, I didn't notice. I only caught a glimpse of him out of the corner of my eye as I was bending over to dump the water out of the bucket. The only thing I really noticed was the hat. Otherwise I might not have noticed him at all."

Shelby's mouth had turned dry and her palms were becoming increasingly clammy.

"What color was the hat?"

"The same color as my pants. Khaki, I guess you'd call it."

10

Dear Reader,

Do you know what the secret is to a really good pitcher of iced tea? A pinch of baking soda. The baking soda neutralizes the tannins in the tea, making for a much smoother taste. Next time you brew some tea—hot or cold—try it. Just a pinch will do—an eighth of a teaspoon should do the trick.

Shelby felt sick as she walked back to her car after leaving Grilling Gals. The hat Valerie had described sounded exactly like Seth's hat—and exactly like the one found on Travis. Was it possible that two people who had the same hat both happened to be at the wedding? Shelby didn't think so.

Bert was at the house when Shelby got home.

"There you are," she said when Shelby walked in the

back door. "Jessie's here—I sent her out to start weeding the herb garden."

"Thanks." Shelby pulled out a kitchen chair and sat down.

"You look like you saw a ghost."

Shelby took a deep breath. She riffled the edges of the newspaper that was sitting out on the table. If she didn't tell anyone what Valerie had told her, then it didn't exist, right?

"It's nothing. I guess I'm a bit tired, that's all."

Bert looked as if she didn't believe a word of what Shelby said. She began to open her mouth, and Shelby knew she had to forestall further questions or she would certainly cave and tell Bert everything.

"Listen, can you watch the kids tomorrow night? Matt and I are going to the Lovett Diner for dinner."

A huge grin split Bert's face. "You have a date."

"It's not a date," Shelby said, squaring her shoulders, aware that she sounded like a petulant child.

"Is he paying?"

"Yes, I think so. But maybe I should offer to—" Shelby held her hands out, palms up.

Bert shook her head so vigorously her gray curls bounced. "No. If he's paying, it's a date. Don't you go offering to pick up the tab. Next time you can invite him here for dinner and cook him something nice. Maybe that pot roast you make that positively melts in your mouth. I'm sure he'd like that."

"Do you really think . . . I mean, last time we went to dinner, he paid. . . ."

"If you offer to pay, he's going to think that you think he can't afford it, and that's emasculating. Men don't like that."

"If you say so."

"I do. Besides, how much of a tab can a person run up at the Lovett Diner?"

Shelby laughed. "That's true. The most expensive thing on the menu is the cubed steak with gravy and mashed potatoes and that would hardly break the bank."

Bert stared at Shelby, studying her so intently that Shelby began to blush.

"Now you're looking a little perkier. There's nothing like a date to pick up a girl's spirits." Bert rubbed her hands together. "How about we start staking the plot for the eggplant and pumpkins?"

"Good idea," Shelby said, relieved that Bert had dropped the subject of her date with Matt.

But she was wrong.

"Can we call you and Matt an *item* now, as they say in those gossip magazines?" Bert said as she tied string to a stake.

Shelby groaned inwardly. Bert could be like a dog with a bone when she wanted to be.

"We're having dinner. That's all."

"This is your second dinner. I remember when he took you to that place in Allenvale. What was it called?"

"Lucia's," Shelby said through tight lips.

"That's right." Bert gestured to Shelby. "Here's the string. You can tie your end now—mine's done."

Shelby took the string, pulled it taut, and tied it to the stake she'd hammered into the ground across from Bert.

"So the handsome cowboy next door is out of the picture?" Bert said as she pulled the ball of string from her pocket. "And what about Frank? He's in love with you, you know. For a while I thought you two—"

"Bert, please. I'd rather not talk about it."

"Okay. Subject's closed."

Shelby could tell by the stiff set of Bert's shoulders that her feelings were hurt.

"I'm sorry, Bert. I didn't mean to snap. But honestly, it's a subject that has often kept me awake at night." Shelby pulled off her gardening gloves and wiped her forearm across her forehead. The sun was climbing in the sky and the early-morning breeze had died down.

"You have three men interested in you. That's every girl's dream. I don't see what the problem is." Bert grinned to show she was kidding.

"I'm hot. Why don't we go inside and get a cold drink?"

Bert followed Shelby back to the house and into the mudroom, which still retained some of the coolness of the morning air.

"It feels heavenly in here," Shelby said as she opened the refrigerator. "I have iced tea or lemonade." She held up the two pitchers.

"Iced tea for me." Bert stretched her legs out under the table. "So your next-door neighbor is out of the picture. But Frank? I really thought the two of you . . ."

Shelby sighed as she took the seat opposite Bert. She cradled her glass of lemonade in her hands, enjoying the coolness against her palms.

"Frank is . . . Frank. That's the problem. He's not Bill, but he's so much like Bill that it confuses me."

"Certainly they looked alike."

"Exactly. Is my attraction to Frank based on the fact he looks like Bill? He might not be like Bill at all."

"So in order to avoid disappointment, you've ruled Frank out?"

Shelby turned her glass around and around in her hands. "It's not so much that I've ruled Frank out. It's more that I've decided to give Matt a chance."

"I'm not going to argue with you. Just so you haven't

closed yourself off. You're young yet, with a lot of future in front of you. It would be nice for you to have someone to share that with."

Shelby realized she'd better end this conversation before things became too uncomfortable. She started to get up. "Back to work, I guess."

"I'll bet the band could use something cold to drink," Bert said. "I saw one of them getting water from the gardening hose."

"It must be pretty hot in the barn, too," Shelby said, opening the refrigerator. "I'll take them some iced tea."

She pulled a pitcher from the fridge and opened the cabinet next to the sink to retrieve some glasses.

"Do you think any of Travis's band members had anything to do with his death?" Bert said.

Shelby paused with the pitcher of iced tea poised above a plastic carafe.

"As far as I can tell, some of them may have had a motive, but it's hard to picture any of them actually committing the crime."

"That's true," Bert said as she stood up. "They're certainly what my mother would have called a ragtag bunch, but they seem harmless enough."

Shelby finished pouring the iced tea into the carafe and snapped the top into place. It, along with the glasses, went into her wicker basket, and she headed out the door.

"I'll join you in a few minutes." She waved to Bert.

Bitsy and Jenkins trotted along at Shelby's heels, occasionally darting off to chase a butterfly or sniff at a clump of weeds.

Shelby didn't hear any music coming from the barn as she approached. The band must be taking a break—her timing was perfect. As she got closer, she heard voices coming from around the back of the barn. It was hard to make out what they were saying, but Shelby did hear the name *Travis*. Her ears perked up.

She inched closer, trying to keep the glasses in her basket from rattling. For once, there weren't any sounds of tractors plowing or mowers going.

The voices were male and female. Shelby recognized the female voice—it was Jessie. Was it Jax she was talking to? They were quiet for several seconds and Shelby tensed, ready to move away and toward the entrance to the barn.

The conversation started up again, and although Shelby strained her ears to the point where she thought her head would burst, she could catch only intermittent words—*Travis . . . long ago . . . nobody remembers.*

At any moment, they might be finished talking and she would be caught, but Shelby couldn't move. She had the feeling she might hear something important—something that would keep the police from sniffing around Seth and send them off in another direction.

There was a rustling sound and Shelby tensed again. When Jessie spoke, she could tell they were moving closer.

"Do the cops know the whole story?" Jessie said.

Shelby bit her lip in frustration. She couldn't hear the man's response. But then he suddenly got louder, and Shelby recognized Jax's voice.

"And what about you? Do they know about . . ."

Jax lowered his voice again and it was all Shelby could hear. She could tell they were coming closer. Any second now and they would be around the corner.

She quickly moved away and walked through the open door of the barn.

||||||||||||||||||||||||||

Shelby and Bert finished staking out the plot for the egg-plant and pumpkins and by the time they were done, they were ready for another cold drink. They went inside through the mudroom, and Shelby dropped her mud-encrusted gardening gloves on the table she used for potting seedlings and separating plants.

"I'm glad that's done," Shelby said as she retrieved the pitcher of iced tea and filled two glasses. "Thanks for your help, Bert."

"I'm grateful that I can help. It sure beats sitting alone in my apartment, watching the soaps on television."

Shelby smiled. "It sounds like you could use a little romance in your life, too."

"No, thanks. I'm done with that."

"But wouldn't you like some companionship?" Shelby couldn't help teasing Bert.

"I've got Mable, my cat. That's all the companionship I need."

Shelby brought the glasses to the table along with plates and the remains of a blueberry cake she'd made the day before.

"When I was taking the iced tea out to the barn, I overheard Jessie and Jax talking. Something about a story and did the cops know," Shelby said as she cut a slice of cake and passed it to Bert. "Do you have any idea what he might have meant? Do you remember anything about him?"

"I knew who his mother was to say hello to her, but I didn't keep up with her at all. The only story I can think of is the accident that sent Travis's brother to rehab for so long."

"Maybe that's it. Maybe there's something there."

"You're good on the computer. Maybe you can look it up."

"I will," Shelby said. "I definitely will."

‖‖‖‖‖‖‖‖‖‖‖‖‖‖‖‖‖‖

Shelby was itching to get at the computer to see if she could find anything on a story that involved Jax and possibly Travis. She thought back to what she'd overheard. . . . *Long ago . . . nobody remembers* and *Do the cops know the whole story?* And she thought Travis's name had been mentioned, too.

Shelby was about to power up her laptop when the front door opened and then slammed shut and Billy came flying into the kitchen.

"How was school?" Shelby said as he made a beeline for the refrigerator.

Dear Reader, the amount of food that boy consumes is astonishing. I suspect we're in for another growth spurt. His new pants are already almost too short.

"School was okay," Billy said as he bit into an apple.

"What did you do?" Shelby went to ruffle his hair, but he ducked away from her hand.

"Nothing."

It was the same conversation they had every day after school—school was okay and he'd apparently done nothing.

"Can I go out and play?"

Shelby sensed suppressed energy coming off him in waves. Sitting at a desk in a stuffy classroom all day was difficult for a boy his age.

"Sure."

The screen door to the mudroom banged shut and the front door banged open almost in unison.

Shelby saw Billy through the window streaking across the yard as Amelia walked into the kitchen.

"How was school?"

Amelia looked angry—her lips set in a thin grim line, her brows lowered over her eyes like shades that had been pulled down.

"Is something wrong?"

Amelia collapsed into a kitchen chair with a loud sigh. "Kind of."

Shelby positioned herself at the sink with her back to Amelia. Amelia was more likely to talk if Shelby wasn't looking at her. She picked up a sponge and began to wipe down the counter.

"Are you in trouble?" Shelby asked, her mind racing through all the things Amelia might have done. Passing notes in class?

Dear Reader, do kids even pass notes in class anymore like we did? I imagine all messages are sent via text these days.

"No. It's this girl at school."

"Oh?" Shelby scraped at a bit of cheese stuck on the counter with her thumbnail.

"Her name's Lorraine. A lot of the kids pick on her. On the bus today a bunch of boys were calling her Frankenstein."

"That's horrible."

Shelby remembered the girl's picture on Facebook. Her looks were rather unfortunate.

"I told them to stop."

Shelby felt a glow of pride. "Good for you." She turned around and smiled at Amelia briefly.

"Yeah, but now all the kids are going to hate me."

"For sticking up for this Lorraine? Why?"

"You just don't do that, Mom. You don't understand."

"Have you told a teacher about what's going on?"

Amelia looked aghast. "You mean be a narc? You've got to be kidding."

Shelby knew better than to try to argue. "Is there something else you can do?"

"Like what?" Amelia put her head in her hands and stared at Shelby morosely.

"I've read some schools have antibullying campaigns. Maybe you could start one."

Amelia made a sound like a grunt. Shelby wasn't sure if she was agreeing with the suggestion or rejecting it out of hand.

"Maybe you could get some of the more popular kids to join in with you."

This time Amelia snorted. "Why would they do that?"

Shelby leaned against the counter. "I don't know," she admitted. "Maybe you could turn it into something cool to do. Start the campaign off with a big bang."

"Cool?" Amelia stared at her skeptically. "How?"

Shelby thought frantically. "I don't know. Perhaps a contest of some kind?" She snapped her fingers. "Or how about a theme week?"

Amelia raised her eyebrows.

"You could host a pay-it-forward week," Shelby said, getting excited about her idea. "And encourage everyone to do something nice for someone else and post it on a special Facebook page. Then you could have a drawing and the winner gets a prize of some sort."

Amelia wrinkled her nose. But Shelby could tell she was thinking. At least she hadn't rejected the idea out of hand.

"What kind of prize? Where would we get it?"

"You and Katelyn could form a committee and go around soliciting items from local merchants. I'm sure Matt would donate something."

Amelia snorted. "Like what? A case of baked beans?"

"Very funny, smarty pants. He carries some nice wind-breakers. And maybe the school store would throw in a Lovett High sweatshirt." Shelby clapped her hands. "Oh, and perhaps the diner would kick in a small gift certificate. I think you could put together a nice basket."

Amelia's expression was slowly changing. "Oh," she exclaimed. "I've just had the most wonderful idea."

"What is it?"

Amelia's eyes were shining. "I don't want to say anything until I know if we can pull it off. I have to go talk to Katelyn and see what she thinks."

"Not even a hint?" Shelby teased.

Amelia shook her head. "You've been the biggest help, Mom. Thanks."

And she aimed a kiss at her mother's cheek before bolting from the room.

┉┉┉┉┉┉┉┉┉┉┉

As anxious as Shelby was to find out anything she could about Jax and Travis, she had to wait to get back to her research. She had to work on her blog first. She was writing a post on ways to preserve herbs for later use by drying them—or, her favorite method, freezing them in a bit of water in an ice cube tray.

Then it was time for dinner. She was sautéing chicken along with peppers and tomatoes she'd canned from last year's harvest, a chopped onion and her own homegrown garlic. She'd picked some thyme and oregano to add as well.

Chopping released the scent of the herbs, and Shelby closed her eyes for a moment, savoring the delicious smell. There was something calming about the scent of fresh herbs.

She added the thyme and oregano to the chicken simmering on the stove and put on a pan of water to boil for the potatoes. They were almost the last of the crop she'd picked in the fall, and she wanted to enjoy delicious buttery mashed potatoes one more time. Soon there would be corn from a neighboring farm to be grilled and eaten off the cob.

Amelia was in considerably better spirits when she came down to dinner. Billy never said much while they ate—he was too busy putting away the meal so he could go back outside and play. The days were long, and it was hard to get him to come inside for his bath and bed. Shelby had to keep reminding him that school would be out soon and then he'd have all the time he wanted to spend outside.

Finally Billy was in the tub and Amelia was back on the phone in her room with Katelyn, planning their upcoming antibullying campaign.

Shelby powered up her laptop again and brought up her favorite search engine. She'd already seen a lot of the articles that immediately came up about Travis. They all concerned his music career or were sanitized versions of his brief biography.

Shelby continued to dig until she came to a story from the Michigan Live Web site. It was dated the year Shelby's husband died, which would explain why she didn't remember the story.

The piece was about the accident involving Travis and his brother. Jax had sustained a head injury as well as several broken bones, and an unnamed medical source had predicted he would need rehabilitation for months.

Travis had been luckier, having suffered a broken collarbone and two broken ribs—certainly painful enough but much more easily healed.

The story went on to explain the accident with numerous

quotes from witnesses on the scene and police personnel as well as professional accident investigators.

None of this seemed particularly relevant to Travis's murder. Shelby was about to leave the site—she had her finger on her mouse—when she got to the last paragraph. She read it through twice to be sure she was understanding it correctly, although the words and language were plain enough.

Paislee had told her that Jax was driving the car when the accident occurred. Or maybe she simply assumed it. But he hadn't been. Travis had been behind the wheel.

So not only did Travis leave his brother behind in his rise to stardom—he was the cause of the accident that had stripped Jax of his chance at a music career.

She wouldn't blame Jax for being mad. But had something pushed him over the edge to murder?

11

Dear Reader,

Have you ever noticed how the first pancake almost never turns out as well as the rest of the batch? There are a couple of things that contribute to that, like your griddle not being hot enough or using too much grease. Your griddle should be hot enough that a couple of drops of water will sizzle and dance when dripped onto the surface. It's also a good idea to have your batter at room temperature—otherwise it will cool down the surface of your griddle too quickly. And no peeking! Don't lift the pancake to check the underside until it's been cooking for two to three minutes, the top is bubbling, and the edges are dry.

Shelby was up early—there was no such thing as sleeping late on a farm. She pulled on a pair of jeans and a sweatshirt—mornings were still cool enough to warrant one.

She tiptoed downstairs and out the back door, with Bitsy and Jenkins at her heels. A swirl of mist still clung to the dew-covered grass, and the sun was barely above the horizon. It was quiet—only a few birds chirped from their perches in the trees, and the insects were not yet humming their daily song.

The wet grass brushed at Shelby's ankles as she walked toward the old red barn. The only pieces of wedding decor left were the strands of lights hanging from the rafters. Brian had negotiated with the rental company to keep the generators until the band was no longer using the barn for their practice sessions.

The sun was not yet strong enough to illuminate the inside of the barn, so Shelby flipped on the lights, which twinkled above her like stars in the sky.

She filled her old dented and rusted metal pail with chicken feed from the bag propped in the corner—the same pail her parents had used and possibly even her grandparents—and went back outside, where the chickens quickly gathered around her ankles.

She yawned as she scattered seed across the bare ground. The chickens scurried from spot to spot, pecking up the feed. Off in the distance, Jenkins and Bitsy were running in circles, burning off the energy they'd accumulated during their sleep. In another hour they would be dozing inside in the warmth of a sunbeam, having their first nap of the day.

Shelby returned the pail to the barn and walked back toward the house, breathing deeply and savoring the peace of the morning. It was hard to believe a murder had recently been committed right here on her property. She pushed the thought away as she held the screen door open for Bitsy and Jenkins, who were now ready for their own breakfast.

Shelby had to ease the dogs away with her leg so she could pour their food into their bowls. They watched eagerly, their tongues hanging and saliva bubbling at the corners of their mouths.

Shelby retrieved her griddle from the cupboard and started it warming on the stove while she went to call Billy and Amelia. She waited by the stairs until she heard Billy's feet hit the floor, then went back to the kitchen to retrieve the pancake batter she'd made the night before from the refrigerator.

Shelby was flipping over the first batch of pancakes when Billy appeared, his cowlick standing up like a rooster's comb on the top of his head, his eyes still swollen with sleep.

Shelby pulled a plate from the cupboard, stacked three pancakes on it, and slid it in front of Billy, who grunted before picking up the bottle of syrup and flooding his plate.

Shelby had a family friend in northern Michigan who tapped his maple trees in March, when the nights were below freezing and the days warmer, and always sent her several bottles of the precious liquid.

Once Billy and Amelia were out the door and off to the school bus, Shelby did the dishes and tidied up the kitchen.

Shelby was opening up her laptop when she thought of Mrs. Willoughby. The specter of Mrs. Willoughby finding her wanting hung over Shelby's head. She decided she ought to put a little more time into investigating Isabel Stone. Not that she expected to unearth much of anything about the woman, but if it would set Mrs. Willoughby's mind at rest, it would be worth it. Reverend Mather would no doubt appreciate having Mrs. Willoughby's mind laid to rest, too.

Shelby stretched her arms out in front of her at shoulder height, the fingers of both hands laced together. But how to investigate? She dropped her arms and drummed her fingers on the table. Maybe she could contact that company Isabel used to work for. With any luck, someone there might know a little more about Isabel.

Shelby jiggled her mouse and her laptop screen lit up. She went to Facebook, pulled up Isabel's profile, and checked the name of the Canadian company where she'd worked as a secretary. Glide—that was it.

Shelby found Glide's Web site easily enough and jotted down their contact number. She hesitated with her hand on the phone—what excuse was she going to give for asking all these questions? She was terrible at lying, but she'd have to give it a go and hope for the best.

"Hello. This is Glide Corporation, Carol Davis speaking. How may I help you?" The woman's words ran all together.

Shelby twisted the telephone cord around her finger. "Carol, I'd like to verify the employment of an Isabel Stone, please."

"Isabel? She no longer works here, I'm afraid."

"I only need to verify her employment and ask you a few questions," Shelby said, feeling her face turn red at the lies sliding from her mouth so easily.

"Oh, it's human resources you'll want, then. You can speak to Dotty Polsky. She'll be able to help you."

And before Shelby could even say *thank you*, her call had been transferred and another phone was ringing. Dotty Polsky picked up on the third ring.

Shelby had to clear her throat twice before any words came out.

"I'm trying to verify the employment of an Isabel Stone who said she used to work for Glide Corporation."

"Oh my goodness, Isabel!" Dotty said. "How is she? It's been ages since we've heard from her."

Shelby hesitated. "She's . . . she's fine."

"Oh, good. Such a nice lady. We were really sad to see her go."

"So you knew Isabel?"

"Yes. We weren't close, but we would chat whenever we ran into each other, if you know what I mean." There was a pause and the sound of rustling papers. "We were all so happy for her when she got rid of David. He was a real piece of work."

"David?"

"Her ex. Treated her very badly, if I must say so myself. She was too nice and took it for far too long. After she divorced him, he took off with some Vegas showgirl. And good riddance, I say."

"Did they have children?"

"No. I think Isabel saw the writing on the wall and decided against it. Good thing, too."

"So Isabel worked there as a secretary?"

"Executive secretary," Dotty corrected quickly. "She worked for George Hastings, the president of Glide. He often said he didn't know what he'd do without her."

Shelby's shoulders sagged. So far, all she'd managed to do was confirm information she already knew.

She cleared her throat again. "What was Isabel Stone like?"

"Like?" Dotty repeated. "Well, she was efficient, always on time, a hard worker. Everything you'd want in an employee."

All admirable qualities, Shelby thought. But would that satisfy Mrs. Willoughby? Shelby suspected Mrs. Willoughby wouldn't like Isabel Stone even if she found out the woman was about to be canonized as a saint.

"So you and Isabel were friends?"

"Not friends exactly—like I said, we'd chat whenever we could. Isabel never wanted to come out to lunch with the rest of us gals. Not that she was standoffish—I don't want you to get the wrong impression. But she always said she had work to do. We'd all be going out for a bite and she'd stay at her computer, typing away at something. One time I saw her with this huge stack of papers in front of her."

"Oh?"

"When I asked her about it, she positively blushed. Said she hoped to be a writer someday. Took us all by surprise."

The sound was suddenly muffled as if Dotty had put her hand over the receiver. Shelby heard her saying something to someone in the room.

"Where was I?" Dotty said when she came back on the phone. "I wonder if Isabel is still writing. Whenever I'm in a bookstore, I look to see if she's had something published. But I suppose it isn't that easy."

"I wouldn't think so," Shelby said. She unwrapped the phone cord from around her finger. "You've been very helpful. Thank you so much."

Shelby hung up and stared at the phone. So she knew a few things about Isabel now. She was divorced—no kids—she'd been an executive assistant to the president of her company, she was a hard worker, and she wanted to be a writer.

That was quite a lot from one conversation. But would Mrs. Willoughby think it was enough?

||||||||||||||||||||||||

Shelby fluffed her hair in the bathroom mirror and retrieved her knitting bag from beside the living room sofa. Although to call what she was doing knitting was an exaggeration. It was time for her knitting group at St. Andrews. Shelby was sorely tempted to give up knitting, considering her lack of success. However, quitting wasn't in her nature, but stubbornness certainly was.

The band's van had already pulled into the driveway and was parked alongside Shelby's car. As she walked around it, she could feel it was still warm—they must have recently arrived.

Shelby was opening her car door when she hesitated. Was she being foolish in letting the band practice in her barn? What if one of them was the killer? She thought of each of them in turn—Brian, who was so businesslike and polite; Jax, who still seemed like a boy even though he was well into his twenties; Cody, who worked so hard; Paislee, who didn't look as if she would hurt a fly; Peter, who was so earnest—and besides, he was Kelly's cousin.

Some of them might have had a motive for hating Travis and maybe even a motive for killing him. But had they?

Shelby didn't know. What she did know was that she couldn't put Billy and Amelia at risk. They were in school during the day, so that was okay. But she'd have to tell the band they'd need to leave the farm before the kids got home.

Shelby opened her car door, threw her knitting bag onto the passenger seat, and slid behind the wheel. Her car was so old it was in danger of becoming a classic, and Shelby always said a short prayer when she turned the key in the ignition.

The car sprang to life and she breathed a sigh of relief, but then it sputtered, it jerked, and the motor went dead. Shelby tried to start it again, but besides making a groaning noise, as if it were in pain, the engine refused to turn over.

Shelby heard a sound and glanced in her rearview mirror. Another car was barreling down the drive, kicking up bits of loose gravel as it went. It pulled up in back of the van and Jax got out.

He leaned his elbows on Shelby's car and peered in her open window.

"Having some trouble?"

Shelby made a face. "It's not starting. I don't know what's wrong."

Jax's mouth crinkled into a smile, and Shelby realized how attractive he was. He wasn't as ostentatiously good-looking as Travis had been—his attractiveness lay more in the laugh lines around his eyes, in his generous smile, and in the regularity of his features.

"You do have gas, don't you? That's the main reason why cars don't want to start." He grinned to show he was kidding.

"I certainly don't have much, but I think there are some fumes left in the tank."

"Let's take a look under the hood, then."

"I don't want to be a bother. . . ."

"It's no bother. I happen to know a bit about cars. Hopefully I can diagnose your problem."

Shelby felt guilty—she'd just been wondering if Jax had killed his brother and now she was letting him fix her car.

Dear Reader, it's only because I can't afford a repair bill right now.

Shelby got out of the car and followed Jax around to the front. She noticed that while Travis had been tall and on the lanky side, Jax was more muscled with tight, controlled movements.

He lifted the hood of the car, put his hands on the edge, and leaned in. Shelby joined him. Not that she knew anything about the interior workings of a car. It was a gap she kept meaning to remedy—a successful farmer knew how to maintain and repair her own equipment—but so far she'd been happy to take Jake up on his offer of help when she needed it. She did know how to fill the oil and the washer fluid and put gas in the tank, but that was about it.

Jax pointed toward one of the parts nestled under the hood of Shelby's car.

"That's your problem there."

"Where? What?" Shelby leaned closer, but she still had no idea what Jax had found.

"That's your drive belt right there." He pointed again at a part. "I'm afraid it needs replacing."

Shelby sighed. It sounded like a potentially expensive repair.

"I've got some time," Jax said. "There's an auto supply shop out by the highway. I can pick up a new belt, and I'll install it for you."

Shelby didn't know what to say. Relief washed over her. Surely the belt itself couldn't cost that much. As far as she could tell, it wasn't much more than a length of rubber.

Shelby realized she'd never offered Jax her condolences on the death of his brother. "I'm sorry for your loss," she said, hoping that would remedy the omission.

Jax glanced at her quickly. "Thanks. It's still hard to believe. Travis and I used to be so close. We shared a bedroom growing up, were in Scouts together, hung out with the same people in high school. . . ." His voice trailed off.

"But then it all changed," he said, pulling a handkerchief from his pocket and wiping his hands. "Travis changed."

"When he went on *America Can Sing*?"

Jax nodded his head. "That's when it started, yes." He glanced at Shelby again. "And it only got worse as time went on."

Jax slammed the hood of Shelby's car closed. "Then, of course, there's what he did to Jessie."

Shelby frowned. "What did Travis do to Jessie?"

"You don't know?"

"No. I never met Travis before Saturday."

Jax ran a hand through his hair, leaving it boyishly ruffled. "I'm sorry. I thought you knew." He leaned against the hood of Shelby's car and crossed his arms over his chest. "Travis and Jessie were engaged. They met while Travis was in college. She worked in a bar off campus, and they began dating."

Jax kicked at a piece of gravel. "It got serious real fast. Jessie took Travis to meet her parents and a couple of months later they got engaged. Then Travis won that contest to go on *America Can Sing.*" He ran a hand around the back of his neck. "The wedding was all planned out. I was Travis's best man, and a couple of the guys he knew from college were also in the wedding. The night before, we threw him the obligatory bachelor party."

Jax grinned. "We had a great time. Tommy—he was one of Travis's friends—found a girl willing to jump out of a cake." He gave Shelby a sheepish look. "She was wearing a bikini—pretty tame compared to a lot of what goes on these days."

Shelby had read about some of the antics guys got up to at their bachelor parties. Girls, too. Bill's friends had taken him down to the Dixie Bar and Grill for a couple of beers, and her friends had thrown a party in the church hall with cake and lemonade. No strippers or margarita fountains, like some girls had now.

"It was raining the day of the wedding. Jessie was already at the church when I got there. She looked beautiful.

I was in charge of passing out the boutonnieres to the groomsmen, and of course I had the ring safe and sound in my pocket."

"What happened?"

"Travis never showed up. He was supposed to ride to the church with Tommy, but he told Tommy to go ahead and that he'd drive himself. Said he had something to do first." Jax shook his head. "Instead, he bolted."

"Poor Jessie!" Shelby said.

"Yes. Can you imagine? Not only was she heartbroken—which was bad enough. She was mortified on top of it."

"So, you and Jessie . . ."

"Yes. We fell in love and"—Jax shrugged—"the rest is history, as they say."

━━━━━━━━━━━

Jax wasn't gone more than a half hour before he returned with Shelby's new drive belt. Once it had been installed, her car started up without a hitch. It was too late for her knitting group—Shelby grinned to herself—so at least one good thing had come of her car trouble.

The air had warmed up considerably, and Shelby went inside to change into a pair of shorts. She wanted to start planting the eggplant in the patch she and Bert had staked the day before.

Shelby was coming back downstairs when there was a knock on the screen door to the mudroom.

"Hello? Anybody home?"

"In here, Kelly," Shelby called from the kitchen, having recognized her friend's voice.

"I thought I'd stop by on my way back from the Schmidts' farm. They have a couple of new calves that needed their pneumonia vaccine."

Kelly plopped into one of the kitchen chairs. She'd brought the smell of manure inside along with several bits of hay that clung to her hair and T-shirt. She'd kicked her boots off by the back door and was wearing a pair of thick white socks.

Shelby looked her friend over. Kelly looked tired with dark circles ringing her eyes, but Shelby supposed she wasn't getting much sleep under the circumstances. On the other hand, there was a strange glow about her that was at odds with her obvious fatigue.

"Coffee?" Shelby paused by the coffee machine.

"No, thanks. I'm fine."

"You look tired." Shelby pulled out the chair opposite Kelly.

"I am." Kelly coaxed a ladybug that was crawling up the front of her T-shirt into the palm of her hand and went to the back door to release it.

"Do the police still consider Seth a suspect?" Shelby said when Kelly sat back down.

"I hope not. They haven't been by to ask any more questions. Although I don't know if that means anything. Who knows what they're doing behind the scenes?" Kelly twirled Shelby's saltshaker around and around. "I can't believe we should be in Niagara Falls on our honeymoon right now." She gave Shelby a sly smile. "Have you learned anything interesting?"

"Me?" Shelby said, pretending to be affronted. "Why would I know anything?"

"Come on, Shelby. You know you can't resist playing amateur detective."

Shelby grinned. "Well, I did learn something interesting today."

Kelly leaned forward eagerly. "I'm all ears."

Shelby put her hands on the table. "Travis was once engaged to Jessie."

"Jax's wife?"

"Yes. And get this—he left her at the altar."

"You mean literally as in—"

"Yes. She was already dressed and at the church with the bridesmaids and groomsmen all assembled. And Travis didn't show up. He bolted."

Kelly gasped. "How awful." She stopped twirling the saltshaker.

"Jessie must have hated Travis for what he did to her. Maybe she hated him enough to kill him."

"You could be right." Kelly paused for a moment. "Don't you think it's odd that Jax told you about this?"

"Why? I suppose it's common knowledge among the people who know them."

"But things are different now and he's just given his wife a motive for murder."

"I hadn't thought of that. But I can't picture Jessie killing anyone. . . . Besides, she's happily married to Jax now. She's probably put the whole thing behind her."

"I don't think I'd be able to put it behind me. I'd still be mad if someone did that to me."

"Must be your redheaded temperament." Shelby glanced down at the table. "Speaking of redheads . . ."

Kelly raised her eyebrows. "Yes?"

"I know your cousin Peter is in the band—that's why I agreed to let them practice in my barn."

"Plus they're paying you," Kelly said dryly. "Peter told me," she added.

"True. And the money is definitely coming in handy. But I'm worried. . . ."

"About what?"

"What if one of the band members killed Travis? That would mean there's a killer running around on my farm."

Kelly took a deep breath. "I see what you mean. But we're not dealing with a serial killer here. I mean, this person had to have killed Travis for a specific reason. Maybe in a fit of anger even. They're not likely to kill again."

"You've got a point." Shelby tapped her finger against her chin. "I am going to tell them they have to leave before the children are home from school. I can't expose Billy and Amelia to any potential danger."

"There!" Kelly said triumphantly. "You've solved the problem." She leaned forward and grabbed Shelby's hands. "But I didn't stop by to talk to you about this, though. I have something else to tell you."

"What?"

Kelly laughed and her face brightened. "I'm pregnant."

"That's fantastic." Shelby jumped up, ran around the table, and hugged her friend. "How far along—"

"Not very, so we're not going to say anything just yet, but I couldn't wait to tell you."

"I'm so happy for you." Shelby couldn't stop smiling. "You're going to be a wonderful mother."

Suddenly Kelly's face fell. "I just hope the baby's not going to grow up without a father because Seth's in jail." She burst into tears.

12

Dear Reader,

Do your children like vegetables? Or do you have trouble getting them to eat them? Fortunately Amelia and
Billy, having grown up on a farm, are willing to eat
their share. However, if you are having trouble getting
some vitamins into your children's diets, there are ways
to sneak in some of the green stuff without their knowing it.

Take macaroni and cheese—something virtually
every kid likes. Add small pieces of cut-up broccoli,
and I'm willing to bet they won't complain. Zucchini
bread, warm from the oven and dripping with butter,
is delicious. No need to tell anyone there's a vegetable
in it! Carrot muffins with cream cheese frosting are
another sneaky way to make sure they get some beta-
carotene. It works with picky husbands, too!

Shelby reassured Kelly as best she could that the police wouldn't accuse Seth without evidence, and since Seth was innocent, there would be no evidence to be found.

Kelly had finally calmed down and had left to continue on her rounds, her next stop being at the Braxtons' farm for more vaccinations.

Kelly certainly didn't need this stress, Shelby thought. Pregnancy was demanding enough—not just the physical symptoms, but also the hormonal swings. She remembered it well. She smiled to herself. One time she had had a crying jag when she discovered the general store was out of rocky road ice cream, her favorite. She'd eaten so much of it while pregnant she was half-afraid she would give birth to a giant ice-cream cone.

The same thing was obviously happening to Kelly. She would probably settle down in another month or two. Of course by then she'd have heartburn and swollen feet, and Shelby wasn't sure that was much of a trade-off.

She headed outside to tackle planting the eggplant, which had been her plan earlier. Jessie had asked for the day off, and Bert was at the gastroenterologist's, discussing her gallbladder surgery.

Shelby enjoyed working alone occasionally. She took her time, relishing the feel of the earth between her fingers and lovingly mounding it over the seeds.

She was almost finished when the smell of cigarette smoke drifted over on the slight breeze. Shelby sniffed. Where was that coming from? She looked up to see Paislee walking toward her, a cigarette dangling from her slender fingers.

"Hey," Paislee said, brushing away a strand of hair that had blown across her forehead. She gestured toward the cigarette and made a face. "I know I should quit, and I did quit at one time, but whenever I'm stressed, the urge comes back."

"I understand it's a hard habit to break."

"Travis didn't like it when I smoked. He said it made my hair and clothes smell. That's why I quit in the first place. But now . . ." Her voice trailed off, and she took a puff on her cigarette. "I guess it doesn't matter anymore. No one else minds the smoke."

Dear Reader, I could tell her that quitting would benefit her more than anyone else, but I'm pretty sure it wouldn't make any difference.

Shelby stood up with a grunt. "How are your practice sessions going?"

Paislee shrugged her narrow shoulders. "Fine. We're working on a new song, and I'm getting used to singing with Jax instead of Travis."

"That's wonderful that Jax could step in like that."

"To be honest with you, Jax is a lot easier to get along with than Travis was."

"Really?"

"Travis treated everyone as if they were beneath him. All because he won the *America Can Sing* competition. He loved lording it over Cody. Cody's a decent guy. It wasn't fair."

Paislee's cigarette had burned down to the filter, but she continued to hold it, pinched between her thumb and index finger.

"Cody was eliminated in the first round of *America Can Sing*." She looked at Shelby. "But he's really a good guitarist, you know. He choked, that's all. It happens."

"I'm sure it does." Shelby swatted at a fly that kept trying to land on her ear.

"It wasn't fair that Travis wanted to get rid of him."

"What?" Shelby stopped fussing over the fly and stared at Paislee, openmouthed. "Travis was going to fire Cody?"

"Yes. I tried to talk him out of it."

"Did Cody know this?"

Paislee brushed at the hair blowing across her forehead again. "I don't know. I think so."

That was certainly interesting, Shelby thought.

"Paislee," a voice called.

Shelby and Paislee both turned around. Cody was standing outside the barn door, gesturing toward Paislee.

"I'd better go." She gave a quick smile. "Break's over, I guess."

"Listen." Shelby put a hand on Paislee's arm. "I'm sorry about this, but I'm going to have to ask you to wind up your practice sessions by three o'clock."

Paislee looked startled. "Why? Have we done something? We've tried not to be a bother."

"You haven't been. It's just that I think it would be better if you were gone by then."

Paislee looked confused, but then Cody called her name again. She glanced back toward the barn.

"I'd better go. I'm sorry if we're bothering you. I'll tell the rest of them."

Shelby watched as Paislee picked her way across the field. Cody walked toward her, meeting her halfway. He put his arm around her as they walked, their two heads close together.

Shelby shoved her hands in her pockets. She felt bad that Paislee thought the band was being a bother, because that certainly wasn't the case. Shelby hardly knew they were there.

She looked out across the field. Paislee and Cody were about to walk back into the barn when Cody turned around and stared straight at Shelby. He stared long enough for her to become uncomfortable enough to turn away.

Shelby shivered despite the warmth of the sun. Why had Cody turned to look at her like that? Was it something Paislee had said to him? His expression had been almost . . . menacing. Was it because she wanted them to leave the farm early?

Somehow she didn't think so.

━━━━━━━━━━

Shelby was having a late lunch when Billy got home from school. Shelby barely had time to shove a piece of her home-made string cheese into his hands before he was out the door to play. Amelia got home shortly afterward. Her cheeks were red and her face was flushed with what looked like excitement. Shelby wondered what had happened in school that day. Had some boy she had a crush on suddenly noticed her? Shelby felt a pang at the thought. The road was rocky ahead—she remembered her own adolescence and the moments of great exultation as well as those of dark despair.

But judging by Amelia's face, today had been one of the good days.

"How was school?" Shelby said as Amelia dumped her backpack on a kitchen chair and foraged in its depths.

"Wonderful," Amelia said, grinning and clutching her social studies textbook to her chest.

"That good, huh?" Shelby smiled at her daughter. Seeing Amelia happy made her happy—a sentiment only parents could really appreciate. "So what's put you in such a good mood?"

"The kids at school are getting excited about our anti-bullying campaign. Katelyn and I have invited a few people to join our committee. Even Bailey O'Keefe has agreed to be on it."

"And who is Bailey O'Keefe?" Shelby said as she began folding the bundle of towels she'd pulled from the dryer and piled on the kitchen table.

Amelia rolled her eyes. "She's Luke Armstrong's girl-friend."

"Isn't he the new quarterback?"

"Yes. Can you believe it? Bailey's practically royalty."

"Just because she's dating the quarterback? Surely she has some merits of her own." Shelby added a folded towel to the growing stack on one of the kitchen chairs.

"Of course she does." Amelia got a glass from the cupboard, filled it at the tap, and took a gulp. "Today at lunch, someone threw a meatball at Lorraine. It would be one thing if they started throwing meatballs at everyone and it was only a random food fight, but they didn't—just Lorraine. I got up to tell them to stop and Katelyn stood up with me. Then Bailey jumped up. I couldn't believe it. Then Roger Peacock—he's in my English class—stood up, too. Pretty soon there were ten of us standing up for Lorraine. They wouldn't have done it if Bailey hadn't done it first."

Dear Reader, talk about sheep mentality. It pretty much describes teens.

Amelia took another drink of water and wiped her mouth with the back of her hand. "This campaign is going to be positively epic."

"So how is your brilliant idea for the kickoff shaping up? Still not going to give me any hints?"

"It's going great. I'm just waiting for them to—" Amelia clamped her mouth shut. "I'll tell you about it when it's all set."

"Somehow I don't think it has anything to do with the theme week and the raffle I suggested."

Amelia didn't say anything. She pulled open the fridge, retrieved a can of pop, and grabbed a granola bar. Clutching both in her hands, she started toward the door.

Shelby was left feeling decidedly uneasy although she couldn't quite put her finger on why.

llllllllllllllllllllllllll

"What's that you're making? I thought you were going out to dinner." Bert walked into the kitchen, her beige patent leather purse—what she thought of as her *summer bag*—swinging from the crook of her arm.

"I am, but the kids have to eat, don't they?"

"I could have put something together for them."

Shelby stopped with her wooden spoon in her hand. "You're already doing enough for me, Bert. I can't ask you to do that, too."

"I could have ordered a pizza for them. There's that new place out by the highway that delivers. The kids would like that."

"I'm sure they would," Shelby said, continuing to stir the macaroni and cheese bubbling on the stove. "But they get pizza for lunch at school now, believe it or not, and I try to make sure they're getting at least one healthy meal a day. I've put some cut-up broccoli in here, so they get their veggies as well as a boatload of fat and carbs."

"Pizza for lunch? We had to make do with what our mothers sent in our lunch sacks. I remember having butter sandwiches, because that was all my parents could afford, although my mother, bless her heart, would cut the bread into fancy shapes, which made all the other kids jealous."

Shelby glanced at the clock. She could feel the steam

from the pot of boiling water curling the hairs around her face. She hoped she would have time to wash her face, put on some fresh makeup, and maybe take a flat iron to her hair.

"Why don't I keep an eye on that while you get ready?" Bert said almost as if she could read Shelby's mind.

Shelby's shoulders sagged in relief. "Thanks, Bert."

"I'm sure you want to spend some time primping for your date."

Shelby was about to open her mouth to protest it wasn't a date—at least not a date date—but if it pleased Bert to think it was, why should she be the one to snatch her happiness away?

Bert took over supervision of the pot of macaroni and cheese, and Shelby dashed upstairs to make herself presentable as quickly as possible.

Shelby grabbed a blue-and-white flowered sundress from her closet and slipped into it, then nearly changed her mind. She didn't want to appear as if she was trying too hard. But she had to admit, the dress did good things for her—it brought out the auburn highlights in her dark hair and looked attractive against the tan she'd acquired working outside.

After fussing with her hair for ten minutes, Shelby decided it would have to do. She had achieved some semblance of neatness and that was about all she could hope for. She powdered the shine off her nose, swiped on some lipstick that left a berry-colored stain on her lips, flicked off the light in the bathroom, and went downstairs.

Bert had put out the place mats and was rummaging in the kitchen drawer for silverware.

Shelby peered into the pot of macaroni and cheese. She picked up the spoon and gave it a couple of stirs.

Bert took the spoon out of her hand and glared at her. "I've been cooking since before you were born, missy, so no need to go worrying about the kids' dinner."

Shelby put her hands up in surrender. "I can see you've got it under control."

The doorbell rang just then, and Shelby's heart jumped.

Bert gave her a slight push. "Have a good time."

"Thanks," Shelby called over her shoulder as she headed toward the foyer.

"Hey," Matt said when Shelby opened the door.

He was wearing a pair of khakis and a blue-and-white-striped shirt. He smelled of laundry starch and crisp men's cologne and Shelby was glad she'd taken the time to put on a dress.

"Shall we go?"

Matt led Shelby to his car and opened the door for her. "I'm sorry it's only the diner for dinner. You have to promise to let me take you to Lucia's again soon."

"I will."

Half a dozen cars were parked in the diner's lot. Most locals had already been in for their main meal and were headed home to catch the evening news. Dining out wasn't something Lovett residents did on a regular basis, but every now and then even the thriftiest of farmers made a trip to the diner for lunch or dinner or to the Dixie Bar and Grill for a greasy hamburger and fries and a cold beer.

"Let's sit in the back away from the fan." Matt pointed to an industrial-sized freestanding fan that stood in the corner by the front door.

He led Shelby to a table and waited while she slid into the booth.

Matt picked up the menu and laughed. "I don't know why I look at this." He waved the plastic-coated paper in front of Shelby. "I know perfectly well everything that's on it."

"I don't think it's changed since they opened this place," Shelby said, setting her menu aside.

The waitress, a harried-looking older woman with dyed red hair and a pencil stuck behind her ear, appeared at their table.

"Coffee?" she said, arching severely plucked brows as she turned over their coffee cups and held a coffeepot over them.

Both Matt and Shelby nodded.

"Has there been any news about that poor fellow's murder?" Matt said as he stirred cream and sugar into his coffee.

"Not really. I haven't talked to Frank since shortly after it happened." Shelby picked up her empty sugar packet and began to pleat it. "It seems Travis had a fair number of people who had reason to dislike him—both in the band and here in Lovett."

"But to kill someone." Matt shook his head. "You'd have to be plenty mad."

"True. It's hard to imagine."

The waitress returned with a pad and pencil. "Ready to order?"

Shelby and Matt ordered and were quiet until the waitress moved away to wait on the table by the door.

"Who are your suspects?" Matt said, and grinned.

Shelby put up a hand. "I'm staying out of this one, believe me."

"Mmm-hmmm." Matt made a noncommittal sound.

"Seriously," Shelby protested.

Matt fiddled with his spoon. "You must have an opinion, though. Who's your chief suspect?"

Shelby thought. "I don't know. Maybe Jessie? Travis left her at the altar—literally—and that's bound to leave a deep scar. Of course she seems happily married now, so maybe not." Shelby blew on her coffee—the diner prided itself on providing a scalding-hot brew for its customers—and took a sip. "Of course Jax—he's Travis's brother and Jessie's husband—has a motive as well. Travis was driving when they were in an accident that put Jax in rehab for months and cost him his singing career."

"Isn't he the fellow who's taken Travis's place in the band? That would certainly strengthen his motive."

"I agree. Plus maybe there's some lingering resentment over Travis's treatment of Jessie? I don't know."

The waitress appeared at their table with a huge tray balanced on her shoulder. She slid a plate of chicken-fried steak and mashed potatoes drowning in gravy in front of Matt and a potpie in front of Shelby.

"So," Matt said when he'd almost finished his meal. "What about us, Shelby? Where are we going with this?"

Shelby looked up, startled. "I . . . I . . . What do you mean?"

Matt pushed his plate away and rested his folded hands on the table.

"I mean you and me. I think you like me." He gave a crooked, self-deprecating grin. "And I know I like you."

"I do like you," Shelby blurted out, feeling her face get hot.

"I'm not getting any younger," Matt said. He laughed. "I never thought I'd hear myself say that." He reached out and took Shelby's hand. "But I mean it. I've been through a lot, but I've made my peace with it, and I'm ready to settle down." He looked away from Shelby. "I'd like a family to come home to at night."

"I don't know what to say," Shelby stammered.

Matt squeezed Shelby's hand. "You don't have to say anything. I just need to know that that sort of relationship isn't out of the question someday. Will you think about it?"

Shelby took a deep breath. "Yes. I'll think about it."

llllllllllllllllllllllllll

The sun was setting when Matt dropped Shelby off at home. The shadows in the corners had deepened and a light shone through the front window of the house.

Shelby was walking up the front path when she noticed a figure standing at her front door. It was Frank.

She was embarrassed that he had seen her with Matt, although she knew it was perfectly reasonable for her to be out with a man. She was no longer a wife, after all—she was a widow.

"Hello," Shelby called as she approached the front door.

Frank watched her as she walked toward him.

"I'm sorry. I didn't realize you were out." Frank kicked at a loose pebble with the toe of his boot. "I wanted to check on you and the kids. Make sure you're okay."

"Come on in." Shelby pulled open the screen door, and it squeaked loudly.

"You should let me oil that for you. A good squirt of WD-40 and it won't make a sound."

Bert was asleep in a chair in front of the television, her knitting abandoned in her lap.

Shelby smiled and put a finger to her lips. "Shhhh."

Frank grinned back.

"Coffee?" Shelby asked as she led Frank down the hall to the kitchen.

"Sure." Frank massaged his forehead between his eyes. "I've been up since four a.m. Bad accident out by the Dixie.

Your neighbor Jake was called out, too. He had to use the Jaws of Life to extricate one of the victims."

"What happened?" Shelby filled the coffee carafe with water and poured it into the machine.

"It's still under investigation, but as near as we can tell, the driver of the Durango was texting on his phone when he ran a stop sign and T-boned a Chrysler Sebring. Not the sort of car you usually see out here." Frank shook his head. "It wasn't pretty."

Shelby could imagine. She lived in fear of the moment when Amelia got her license. She was sure she'd never have a moment's peace again.

The coffee machine had stopped gurgling, and Shelby retrieved two mugs from the cupboard. They didn't match, but she figured they would hold the coffee all the same.

"Was the driver drinking?"

"I don't know. He had to be airlifted to the hospital, where they'll run some tests, of course. But one of the patrolmen thought he smelled marijuana."

Shelby shuddered. She handed Frank his mug of coffee.

"Texting, drugs, and driving are a deadly combination."

Shelby pulled out a chair and sat down. She took a sip of her coffee. It was hot and burned going all the way down.

"Any news on the murder investigation?" Shelby said when she could talk again.

"Nah. Not much. We're following up a couple of leads, but so far all the leads we've had have taken us nowhere." Frank stirred his coffee absentmindedly. "No one saw or heard anything, it seems."

Shelby thought about Valerie of Grilling Gals seeing someone in Seth's hat—she refused to believe it was Seth himself. Valerie had said she'd told the police about the hat—if Frank really thought Seth was the person Valerie had seen, surely Seth would have been arrested by now.

Frank was quiet, stroking the side of his mug with his thumb.

"Did you have a nice time tonight?" he said finally. He didn't look at Shelby but stared into his coffee mug.

It wasn't what Shelby had expected. "Yes," she said after a long pause. She picked up her coffee, hoping the mug would hide her face.

"Wasn't that Matt from the general store?"

"Yes, it was."

Frank smiled. "He's a good guy."

"Yes," Shelby said again, not knowing what else to say.

Her heart was practically beating out of her chest as she looked at Frank. He was so like Bill, she longed to reach out and touch his face and run her fingers over his lips. She shook herself. She'd decided Frank was off-limits. How would she ever know if she really loved him? It wasn't fair to him. It was time for her to move on—Matt was part of her future; Frank was part of her past.

Frank must have sensed her change in mood because he pushed back his chair, scraping it across the linoleum with a loud screech.

"I'd better be going. I wanted to make sure you and the kids were okay." He shrugged. "You know, given that someone was murdered right here on your farm."

"I appreciate that, Frank. I really do."

"I'll be going, then."

"Frank?" Shelby called after him.

He turned around, a hopeful look on his face.

"Thanks."

13

Dear Reader,

Did you know there are different types of dawn? Twilight, too. Civil dawn is the brightest and occurs when the center of the sun is six degrees below the horizon. At nautical dawn, the center of the sun is twelve degrees below the horizon. The sky is completely dark before astronomical dawn, which is when the center of the sun is still eighteen degrees beneath the horizon.

At civil twilight the sky is still light enough for outdoor activities to be carried out. It's not unusual to find farmers still out in their fields working until the sun finally dips lower in the sky.

Shelby slept uneasily that night with images of Frank, Bill, and Matt invading her dreams. When she woke, the bedclothes were in a tangle, and her nightgown was damp with perspiration.

No sun was peeking around the edges of the blinds. Shelby glanced at her alarm clock. It was only five in the morning. She swung her legs over the side of the bed and grimaced when they hit the cold floor. Nights were still cool, although during the day it was warm enough to go swimming if you were courageous enough to brave the chilly waters of the lake.

The chickens would be fed early this morning, Shelby thought as she slipped into the jeans and T-shirt she'd left on her chair the day before. But she knew she wouldn't hear any complaints from them.

Shelby flicked on the kitchen lights and winced slightly at their brilliance. She'd gotten dressed in the dark and her eyes had yet to adjust.

It was dark out, but there was the suggestion of the faintest light at the edge of the horizon. It didn't matter—Shelby knew the way to the barn with her eyes closed, every bump, twist, and turn.

Shelby pulled open the barn door. The customary squeak had been remedied with some WD-40 before the wedding. Matt had helped her drag the feed bags and farm implements back to their usual places. They looked at odds with the musicians' amplifiers, cords, and microphones.

Shelby filled her pail and, with the chickens squawking around her ankles like a gaggle of unruly children vying for her attention, distributed their feed.

The sky was getting lighter as she walked back to the farmhouse. The children would be asleep for another hour and that would give her time to work on her blog.

Today she was writing about Kelly's wedding. She'd promised her readers a detailed description of the events. Shelby bit her lip. What to do about the murder? Her readers might have seen the story in the newspaper and would wonder why she hadn't mentioned it. Perhaps she could touch on it only lightly and that would be satisfactory. She hoped that someday she could think about the joy and beauty of Kelly and Seth's wedding without also having Travis's murder come to mind.

Shelby heard Billy's alarm go off as she was finishing up her blog entry. Minutes later, Amelia's alarm went off. Shelby listened carefully, making sure she heard two pairs of feet on the floorboards and didn't need to go to the bottom of the stairs to call them.

Shortly afterward, Billy came stumbling down the stairs and into the kitchen. He wanted to eat his bowl of cereal in front of the television, but Shelby nixed that idea. He would spend more time watching than eating and would miss the school bus again.

Amelia came downstairs at the last possible minute and grabbed one of Shelby's homemade granola bars on her way out the door. Billy wasn't far behind. Quiet settled over the house, and Shelby took a moment to savor it. As much as she loved her children, she wasn't averse to some peace occasionally.

Today she was holding a cooking class in the church kitchen as part of Lovett's adult education program. Shelby had accepted the assignment in a weak moment during the winter, when the days had seemed so long without as much work to do on the farm.

They were going to learn how to spatchcock a chicken and bake it with lemon and herbs. It was a simple but delicious recipe.

Shelby filled her basket with the fresh chicken she'd purchased from the Comstocks' chicken and turkey farm down the road, along with thyme and oregano from her own garden, a couple of lemons, and a bottle of olive oil.

The church kitchen was well equipped with pots and pans, but the quality of their knives was questionable, and Shelby seriously doubted that she would find a zester in one of their drawers, so she tossed both into her basket.

She put Billy's cereal bowl and spoon into the dishwasher, wiped down the kitchen table, and turned out the lights.

||||||||||||||||||||||||

Mrs. Willoughby was the first to arrive for class—not unexpected since she was the church secretary and had to only come down the stairs. Isabel Stone was next with Coralynne not far behind. Liz Gardener had signed up, but Shelby knew from experience that she was likely to cancel at the last minute, so she was surprised when Liz appeared at the door.

The ladies arrayed themselves around the kitchen island—both Mrs. Willoughby and Coralynne keeping an obvious distance from Isabel Stone, whom they both deemed unworthy of Reverend Mather's attentions.

Shelby smiled to herself. Isabel was overdressed as usual in a white silk blouse and a floral printed skirt. Shelby urged Isabel to come stand by her, a move that made both Mrs. Willoughby and Coralynne frown slightly.

Shelby waited till everyone was settled to begin.

"Today we are going to spatchcock a chicken."

There was a barely audible gasp from Mrs. Willoughby and a clearly disapproving look on her face.

"It means to butterfly a chicken or spread it open," Shelby added hastily, demonstrating with her hands. She could only imagine what Mrs. Willoughby must have been picturing.

"Then why not say so in the first place?" Coralynne sniffed.

"You may find a recipe that refers to it as spatchcocking—particularly if it's an English recipe."

"American recipes are perfectly good enough for me," Mrs. Willoughby said, her many chins wagging in disapproval.

Shelby sighed. She placed the chicken, which suddenly looked obscenely naked, on the cutting board and grabbed her knife and kitchen shears.

"It's really quite easy," Shelby said as she spread the chicken out flat. "And it cooks so much faster this way. You can grill it or bake it—it's delicious either way."

The fresh scents of lemon and herbs perfumed the air as Shelby set about zesting and chopping. Her audience watched with rapt attention.

"What if I don't want to use thyme or oregano?" Isabel asked. "Daniel doesn't care for herbs."

Mrs. Willoughby and Coralynne exchanged knowing glances.

"You can make the dish with lemon, salt, and a little pepper then," Shelby said. She poured some olive oil into a bowl and added the lemon zest and the chopped herbs.

Liz looked around the room. "I'm going to say it if no one else is. Is there anything new about the murder?" She crossed her arms over her chest. "I haven't seen anything in the paper lately. There was nothing in our little local paper and nothing in the daily paper either."

Shelby decided to ignore the interruption. "Now you put the spatchcocked chicken in a dish and pour the herb-and-lemon oil over it. Be sure to rub it in really well."

Shelby looked up and sighed. No one was listening.

"Doreen is in my Bible study group," Mrs. Willoughby

said. "She works over at the police station. She said the poor man was drowned in a trough that was filled with water."

Everyone gasped.

Shelby thought the police were keeping that information quiet. Obviously if they wanted to keep details of their cases under wraps, someone was going to have to figure out how to keep Doreen quiet.

"That's absolutely terrible," Isabel said in her husky voice. "Who would do such a thing?"

"It seems the police don't have a clue," Mrs. Willoughby said authoritatively.

"They must have some idea," Liz insisted. "Weren't there clues at the scene?"

Shelby thought of Seth's hat and clamped her lips shut—not that she would say anything, but just in case something burst out of her mouth.

"How on earth could someone drown in a trough?" Coralynne asked, her eyes wide. "That doesn't seem possible."

Mrs. Willoughby looked at Coralynne as if she had just asked whether the earth was flat or round.

"The murderer"—she said the word with great relish—"obviously held the poor man's head underwater. There's no other way."

Coralynne looked spooked, her eyes the size of saucers. "I do hope there isn't a murderer running around loose in Lovett."

Shelby hastened to reassure them. "I'm sure the motive was personal and we're all perfectly safe."

"I hope so. I saw a television show the other day about a serial killer who went around targeting older women with cats. It scared me half to death."

"But a television show is hardly real, is it?" Mrs. Willoughby said. "It's all made up. Things like that don't happen in real life."

Shelby opened her mouth but then shut it again. No need to alarm Coralynne any further.

"But don't you think—," Liz said, pausing as if she was thinking. "Don't you think that the killer would have gotten wet? It seems unlikely that the poor, hapless victim simply allowed himself to be drowned. He must have struggled."

"What a ghastly thought," Mrs. Willoughby said.

Liz shrugged. "It's true."

Liz was right, Shelby thought. Surely the killer got water on him. Or her, she added to herself. She should have thought of that herself. She tried to think, but she couldn't remember whether she'd seen anyone wearing clothing with wet spots. It just hadn't occurred to her at the time.

Maybe someone else would know? The band was still using the barn for practice. Perhaps she'd feel them out and see how they responded.

Mrs. Willoughby stayed behind to help Shelby clean up the dishes. She sidled up next to Shelby, who was elbow-deep in sudsy water, and asked in a whisper, "Have you discovered anything about Isabel yet? Surely you must have found something on the computer."

Shelby closed her eyes and sighed. She'd thought she was going to get away without an inquisition from Mrs. Willoughby. Perhaps the best plan of attack was to try to make the little information she'd managed to glean from Dotty sound as enticing as possible.

"Well." Shelby paused dramatically. So dramatically that Mrs. Willoughby held her breath and looked as if her eyes were going to bug out at any second.

Finally Shelby took pity on her. "I did find out a few things," she said in a conspiratorial and tantalizing voice.

"What?" Mrs. Willoughby was practically licking her lips in anticipation.

"Isabel is from Canada." Shelby pronounced this as if it were terribly exotic—on a par with being from Nepal or Mozambique.

Mrs. Willoughby's eyes got bigger. She was falling for it.

"And she had a very high position in a company called Glide. In fact, she was second only to the president of the company."

It was a bit of an exaggeration, but Mrs. Willoughby's indrawn breath told Shelby she was impressed.

"She's divorced." Mrs. Willoughby frowned and Shelby hastened to add, "But he was a terrible man and she had no choice."

Mrs. Willoughby's expression softened.

"No children," Shelby added.

Mrs. Willoughby nodded.

Shelby leaned a little closer to Mrs. Willoughby. "But a hard worker and very well liked."

Dear Reader, take that, Mrs. Willoughby! Isabel appears to be a fine, upstanding citizen, if a bit mysterious.

Mrs. Willoughby sniffed. "Perhaps she's not as frivolous as her high heels and flowery perfume would suggest."

"And," Shelby said, employing another dramatic pause, "she wants to be a writer."

"Well, I never," Mrs. Willoughby said. "I honestly don't know what Reverend Mather would make of that."

||||||||||||||||||||||||

Shelby took the chicken home with her—there wasn't time to bake it during the class—and stowed it in the refrigerator for dinner that night. She made herself some lunch, then headed outside to do some weeding before her herb patch was taken over with the pigweed she'd spotted earlier. It had to be removed before it flowered, or you'd be battling it forever.

Shelby knelt between the rows of thyme and oregano and began yanking weeds. She thought her conversation with Mrs. Willoughby had gone rather well. At least until the end. Perhaps she shouldn't have told Mrs. Willoughby about Isabel's ambitions to become a writer. No doubt that was something she would find unseemly in a rector's wife.

Music was coming from the open doors of the barn. The band was playing the song she'd heard the other day—the one with the haunting melody. Once again, Jax's and Paislee's voices blended beautifully together. Shelby stopped to listen, her head cocked to one side. She wondered if they would be recording the piece. It seemed as if Jax had permanently stepped into Travis's place in the band. Had he possibly murdered his brother to achieve just that?

And what about Cody? Was he still hoping to start a relationship with Paislee? With Travis out of the way, it was possible she would turn to him.

Shelby sighed as she sat back on her heels and surveyed her herb garden. She'd certainly uncovered enough motives for Travis's murder, but she was no closer to uncovering the killer.

‖‖‖‖‖‖‖‖‖‖‖‖‖‖‖‖‖‖‖‖‖‖

Shelby was carrying a bag of dog food from her car to her house—she'd been to the Lovett Feed Store to stock up—when Brian, the band's manager, pulled into the driveway in his Taurus.

He waved to Shelby as he got out of his car.

"Looks like you could use a hand with that," he said, taking the bag of dog food from her.

Shelby had carried similar bags of dog food into the house by herself many times before, but she wasn't the sort of woman to turn down an offer of help. In her mind, she had nothing to prove, so why not let someone else lend a hand?

Brian hefted the bag as if it were weightless, shifting it into the crook of his arm.

"Thanks," Shelby said, falling into step beside him. "The dogs seem to be out of food every time I turn around."

Brian smiled. "I imagine that mastiff of yours eats her fair share."

Brian had a nice smile, Shelby thought. It changed his face—he no longer looked so stern, which had been her first impression of him. He had attractive blue eyes as well.

"Where would you like me to put this?" he asked when they were inside.

Shelby led him into the mudroom. "You can put it over there, if you don't mind." She pointed to the far corner.

Brian leaned the bag against the wall.

"Thank you," Shelby said. "Can I get you a cold drink?"

"That would certainly hit the spot."

Shelby retrieved a pitcher of iced tea from the refrigerator and filled two glasses.

"Thanks." Brian took the glass, leaned against the kitchen counter, and took a sip.

"Had you known Travis long?" Shelby said.

"Not very, no. I met him when he was on *America Can Sing*. I knew right away he had talent, and I decided I wanted in."

"Hitching your wagon to his star, so to speak?"

Brian laughed. "It doesn't sound very nice when you put it that way, does it? But look at it this way. His job was to do what he did best—sing. My job was to do everything else so he didn't have to."

Dear Reader, wouldn't that be nice?

Brian finished his iced tea but seemed in no hurry to leave.

"How lucky for you that Jax has been able to take Travis's place so easily," Shelby said.

"Jax is every bit as talented as Travis was. It's too bad about that accident. But he worked hard in rehab, and they managed to put him back together." Brian put his glass down on the counter. "He wanted to pick up where he and Travis had left off, but Travis wouldn't hear of it. He'd made a solo career for himself, and he wasn't giving it up."

"You mean Jax asked Travis if he could join the band as originally planned?"

Brian pointed a finger at Shelby. "Bingo."

"Jax must have been furious. Especially since the accident was Travis's fault."

"Furious is right. I'd say he was beyond furious." Brian hooked his thumbs through his belt loops and crossed his ankles. "Someone had to have been pretty darn furious to do what they did—drowning Travis like that." He shook his head. "Awful way to go."

"So you think Jax killed Travis?"

Brian shook his head vigorously. "No, no, nothing like that. I didn't mean for you to think . . ."

Shelby thought about what Liz had said during the cooking class.

"Whoever murdered Travis had to have gotten wet, don't you think? I mean, I doubt Travis let them hold his head under the water without so much as an attempt to struggle."

Brian raised his eyebrows. "Good point. I hadn't thought of that."

"Did you happen to notice anyone coming back into the barn with wet clothes?"

Brian rubbed a hand over his face. "Not that I can think of. But I don't know if I would have even noticed. We were all occupied with the performance. I doubt the person would have been dripping wet. That I would certainly have noticed."

Brian uncrossed his ankles and pushed away from the counter. "I should get back. We have a couple more hours of rehearsing ahead of us. We want to record that new song with Jax and Paislee before word gets around about Travis's death and people assume we're all washed up." Brian laughed. "Washed up," he repeated. "Perhaps not the most fortunate choice of words, I'm afraid."

14

Dear Reader,

They say that revenge is a dish best served cold. Of course, most people act in the heat of the moment—striking out either physically or by saying something they soon regret. I think it takes a special kind of person to be able to bide their time and strike when their enemy least expects it. I can't help but wonder if that's what Jessie did.

She certainly had good enough reason to hate Travis. Of course, they also say that living well is the best revenge. She had a new life with Jax—but was that enough for her?

"How are you feeling?" Shelby said.

She and Kelly were sitting on Shelby's porch in a pair of rocking chairs with cold glasses of lemonade by their sides.

The air was cooler than it had been earlier and a faint breeze had picked up. It was quiet—the only sounds the vibrating buzz of insects hidden in the plants and trees and the faint *rat-a-tat-tat* of a woodpecker in the distance.

"Meh," Kelly said. "I'm not really nauseated, but at the same time, the smell of manure is beginning to put me off. And I've been craving cornflakes like you wouldn't believe. And sleeping! I fell asleep in my truck yesterday between appointments." She rocked her chair back and forth. "Seth says that's normal and will go away after the first three months."

"And return the last month or two," Shelby said, thinking about her own pregnancies. "Get as much rest as you can. You won't be getting much sleep once the baby is here."

Kelly groaned. "So I've heard." She circled the rim of her glass with her finger. Rivulets of condensation ran down the sides. "I think I'd feel a lot better if Seth wasn't under suspicion for murder."

"The police don't really suspect him, do they?"

"I don't know. Has Frank said anything?"

Shelby shook her head. "Not to me." She ran her fingers over the arm of her chair—the wood was splintering from exposure to the sun and the rain. She'd have to refinish the pair of them soon. "There are plenty of other, more likely suspects. I mean, Seth would hardly kill Travis because of something that had happened in college."

"I know he wouldn't. He wouldn't kill anyone . . . period."

"There are other people who have a lot more to gain from his death. Take Jax, for instance." Shelby stopped rocking and turned to Kelly. "With Travis dead, he's moved into the lead spot in the band. And heaven knows, he had plenty of reasons to resent his brother. Not only did Travis cause the accident that sent Jax to rehab, but when Jax got better, Travis refused to let him join the group."

"So Travis didn't want to share the limelight?"

"It seems that way. And Jax is good. He might even be better than Travis." Shelby began rocking again. "Then there's Cody. Travis treated him like a gofer and apparently was about to fire him."

"That sounds like a good reason to get mad." Kelly leaned her head back against the chair. "What about the girl?"

"Paislee? I don't think she had anything against Travis, but Jessie certainly did."

"Jessie?"

"She's the one who is married to Jax, and she's helping me out here on the farm. She's nice enough, although a little shy. She's the girl Travis was engaged to and left standing at the altar."

Kelly stopped rocking. "I don't know what I would have done if Seth had done that to me."

"Seth would never do something like that."

"You're right," Kelly said. "And he would never murder someone either."

||||||||||||||||||||||||

Shelby couldn't help thinking about what Liz had said during Shelby's cooking class—that the killer must have gotten wet, because surely Travis had struggled. Maybe she would ask the band if they'd noticed anything. It was possible they had. And if one of them was guilty, he might react to the question and perhaps she would pick up on it.

Shelby headed across the field with Jenkins and Bitsy following in back of her with occasional detours to check out an intriguing smell or a curious noise.

She heard someone call her name and looked over to see Jake, her neighbor, mending the fence between the pasture he rented from her and her field. He was wearing a T-shirt that did nothing to conceal his muscular chest and upper arms. Shelby had to admit, he was a very attractive piece of eye candy.

Shelby waved and continued on. She stopped for a moment and listened. There was no music coming from the barn. All she could hear was the rustling of the leaves on the apple tree as the breeze picked up and the sound of Bitsy panting, her large pink tongue hanging out the side of her mouth.

Perhaps she'd missed them. It was almost three o'clock— the time she'd asked them to leave.

Shelby peered around the edge of the open barn door. At first she saw no one, just the band's equipment—microphones, amplifiers, and yards of tangled wires. They must have already left.

She was about to turn away when she heard a noise coming from behind one of the pieces of equipment. A moment later, a head appeared, popping up over the top of the amplifier. It was Cody.

He looked almost as startled as Shelby.

Then he smiled. "I'm sorry. I didn't hear you come in." He pointed to the amplifier. "I was fixing the connection— it was loose. I'll be out of here in a minute."

"Don't worry about it. I didn't mean to disturb you."

"You're fine. I'm almost done. Everyone has gone to the Dixie for a hamburger and some beers. I wanted to get this taken care of before I did anything else."

Travis might be dead, Shelby thought, but it seemed as if Cody was still being used as the group's general dogsbody.

Cody began winding up one of the electrical cords that lay in a heap on the floor. "By the way," he said, "has there been any news about the police investigation? We've had to cancel a bunch of concert dates already. I gather that that detective is a relative of yours."

"My brother-in-law," Shelby said. "But I haven't heard anything from him recently." She hesitated. "One thing did occur to me—and this is what I came out here to ask you— the person who killed Travis must have gotten wet when he held Travis's head underwater. Travis would have struggled. . . ."

Cody shivered. "That's a horrible thought."

"Did you happen to notice anyone whose shirt or pants were wet? You might not have thought anything of it at the time."

Shelby realized she could be putting herself in danger with this question if Cody was the person who'd murdered Travis, but Jake was outside, close by, and would surely hear her if she yelled.

Cody gave Shelby a startled look and became very still.

"No," he said a little too loudly. "I didn't. I think you're barking up the wrong tree if you think one of us did it."

"I'm sorry. I didn't mean to imply . . . I'm sorry if I've offended you."

Cody gave a strained smile. "No offense taken." He patted the amplifier he was sitting on. "Now, if you don't mind, I'd better finish up so I can get out of here. There's a tall, cold glass of beer at the Dixie calling my name."

"Sure. Enjoy your beer."

As she was walking toward the door, she turned around briefly. Cody was staring at her with a very odd expression on his face.

IIIIIIIIIIIIIIIIIIIIIIII

She had certainly picked up a strange vibe from Cody, Shelby thought, as she chopped an onion for the chicken dish she was making for dinner—especially when she'd mentioned the fact that the person who'd killed Travis must have gotten water on their clothes.

She had the feeling Cody knew something, and it was something he wasn't about to share with her. Or was it that he was the guilty party? Shelby had no idea, but the thought that she might have been out in the barn alone with a killer made her shiver.

She put the chopped onion into a pan where olive oil was heating over a low flame, and added some minced garlic. When the onions were softened and the garlic was beginning to brown, she added some chicken pieces. Once the skin was nice and golden brown, she added the tomatoes she'd canned last summer, some orzo, and some chicken broth. She lowered the heat, put a lid on the pan, and let it simmer.

While it cooked, she would work on her blog, although her inclination was to plop into a chair in the living room, put her feet up on an ottoman, and leaf through her pile of seed catalogs.

Shelby sat at the kitchen table and powered up her computer. First she would scroll through the comments on her previous post. She always tried to respond to any questions readers might have had, as well as to engage as many of them as possible in a friendly dialogue. She found it helped to build her audience and bring people back to her blog again and again.

Shelby smiled—some of her regulars had left comments. There were some people she could always count on to read her latest entry, and she'd come to think of them as friends.

She read the second-to-last comment and then went on to the final one. As she read, her hands slowly tightened on the hem of her shirt, and her heart rate sped up until her heart felt as if it were going to jump out of her chest.

It wasn't actually a comment at all—it was a threat. Shelby read it again to make sure she hadn't misunderstood it, but there was no misunderstanding the menace in the commenter's tone.

It read: *Why don't you stick to cooking and gardening and stop poking your nose into other people's business? If you don't, someone else is bound to get hurt, and that someone will be you.*

15

Dear Reader,

Have you ever noticed how in British novels and movies when someone has had a bad shock, they always give them a cup of tea? I used to think that was simply a tradition unique to the British, but it turns out that offering someone tea under those circumstances actually has merit.

The warm beverage helps to get the blood flowing and combats the shaking and shivering that often accompany a bad shock. Adding plenty of sugar is a good idea, too—the sweet will help keep the person's blood sugar levels up until they are feeling normal again.

The kitchen was warm with the stove on and the last rays of sun coming in the kitchen window, yet Shelby felt chilled to the bone. She sat and stared at the message, half-expecting that it was a figment of her imagination and that at any minute it would disappear.

She was surprised to discover her hands were shaking. She had no idea whether this person was some random lunatic who had found her blog by accident or someone who knew about Travis's murder and the investigation.

She ought to tell Frank about it. She couldn't take the chance that the threat was real and that the person might try to harm her or her children.

Shelby picked up the telephone, then hesitated. Frank was busy and worked long, hard hours. Should she really be bothering him with something that might turn out to be a big nothing in the end?

Yes, Shelby decided. Frank would want to know.

She dialed Frank's cell phone. He picked up on the second ring.

"Shelby—is something wrong?"

Shelby heard indistinct scratchy voices coming over Frank's radio and a horn blaring. He must be in his car. She explained about the comment on her blog.

"I'm turning around. I'll be there in ten minutes."

Shelby felt conflicted. Was she wasting Frank's time?

Steam was coming out from under the lid of the pot on the stove. Shelby lifted it and gave the contents a stir. The orzo had absorbed nearly all the liquid from the chicken broth and the tomatoes. A few more minutes and it would be done. She replaced the lid and turned down the flame to a bare simmer.

She heard Frank's car coming down the driveway and her feeling of relief surprised her. She looked out the window, waiting for his truck to appear, then hastily turned away and began to set the table so he wouldn't catch her watching for him.

She debated setting a place for Frank—the kids would love it if he stayed for dinner—but she didn't want him to take the invitation the wrong way or to feel obligated. She stood by the table, the extra plate in hand, and nearly dropped it when Frank rapped on the back door.

"Come in." Shelby rushed over to the counter, put the plate in the sink, and pretended to be washing it.

"Sure smells good in here," Frank said as he walked into the kitchen. He pulled off his baseball cap and ran a hand through his hair. "Somehow those microwave dinners I make never smell quite this good."

"Why don't you stay for dinner?" Shelby blurted out, and instantly regretted it.

"You sure it's no trouble?"

"No trouble at all," Shelby said. "There's plenty."

Frank seemed to take up all the space in her tiny kitchen. And all the air, too, because she was having trouble breathing.

Frank's expression turned serious. "Tell me about this threat you received."

"It wasn't actually a threat," Shelby said, moving her laptop to the counter. "It was a comment on one of my blog posts."

Shelby turned the computer so Frank could read the entry. He exhaled loudly and pointed at the screen. "If it walks like a duck and talks like a duck . . . well, you know the rest. This person—whoever they are—is very clearly threatening you." Frank turned toward Shelby. "The question is why. Why do they think you're poking your nose in other people's business, as they put it?"

"I don't know." Shelby forced herself to meet Frank's eyes. "All I've done is talk to people. It's not my fault if they tell me things."

"What sorts of things?"

Shelby went to the stove to buy time to think. She lifted the lid on the chicken and orzo. Fragrant steam filled the air.

Frank put his hands on Shelby's shoulders and spun her around to face him.

"What sorts of things have people told you?"

"Nothing, really."

"It can't be nothing. You've worried someone enough for them to threaten you. There has to be something."

"I did happen to mention that someone must have gotten wet while they held Travis's head underwater."

"Who did you say that to?"

"Brian—he's the band's manager. And Cody."

"That's all?"

"Yes."

"I'd feel better if you didn't have these people around, at least until we nail down the killer. Can't you tell them to leave?"

"I would, but they're paying me, and I need the money. Besides, Peter—he's one of the guitarists—is Kelly's cousin. So it's not like they're complete strangers."

"Look . . . about the money. I've told you I can help you out if need be."

Shelby felt her face turn to stone. She had no intention of letting herself become a charity case.

"Thank you," she said through stiff lips. "But we're doing fine."

Frank grunted. "Please don't put yourself in a position where you're alone with any of these people, okay? Don't let them in the house or around the kids."

"I've told them they have to leave before the children get out of school."

"Good. That's something at least."

Shelby thought about being alone in the barn with Cody and shivered.

"What's the matter?" Frank asked. "Did something happen?"

"No, no. I just got a chill for some reason."

Frank didn't look convinced and Shelby was relieved when Billy appeared in the door.

"Uncle Frank, Uncle Frank," he cried, dashing over to Frank and hopping on one foot and then the other in front of him. "Will you play ball with me? Please?"

Frank ruffled Billy's blond hair, making his cowlick even more pronounced. "I think it's time for dinner, sport."

"Awwwww," Billy whined.

"Go wash your hands," Shelby said, giving him a push toward the powder room.

"Not fair," Billy muttered under his breath.

Soon they were all seated at the table, passing the platter of chicken and orzo along with a bowl of fresh buttered green beans.

Shelby looked around the table. With Frank there, it felt complete. Had she made the right decision in putting Frank off? Suddenly it didn't feel like it.

|||||||||||||||||||||||||||||||

Shelby squirted a hefty dose of dishwashing liquid into the sink, then turned on the hot-water tap. When the sink was filled with bubbles, she slid the dirty frying pan into the foam and began to scrub it.

Shelby might have been standing in her own kitchen, but her mind was elsewhere. She kept going back to that scene with Cody in the barn. What a strange look he'd given her and when she'd commented on how the killer must have gotten wet—he'd looked positively startled.

If he was the killer, then perhaps it had never occurred to him that something as simple as some splashes of water on his pants or shirt might have given him away. Whoever killed Travis was lucky the day was warm enough for their clothes to dry almost immediately.

Shelby finished washing the few dishes that wouldn't fit in the dishwasher, dried them, and put them away.

She sat down at the table again and powered up her laptop. She was half-afraid to look at her blog for fear of finding another threatening comment, but she breathed a sigh of relief when there were none.

She did have a new e-mail, though. The e-mail address wasn't familiar to her, and Shelby was fearful that it would be another threat. She opened it reluctantly.

The expression *knock me over with a feather* was familiar to her, but she'd never really experienced it before. Until now. She read the e-mail a second time to make sure her eyes weren't deceiving her or her brain wasn't making up things that weren't there.

Apparently Lucia's, the fancy restaurant Matt had taken her to in Allenvale, had recently hired a new chef. The chef—Michelle Martini—was a huge proponent of using locally sourced, fresh ingredients in her dishes.

Shelby had read enough issues of *Bon Appétit* magazine to know that the locavore movement—eating locally grown or produced food—was a fast-growing trend. People were acting as if the concept had recently been invented when Shelby and her family, along with all the farmers she knew, had been eating that way most of their lives. Her kitchen garden provided vegetables and fresh herbs in the warmer months and home-canned produce in the winter. Their milk, and the cheese she subsequently made from it, came from Jake's dairy farm next door, and their eggs from the chickens scratching around out by their barn. Even their meat came from nearby sources.

Apparently the local news was anxious to cover the story of the newly hired chef, and some public relations person had dreamed up the idea of having Michelle go to a local farm, pick produce and other items, and do a cooking demonstration on the spot.

And they were asking if they could film at Love Blossom Farm.

And they were willing to pay for the privilege.

Shelby blinked a few times, but the e-mail didn't disappear.

Wait till she told Amelia about this! Now she couldn't possibly say that nothing exciting ever happened on the farm.

IIIIIIIIIIIIIIIIIIIIIIIIIII

Shelby woke to the sound of rain pinging against her window. The temperature had dropped, and the floor was cold under her bare feet. She pulled on a pair of jeans and rummaged in her drawer for a clean sweatshirt.

She'd decided to wait to tell Amelia about the news segment being filmed at the farm until she had more details and it was signed, sealed, and delivered. No sense in disappointing her daughter if things didn't work out.

Shelby realized she herself would be equally disappointed if things fell through—and it wasn't only because of the money. While she loved working Love Blossom Farm and her life in general, a little something out of the ordinary wouldn't be amiss.

Billy and Amelia had just caught the school bus when

Shelby noticed the band's van coming down the driveway. The rain had turned the dust to spatters of mud, and the windshield wiper on the passenger side was trailing a piece of shredded rubber. It zoomed past the farmhouse and headed down the dirt path to the barn.

Earlier in the morning, Jake had dropped off several bottles of milk, and Shelby was bringing them into the kitchen two by two when she saw someone running from the barn toward the farmhouse.

It looked like Paislee, but the figure wasn't close enough yet for Shelby to be sure. Cody wasn't much taller than Paislee and was equally slender, so it could be either of them.

Shelby waited by the back door, holding it open with her shoulder, wondering what the person wanted. Probably the bathroom—the portable toilets had been picked up by the rental company.

As the figure got closer, Shelby saw that it was definitely Paislee. The rain had flattened her long hair around her face and had plastered several strands across her forehead like a bald man's bad comb-over. She had on a thin white blouse with colorful embroidery on the front. The wetness had rendered it nearly transparent and it stuck to her as if it were glued on. She must have been cold, because she had her arms clasped across her chest and was shivering.

She was nearly to Shelby's door when she stumbled and fell to her knees. Shelby rushed out to help her up, supporting her the rest of the way to the mudroom door.

Paislee was shaking violently and leaned heavily against her as Shelby maneuvered her inside and into a chair in the kitchen.

"What's wrong? What's happened? Are you ill?"

Paislee's eyes were glazed and out of focus. She didn't answer.

Shelby bustled around, putting a mug with water in the microwave and getting out a tea bag and the sugar bowl. She didn't try to talk to Paislee until she'd steeped the tea and added plenty of sugar. She passed the mug to Paislee, who clutched it with both hands.

Shelby knelt beside her chair. "Can you tell me what's happened? Something is obviously terribly wrong."

Paislee opened her mouth, but no words came out. Instead she gave a loud wail that ended in racking sobs.

Shelby waited patiently. She realized she'd promised Frank that she would keep the band members out of the house, but surely Paislee didn't count. She'd obviously come to Shelby because she was upset and not because she planned to commit murder.

Paislee's crying finally slowed and then shuddered to a stop. Shelby grabbed a clutch of tissues from the box on the counter and handed them to her.

"Thank you," Paislee said, mopping her eyes. She blew her nose.

She didn't say anything more, and Shelby did her best to quell her impatience to find out what was wrong.

"Cody's dead," Paislee said finally, her voice flat.

Shelby stopped in her tracks and was so still she might have been a statue. She couldn't process Paislee's words. It was impossible.

"What?" Shelby said finally. "What do you mean?"

"Cody's dead," Paislee repeated. "I guess we need to call the police."

"What do you mean? What about an ambulance? Are you sure he's dead?"

"Yes." Paislee's eyes were still glazed—her gaze far off in the distance somewhere.

Shelby grabbed the phone and dialed 911. She spoke to the dispatcher, then ended the call.

"The police are on their way," she said. Paislee nodded listlessly.

"What happened? Was it an accident?"

Paislee didn't answer.

"Do you want to stay here? I'd better go outside and wait for the police. They will need to know where to go." Shelby began to shiver herself and grabbed her fleece from the back of one of the kitchen chairs and pulled it on. "Is anyone else with . . ." She paused. She didn't want to say *the body*. "With Cody?"

The hot tea seemed to be having a modest effect on Paislee. She'd stopped shaking and her eyes looked less vacant.

"Yes. Brian's there and so is Jax. And Peter, too."

"Did Cody come with you this morning? I saw your van go by. It's only been a few minutes since you got here. How could Cody possibly be dead?"

Paislee shook her head. "No, Cody wasn't with us. He didn't answer his door when we knocked this morning. He'd stayed behind last night to fix something with one of the amplifiers, so Brian loaned him his car."

"The Taurus?"

"Yes. And when Brian went out to the parking lot this morning, his car was gone."

"So Cody had to have come here first thing this morning. Before the rest of you were up."

"I guess so." Paislee brushed at one of the wet strands of hair still plastered across her forehead. "But I'm not sure, because I remember I didn't hear him in his room last night. Our rooms are next to each other, and the walls are ridiculously thin." She rolled her eyes. "The place is a dump, if you ask me."

"You would normally hear Cody in his room?"

"With walls like that? Sure. I'd hear the water running in his bathroom. Even the bedsprings squeaking. And he hadn't turned on his air conditioner at all."

"It wasn't very hot last night—"

"The rooms are horribly stuffy. We've had to turn them on every night." Paislee fiddled with the beaded string bracelets on her wrist. "I hope we don't have to stay here much longer."

Dear Reader, I don't want to say anything, but Paislee is likely to be stuck here even longer now.

Shelby heard sirens in the distance.

"Will you be okay?" She touched Paislee on the shoulder. Paislee jumped as if she'd been asleep.

"Yes. Can I wait here?" Her voice was plaintive. "I don't want to have to see Cody again."

"Of course. I'll be back when I know more."

Shelby had no desire to see Cody either, but she had to be there to direct the police. She wondered if Frank had been notified. Probably. Doreen would have filled him in on the situation.

The rain had stopped, but the air was still heavy with moisture. Brian, Jax, and Peter were standing outside the barn, waiting. Brian was leaning against the wall, one leg crossed over the other. Jax was sitting on the damp ground, his head in his hands, and Peter was pacing back and forth, his hands clasped behind his back.

The rain had abated somewhat, but by the time Shelby reached the barn, she was still wet and miserable.

"Where's Cody?" she said as she approached the group standing outside.

Jax lifted his head and jerked it in the direction of the open barn door. "In there. But you don't want to go in there. It isn't pretty."

Shelby shouldered past him and went into the barn anyway. It wasn't curiosity driving her but a feeling of responsibility.

She didn't see Cody at first—just the usual bulky pieces of equipment and jumble of wires. Then she noticed feet sticking out from behind one of the amplifiers.

It was Cody. He was wearing a pair of black running shoes. They looked new—the bottoms were fairly clean. He obviously hadn't walked across the field to the barn this morning. The rain had started during the night and by morning the ground was dotted with puddles and oozing patches of mud. It would have been impossible for him to keep his sneakers so clean.

He must not have left after Shelby had talked to him the day before.

Shelby approached the body cautiously for a better look. Cody's face was contorted and she noticed something around his neck—a string of some kind? It was partly obscured by flesh and she couldn't be sure.

It was clear Cody was dead—his eyes were open and already had a milky film over them. Shelby backed away and ran out of the barn.

She took a few minutes to breathe deeply of the fresh air and to wait for her heartbeat to return to normal.

She felt a strong sense of déjà vu as two patrol cars came barreling down the path and across the field to the barn, skidding to a stop outside the open doors.

Two patrolmen jumped out of the car and trotted over to Shelby.

"We got a call that there's been a fatality? Is that right?" the older one said.

Shelby's voice suddenly deserted her and she pointed to the interior of the barn in response to the officer's question.

As Shelby had suspected, Frank wasn't far behind. He jumped out of his truck almost before it had completely rolled to a stop behind the patrol car. His expression was grim as he walked toward Shelby.

"I don't like this," he said when he reached her. He scowled, tugged at the brim of his cap, and turned to look at the open barn doors. "I wish you and the kids could go somewhere until this is all over."

"You know I can't," Shelby said. "There's too much work to be done. I'd lose everything. This is the most critical time of year for a farm. You know that."

Frank grunted. "I didn't get much out of Doreen over the radio. Another murder?" He pushed his cap back on his forehead.

"Yes." Shelby's voice shook. "It's Cody. He is . . . was . . . a guitarist with the band. He's . . . It's awful."

"Guess I'd better take a look. ME is on the way." He put a hand on Shelby's shoulder. "I'll need to talk to you. Do you mind waiting here? Will you be okay?"

Shelby nodded and Frank walked over to the barn and through the open doors.

Five minutes later Shelby heard the engine of a car. Unlike Frank's pickup or Shelby's own car, it purred smoothly as it negotiated the dirt path and came to a halt in back of Frank's truck.

Frank must have heard the car, because he came out of the barn, his hat in his hands. He motioned to the ME as he picked his way across the field toward the barn.

The ME flashed his gap-toothed smile at Shelby and disappeared into the barn behind Frank.

Shelby decided that if Frank needed to talk to her, he could certainly find her in her own kitchen. He was a detective, after all. And she felt she really ought to check on Paislee. The girl had been terribly distraught. She shouldn't be alone.

Brian, Jax, and Peter continued to hover near the entrance to the barn. Brian had lit a cigarette, holding it pinched between his thumb and index finger. He was now the one pacing back and forth, following the same path with near military precision.

Shelby was pretty sure that nobody noticed when she turned and walked away.

⁗⁗⁗⁗⁗⁗⁗⁗⁗

It was well over an hour later when Frank showed up at Shelby's back door. Paislee had fallen asleep on the sofa in the living room, where Shelby had left her with a second cup of tea. She looked young and so defenseless—her head tipped back, her eyes closed, her long lashes making crescent-shaped shadows on her cheeks, her long hair—still slightly damp—spread out over the cushions.

Shelby hated to wake her, but Frank needed to talk to her. He'd already talked to the rest of the band, and Shelby had heard them leave, going very fast down the drive, the van bouncing and rattling over each rut it hit. They'd obviously forgotten about Paislee in their haste to get away.

Shelby could hear the low voices coming from the living room—Paislee's occasionally rising to a nearly hysterical pitch followed by Frank's soothing tones. She was putting on a pot of coffee when Frank stuck his head into the kitchen.

"I'm giving Paislee a ride back to the motel. Will you be here a little longer? I still need to talk to you."

"Sure."

As soon as Shelby heard the door close, she poured herself a cup of coffee, stirred in some sugar, and sank into one of the kitchen chairs. The horror of everything that had happened suddenly washed over her like a wave, and her hand shook as she raised the cup to her lips.

She didn't know how long she sat there, but suddenly Frank's truck was coming back down the driveway.

Shelby jumped up, debating whether to run into the powder room to comb her hair, when Frank's knock sounded on the screen door.

"Come in." She hoped her voice didn't sound as shaky as she felt.

"Are you okay?" Frank frowned.

"Yes. A little shaken is all."

"I don't blame you. Anyone would be. It still rattles me sometimes."

Shelby couldn't picture Frank rattled.

"Is that coffee I smell?" Frank asked with a smile.

"Yes. Let me get you some."

Shelby was glad to have something to do and she quickly retrieved a mug, filled it, and brought it over to the table.

Frank ran a hand through his hair. "This has been a terrible business."

Shelby sat in the chair opposite. "Do you know what happened? I saw Cody, but I wasn't sure . . . How did he die?"

"Strangulation." Frank ran a finger around his own collar. "There was a wire wrapped around his neck. The medical examiner thinks it's most likely a guitar string."

Shelby found her hand going to her own neck.

Frank sighed and put down his mug. "I gather this Paislee found the body?"

"Yes. This morning—well, right before we called you."

"How did she seem?"

"What do you mean? She was obviously terribly upset. I couldn't get a word out of her until I'd gotten her calmed down a bit."

"So she arrived with the rest of the crew that was here?"

"Yes. With Brian, Jax, and Peter."

"Peter's an odd fellow. Doesn't say much."

"I haven't had a chance to talk with him. He's mostly stayed in the background."

"So they all arrived this morning. But obviously Cody was already here. I assume he was also already dead."

Frank traced the rim of his coffee cup with his finger, his eyes narrowed and his brow furrowed.

"They were all here yesterday, too. Is that right?"

Shelby nodded. "Yes. They were practicing. They all left together, but Cody stayed behind."

Frank looked up sharply. "He did? Why?"

"He was fixing some of the equipment. An amplifier, I think."

"Did they come back and get him?"

"No. Brian left his car—the Taurus—for Cody. Brian was in the van with the others."

"Did you hear Cody leave?"

"No. I didn't see the Taurus when I went to feed the chickens, but Cody usually pulled it around in back of the barn, so I wouldn't have."

"Was Cody in the barn then?"

"I don't know. I didn't see him. The bag of chicken feed is by the door, so I didn't go very far inside."

"Maybe he was outside having a smoke?"

"He couldn't have been. I happened to notice how clean his sneakers were. If he'd been outside, they would have been muddy." Shelby got up to refill Frank's coffee cup. "I think he was hidden by those huge amplifiers and that's why I didn't see him." Shelby smiled briefly. "Besides, I'm never fully awake at that hour. It's possible I didn't notice him."

"So it looks as if he was killed sometime yesterday afternoon or evening." Frank's hand tightened around the mug. "Did you hear anything? A car? Voices? Anything out of the ordinary?"

"I'm afraid not."

Frank pinched the bridge of his nose. "Somebody knew Cody would be out in the barn alone."

"That would be anyone in the band."

"Yes. And at some point one of them came back here to kill him. It can't have been too late at night. They couldn't count on Cody being here that long."

"I'd already told them they had to leave by three o'clock. He was finishing up when I went out to talk to him yesterday."

Frank's eyebrows shot up. "You talked to him?"

"Yes." Shelby looked down at her hands, which were clasped on the table. "Like I told you, I asked him about the day of the wedding and whether he'd noticed that anyone's clothes were wet."

Frank closed his eyes, and Shelby could see the muscles in his jaw working. Finally he opened his eyes again.

"When I think of the danger you put yourself in . . ."

"Well, nothing happened, and Cody said he hadn't noticed anyone." Shelby paused. "But he did get this very strange look on his face."

"Strange, how?"

Shelby held her hands out, palms up. "I don't know. I can't describe it. Sort of like he'd thought of something suddenly."

"So maybe he did notice someone who'd been wet." Frank shook his head, his eyes on Shelby. "Promise me you'll stay out of this from now on? Please?"

"I promise."

Frank turned his coffee cup around and around in his hands. "The killer took quite a chance of being seen. If you'd been looking out your kitchen window . . ."

"If it was one of the band members, they could have said they were only coming to see how Cody was doing. I probably wouldn't have thought anything of it."

"True. Maybe the autopsy will tell us something. Although I doubt it. The manner of death seems pretty obvious to me."

"And the guitar string certainly points to someone in the band." Shelby ran a hand through her hair and was horrified to find how tangled it was.

"Not necessarily. It might have been the handiest thing available."

"Do you think killing Cody was a spur-of-the-moment decision?" Shelby twisted a lock of hair around her finger. "Maybe there was a fight?"

"Could be. Or not. This case is proving to be very frustrating." Frank smiled. "Most of what we deal with around here is pretty straightforward." He sighed and pushed away from the table. "I'd better be going. The medical examiner promised to perform the autopsy this afternoon, and I'd like to be there."

Frank stood up, then paused and put a hand on Shelby's

shoulder. "Be careful, okay? Keep an eye on the kids. Especially Billy. I know he likes to wander all over the farm on his own."

"I will. Don't worry. Billy is going to be under strict orders to keep to the backyard."

16

Dear Reader,

When I was pregnant with Amelia and Billy, the doctor assured me that any pregnancy cravings I might have were perfectly normal. Of course there's the old joke about a woman craving pickles or sending her husband out into a raging storm to buy a carton of her favorite ice cream, but cravings can be quite individual.

It might be sauerkraut for one woman and sardines for another. Most cravings are harmless and make for a good story after the baby has arrived.

But Shelby did worry. She found herself jumping at every sound, even though it was normal noise that she would ordinarily pay no attention to. She'd have been more than happy to leave the farm until this was all over, but that simply wasn't possible. She was counting on the money from the sale of the lettuces and other vegetables that were beginning to grow as well as those she'd just planted. And the vegetables in her kitchen garden would keep them going through the summer and then be canned to tide them over during the winter.

Shelby sighed. She couldn't make sense of Cody's death. He'd had a strong motive for killing Travis. Travis had threatened to fire him, and Travis had wooed Paislee away from Cody. With Travis out of the way, it was quite possible Cody would be able to get Paislee back and secure his place in the band.

Shelby thought about it while she made her bed and vacuumed the living room. The rain had started coming down in sheets again—she'd get no outdoor work done today. The holes that pockmarked the driveway were filled with water that looked to be almost ankle deep.

Shelby was about to fix herself some lunch when the doorbell rang. This time she jumped in earnest. She had to get a grip on herself before the kids got home. If only it weren't raining—some good sweaty outdoor work would take care of her case of nerves.

Shelby pulled open the door to find two people on her doorstep: a young man with elaborately shaped facial hair and a woman who looked to be an extremely—and expensively—well-preserved fortysomething.

"Shelby?" the woman gushed.

Her hair was a shade of red rarely seen in nature and she was so thin Shelby was convinced that if she swallowed a pea or a lima bean, its progress down her esophagus and into her stomach would be visible to the naked eye.

"Can I help you?"

"We're from WXYZ." The woman frowned, then seemed to remember that it wasn't good for her skin and quickly resumed her placid expression. "You did get our e-mail?"

Shelby had forgotten all about the e-mail amidst the morning's drama.

"We did say we were going to stop by to spec things out. I hope it's okay?"

"Yes. Of course. I'm sorry."

Shelby led them into the living room, where she glanced in embarrassment at the sofa and chairs covered in old quilts to keep the dirt from the dogs off.

"We won't take up too much of your time," the woman said. "We need to see where we're going to be filming."

"To work out the camera angles." The young man pointed in the direction of the windows.

"Too bad it's such a filthy day," the woman said.

Shelby realized she recognized her from WXYZ's *The Hive at Five*, a local program offering features of special interest to women.

"You're Felicity Sanchez, aren't you?"

The woman preened, obviously pleased to be recognized. "Do you watch our show?"

"When I have time, and I'm not—"

"We're very excited about this program," Felicity cut in. "It's quite a coup to get chef Michelle Martini on our show."

Felicity walked past Shelby and started toward the kitchen. Shelby hastened to catch up with her.

Felicity leaned against the sink and looked out the kitchen window.

"Is that where it happened?"

"Where it happened?" Shelby repeated. "Oh, you mean the—"

"Yes," Felicity said, her mouth snapping closed as sharply

as a Venus flytrap capturing its victim. "The band was on our show on Friday. I hope you saw it." She raised an eyebrow at Shelby.

Shelby made a noise that she hoped would be taken for a yes.

"I feel just terrible about that young man being murdered. He was quite charming," she trilled in a flirtatious voice. "He insisted on taking me out to dinner and, well . . ." She let the sentence trail off suggestively. "I'd hoped to have him back on the show alone, but it wasn't to be."

Dear Reader, it looks as if Travis was a real player. Did Paislee know?

The cameraman was busy texting on his cell phone and hadn't looked up once since they'd begun talking.

"And now," Felicity said, her tone turning brisk, "let's discuss Chef Martini's show." She turned around to face the kitchen window again, pushed aside the lace curtain, and looked out. The window was running with rain. Felicity rubbed some of the condensation away with her hand.

"My first thought was to set up the cooking table—where Michelle will have all her equipment—on the front lawn with your gorgeous wraparound farmhouse porch in the background." She let the curtain drop back into place and turned around with her hands on her hips. "But then I thought perhaps we ought to film right in the field." She laughed. "Right in the trenches, so to speak."

The cameraman was still busy texting on his phone. "Darren," Felicity said sharply. "What do you think?"

He looked up, blinking like a mole emerging into the sunlight. "What do I think about what?"

"About where we should film," Felicity snapped.

"I dunno. Wherever you want. I can make it work." And he looked back down at his phone.

Felicity looked satisfied—as if that was the answer she'd been anticipating.

"I think it should be in the field, then." She turned to Shelby. "If that's all right with you?" It was clear she didn't expect any argument.

"As long as the plants don't get trampled."

Felicity waved a hand in the air. "We'll be careful. Don't worry." She tapped her fuchsia-colored lips with her index finger. "If we angle the camera correctly, we should be able to capture the barn in the frame. Do you suppose the police will leave the crime-scene tape up until then? It will add an extra little fillip to the segment to have the scene of a murder in the background."

Shelby was horrified but didn't say anything.

"Terrible shame about that young man," Felicity said as if she was continuing their earlier conversation. "We could have had something together." Felicity smiled. "Oh, well. Onward and upward, as they say."

||||||||||||||||||||||||||||||

Shelby sank into a chair after Felicity and Darren left. The woman was a force of nature, Shelby thought. She had a sudden vision of Felicity going head-to-head with Seth's mother, Nancy. Now, that would be something to see. She actually laughed out loud at the picture. It was good to laugh—she'd been so steeped in melancholy lately.

Shelby checked in the refrigerator and found the homemade mozzarella she'd made. Billy and Amelia could use it to make pizzas for dinner. She thought they would enjoy that. The telephone rang and she jumped.

"Shelby? It's Kelly."

"Kelly. Is everything okay?"

"Yes, fine. As long as you don't count Seth being a suspect in a murder." Kelly laughed. "At least I'm getting to the point where I can laugh about it. It really is absurd." Kelly paused. "But that's not why I'm calling. I have a craving—"

This time Shelby laughed. "Starting already, are they?"

"Yes, and it's the strangest thing. I can't stop thinking about the diner's rice pudding. Normally I hate rice pudding, but all of a sudden—"

"I know what you mean," Shelby said. "For me it was rocky road ice cream and fries with malt vinegar. Preferably at the same time."

"Do you want to meet me at the diner? You can't be working outside in this deluge."

"You're right. I'm not. And I'd love to meet you. Give me ten minutes, okay?"

Shelby was more than happy to flee Love Blossom Farm, if only for a couple of hours.

⁕⁕⁕⁕⁕⁕⁕⁕⁕⁕⁕⁕⁕⁕⁕

Shelby didn't see Kelly's truck in the parking lot when she arrived at the Lovett Diner. The rain was still coming down and she could feel splotches of wet on the back of her T-shirt even though she sprinted as quickly as she could to the door of the diner.

She took an empty booth up front so she could easily spot Kelly when she came in. The diner was busy with the voices of the diners and the rattle of crockery creating a discordant din.

Several people were waiting patiently in the take-out line. One young man stood out—tall and thin with shaggy dirty blond hair. Shelby thought he looked familiar and when he turned to leave, she realized it was Jax.

He stopped short when he saw Shelby and smiled shyly.

"Hey," Shelby called to him.

He walked over and stood by Shelby's table, his paper bag of takeout clutched to his chest.

"Hi." He nodded his head. "Listen, do you know if the police are finished with the barn yet? We'd like to get back to practicing, if that's okay with you. We still have some work to do on that new song."

"I don't know. I'm not sure I'm comfortable with it anymore. Under the circumstances."

Jax didn't look surprised. "We were afraid of that. I talked to Brian and he said he would double what he's been paying you."

Shelby hesitated.

"Nothing's going to happen to you. I promise."

Shelby was reluctant. But double the money? She'd be able to put a little aside for the winter when things got pretty lean. It was tempting.

"Please?" Jax gave a big smile.

Shelby sighed. "Fine. But the same rules apply—you have to be out of there by three o'clock."

"No problem. That still gives us plenty of time. I don't know what we'll do if we can't practice."

He gave a lopsided smile. "There's not much to keep us occupied in those motel rooms besides television, and the tension is getting pretty thick. Yesterday Peter and Brian nearly came to blows over who ate the last of the bag of Cheetos."

He shifted the paper bag to his left arm. A large grease stain was forming in the lower right corner.

"And obviously we can't practice at the motel. The management would have the band thrown out in a flash. As it is, I get the impression they'd like us to leave." He frowned.

"It's not as though they're booked up or anything. You'd think they'd be grateful for the business."

"I certainly would think so," Shelby said, thinking of the run-down motel, where there were rarely ever more than a handful of cars parked in the lot.

"But you live in Lovett, right? Can they practice at your place in the meantime?"

Jax looked down at his feet. He mumbled something Shelby didn't quite catch.

"I'm sorry. I couldn't hear you." She made a sweeping motion encompassing the dining room. "It's so noisy in here when it's busy."

"Sorry. I said that I've left our apartment. I've left Jessie. I'm staying at the motel—bunking in with Peter."

"Oh." Shelby didn't know what to say. That certainly explained Jessie's being so upset. "I'm sorry to hear that."

Jax shrugged, but Shelby could see he was hurting. His shoulders tensed.

"Honestly, I could kill Paislee."

Shelby was shocked. She was sure Jax didn't mean that, but this was hardly the time to joke about matters like that.

"Paislee? Why?"

Jax sighed and his shoulders dropped. "I guess I shouldn't blame Paislee. What's that saying? Something about 'Don't kill the messenger.'"

"Something like that."

Shelby waited, hoping Jax would tell her what this was all about. When he remained silent, she realized she'd have to give him a gentle nudge.

"I'm sure Paislee didn't mean to upset you with . . . whatever it was she did."

"You're probably right," Jax admitted. "It's only that I

would rather not have known." He ran a hand through his hair, which immediately flopped onto his forehead again. "Although I suppose it doesn't do you any good to bury your head in the sand."

Dear Reader, what on earth is he talking about? I wish he would get to the point.

"No, it doesn't," Shelby agreed. "I'm sure it can't be all that bad."

Jax's expression changed so rapidly Shelby was taken aback. A slow red flush crept up his neck to his face and to the roots of his hair.

"You don't know what it feels like," he said, the muscle in his jaw working furiously. "To be betrayed—twice—by your own brother and then by your wife."

Shelby heard the tears behind his voice.

"What happened?" she said gently.

Jax shifted the bag in his arms again. The grease stain was growing larger.

"I told you Jessie was engaged to Travis at one time, but he ditched her—left her standing at the altar. You'd think she'd never forgive him, wouldn't you?"

Shelby nodded. She certainly wouldn't forgive a man who had done that to her.

"So then why would she go back to him?"

"Jessie and Travis?" Now Shelby was confused in earnest.

"Paislee told me they were having an affair. It started as soon as Travis came back to Lovett. He came back ahead of the band. Our mother was having surgery—a bypass—and he wanted to be here for it." Jax looked like he was on the verge of tears. "Why would she do that?" He dashed a hand across his eyes. "How could Jessie do that to me?"

Shelby didn't have any answers for him. But she was left with a lot of questions.

||||||||||||||||||||||||

Shelby looked up to find the waitress coming toward her. She gave an apologetic smile.

"I'm waiting for a friend. She should be here any minute."

The waitress nodded and turned on her heel and headed toward another table.

Shelby was still thinking about her conversation with Jax when Kelly arrived, and didn't even notice her come in.

"Hey, you were lost in space there," Kelly said as she slipped into the booth opposite Shelby.

She looked better today, Shelby noticed—she had more color in her face, and the dark circles under her eyes were no longer there. There was still the faintest odor of manure about her, though. Shelby supposed the smell might be ingrained in the soles of the work boots she wore when she was working. Seeing her mud-caked jeans, bleached-out T-shirt, and hair tightly curled from the humidity, Shelby was hard-pressed to reconcile this version of Kelly with the one who had looked so ethereal walking down the aisle just a few days ago.

"So tell me," Kelly said as she unfurled her napkin in her lap. "What were you thinking about? It must have been something good. Interesting, at any rate."

Shelby laughed. "Interesting, yes. Confusing, too."

"Can I help?"

Shelby fiddled with her spoon, spinning it around and around in a circle. "I don't know. Maybe."

"Well, then, shoot."

Shelby wasn't sure where to begin. "I told you about Travis leaving Jessie at the altar?"

"Yes. I remember."

"You'd think Jessie would hate him, wouldn't you?"

Kelly snorted. "I know I would." She looked at Shelby curiously. "Why?"

"Because she started an affair with Travis as soon as he was in town."

Kelly gasped. "You're kidding." She leaned her elbows on the table and put her chin in her hands. "But how do you know?"

"Jax just told me."

"Jax?" Kelly's eyebrows went up with her voice. "But how did he know? Surely they hid it from him."

"Paislee knew and she told Jax."

"The girl singer? But why would she do that?"

"I don't know." Shelby wiggled closer to the edge of her seat. "It sounds so . . . vindictive, don't you think? Maybe Paislee spilled the beans about the affair to get back at Jessie or Travis. Or both. To land them in hot water so she could watch them squirm."

Shelby spread her hands out on the table. "Obviously Paislee didn't care how much she might be hurting Jax in the process," she said. "Paislee and Travis had apparently become an item. But then Travis arrives back here in Lovett and he suddenly takes up again with his former fiancée."

"Who is a fool for taking him back," Kelly said, wrinkling her nose.

"That's certainly true. And imagine how Jax must feel. He's been married to Jessie for a while now. He probably feels he rescued her after she'd been abandoned by his brother."

"Or maybe he was in love with her all along."

The waitress appeared at their table and plunked down two glasses of water dripping with condensation.

"Know what you want?" she said as she slid two plastic-coated menus onto the table.

Kelly's face lit up. "An order of rice pudding for me." She frowned. "No, make that two orders."

The waitress looked Kelly up and down, shrugged, and turned to Shelby. "And you? You want to look at the menu?"

Shelby shook her head. She realized she was starving. "I'll have the turkey club on whole wheat, please. And a lemonade with plenty of ice."

"You've got it," the waitress said, retrieving their unopened menus.

"So Jax had plenty of reasons to hate Travis," Shelby said when the waitress was out of hearing range. "Travis had the singing career that Jax wanted for himself. And because of the accident Travis caused, Jax hadn't been able to pursue his dream."

"Yes," Kelly said, her eyes lighting up as the waitress slid two dishes of rice pudding in front of her.

"I'll be right back with yours." The waitress pointed at Shelby.

Kelly took a bite of rice pudding and rolled her eyes in rapture. "It's like scratching an itch."

"What?" Had she missed something? Shelby wondered.

Kelly laughed. "Satisfying a craving. It's like scratching an itch." She took another bite of her pudding, then pointed her spoon at Shelby. "Poor Jax. Not only was he in love with his brother's fiancée—he had to watch his brother break her heart."

"I wonder why on earth Jessie took up with Travis again. Jax seems like such a nice guy and Travis was . . . well, he was certainly a player, from what I can tell."

"When some women lose their hearts to a guy, their brain obviously follows."

"That certainly seems to be the case here," Shelby said, leaning back as the waitress slid a plate in front of her.

17

||||||||||||||||||||||||||||||

Dear Reader,

This murder that happened here at Love Blossom Farm is getting more and more complicated. Everyone seems to be mad at everyone else! Jessie was mad at Travis for leaving her at the altar, Jax is mad at Paislee for telling him about the affair between Jessie and Travis, and Cody was mad at Travis . . . well, just because. I think this group is going to implode before they ever cut another record!

Shelby was sweeping the porch when Amelia got off the school bus. The rain had stopped, the clouds had been chased away by the strong breeze, and the sun glinted off the puddles dotting the driveway. The air was still heavy with humidity, and Shelby felt her hair sticking to the back of her neck.

She squinted into the distance. Someone was with Amelia, but it wasn't Billy. Billy took a different bus and would probably arrive shortly. It looked as if Amelia had brought home a friend. It didn't look like her best friend, Katelyn. Shelby wondered who it could be.

By the time the two girls had walked the length of the driveway, their cheeks were red and perspiration shone on their foreheads. As soon as she reached the porch, Amelia dropped her backpack on the floor, where it landed with a thud, sending the dust in the pile Shelby had been collecting flying.

"Gosh, it's hot," she said, fanning herself with her hand. She turned to her companion. "Mom, this is Lorraine Spurlinger. We're in math class together."

Shelby held out her hand. "Hi, Lorraine."

Lorraine smiled shyly and shook Shelby's hand.

She wasn't as unattractive as her picture on Facebook had made her out to be. Of course not everyone photographed well. Shelby thought she had a sweet smile but also sensed a vulnerability about her that had probably encouraged the bullies.

"You girls look like you could use a cold drink."

Amelia blew a lock of damp hair off her forehead. "Can we go get ice cream, Mom?"

Shelby glanced down the driveway. "Sure. As soon as Billy gets here."

"Come on," Amelia said to Lorraine. "Let's get something to drink while we wait."

The girls were still in the kitchen pouring lemonade when Shelby heard the front door slam and the thud of Billy's backpack as it hit the floor.

When he walked into the kitchen, his face was as red as Amelia's and Lorraine's had been. His shirt had parted company with his shorts, and his hair was plastered to his head with perspiration.

Billy immediately opened the refrigerator and got out the jar of peanut butter.

"Don't eat that," Amelia said. "Mom's taking us for ice cream."

"You are?" Billy turned toward Shelby with a big grin on his face.

Shelby noticed there was a smudge of dirt in the cleft of his chin and another smudge slashing through his eyebrow like a scar.

"We're going to Koetsier's for ice cream," Shelby confirmed. "But please go wash your face first, okay?"

Billy grumbled but headed toward the stairs.

Amelia rolled her eyes. "He's going to take forever."

"No, he's not. Not with the prospect of ice cream."

Shelby had barely finished talking when they heard the water running in the upstairs bathroom, quickly followed by the sound of Billy's footsteps on the stairs. Shelby wondered if all he'd done was turn the water on and off, but when he reappeared in the kitchen, his face was damp and reasonably clean.

They piled into Shelby's car—Billy with a smile of triumph because he got to sit in the front seat, while Amelia and Lorraine sat in the back. Koetsier's was barely more than a shack located on the main street, just beyond St. Andrews Church. It opened for ice cream when the weather got warm, and during the holiday season sold Christmas trees cut from a nearby farm.

The parking lot was mostly dirt with a scattering of gravel and today, it was quite full. The heat had drawn everyone out, from mothers with children to high school kids sitting on the hoods of their cars eating cones and drinking milk shakes.

Amelia looked over at a group of boys sitting in the back of an open SUV.

Dear Reader, I know exactly what she's thinking. She's embarrassed to be here with her mother. I remember feeling the same way when I was her age.

Shelby went up to the makeshift counter and ordered cones for the girls—cookies and cream—and one for Billy, who had chosen cotton candy. Shelby decided to splurge and got a cup of rocky road for herself.

They sat at one of the wobbly picnic tables. They were left out all winter and the wood was rough and splintered. The girls sat at one end—away from Shelby—and chatted quietly. Billy was engrossed in his cone, and Shelby tipped her face to the breeze that had continued to pick up and was getting cooler. The weather must be blowing in over Lake Michigan, Shelby thought.

She looked around the parking lot. A girl was standing at the counter and from the back she looked familiar—long hair wound into a loose bun, white sleeveless blouse with decorative embroidery on the yoke, and well-worn faded and torn jeans.

When she turned away from the counter, Shelby realized it was Paislee. Shelby looked around the parking lot again and noticed the band's dusty van pulled into a spot in the back. Jax and Brian were leaning against the hood, talking.

When Paislee turned, she must have spotted Shelby, because she walked over toward where Shelby was sitting.

Lorraine stared at Paislee, her mouth hanging open. "Are you Paislee Fields?" she said.

Paislee looked pleased and a slight flush colored her cheeks. "Yes."

"I love your music," Lorraine said, her face turning even redder than Paislee's.

Paislee smiled. "Thank you."

Lorraine continued to stare for a few more moments, but then Amelia tapped her on the arm, and they went back to talking.

"I don't know how much longer I can take this," Paislee said, dropping onto the bench next to Shelby, her voice becoming little more than a whisper.

"Hopefully the police will know something soon."

"I hope so." Paislee broke off a piece of her cone and nibbled on it. "It's awful being cooped up in that motel." She looked down at her hands. "Jax is mad at me," she said.

"Why?" Shelby asked, although she could guess the answer.

"Because I told him about Travis and Jessie," she said without looking up.

"Ah," Shelby said. "Why did you tell Jax? You must have known it would upset him."

Paislee shrugged her thin shoulders. "I guess because I was mad at Travis." She gave a bitter-sounding laugh. "I know that doesn't make much sense, does it?"

Shelby kept her expression neutral. "Why were you mad at Travis?" she asked quietly.

Paislee bit her lower lip. She looked so young, Shelby thought. Shelby herself was barely more than ten years older than Paislee, but everything she had been through—the births of two children, being widowed, raising Amelia and Billy alone after their father died—made her feel as if she were a thousand years old in comparison.

Paislee sighed. "It's hard to explain." She licked the ice

cream that had dribbled onto her hand. "I thought me and Travis were . . . Well, I thought Travis was the one." Her mouth twisted to one side. "People said we made beautiful music together." She spit out another laugh. "I thought it was for real." She looked down and ran a finger over the splintered top of the picnic table, wincing when it caught on a sharp piece of wood. "Then we get here and suddenly he's seeing Jessie again."

She sucked at the drop of blood that dotted the tip of her finger. "He told me about Jessie. Said it was all over between them." She glanced toward Amelia and Lorraine, who were wrapped up in their own conversation. "He said that the night before he and Jessie were to be married—it was at his bachelor party that Jax threw for him—he learned that Jessie and Jax were having an affair behind his back."

Shelby had to stifle a gasp when she heard that.

"One of his so-called friends told him. The guy had had too much to drink and started taunting Travis about it. Said he'd seen the two of them around town when Travis was on tour. There was a fight and Travis stormed out."

Shelby didn't know what to make of this information. According to Jax, he'd swooped in and rescued Jessie after Jessie had been left at the altar. If what Paislee said was true, then he was the reason Jessie had been stood up in the first place. Which one should she believe? She didn't think either of them was above telling lies when it suited them.

"I think they're waiting for me." Paislee gestured toward Jax and Brian, who were leaning against the van. They'd finished their ice cream and were standing with their hands in their pockets. Jax was drawing circles in the dust with the toe of his boot.

Shelby gathered up the used napkins and headed for the

round metal drum that served as a trash can. She heard raised voices as she turned around to head back to the picnic table.

Three boys were standing by the table where Amelia and Lorraine were still sitting. Lorraine had her feet on the seat and her arms wrapped around her knees, which were drawn up to her chest. Amelia had the stormy look on her face that Shelby knew spelled trouble.

The boys—approximately the same age as Amelia and Lorraine—were pointing fingers at the girls, their faces twisted into sneers. Shelby couldn't hear what they were saying, but she could tell by the jeering tone of their voices that it wasn't something pleasant.

Shelby drew in a sharp breath. How dared those boys! Who did they think they were? They were wearing Lovett High School football jerseys and khaki cargo shorts. The one in front with the blond buzz cut seemed to be the ringleader. Shelby thought she recognized him from the pictures that appeared in the *Lovett Chronicle* every weekend the team played a game.

Before Shelby could reach the table, Amelia jumped to her feet, grabbed her half-full paper cup of water, and threw it at the boy closest to her. The liquid hit him straight in the face, momentarily wiping the smirk off.

The boys had now formed a semicircle around the two girls. Amelia was still on her feet, her hands clenched at her sides, the stormy look on her face intensifying.

Shelby strode toward them quickly, her own hands clenched into fists. As soon as the boys caught sight of her, they scattered like pinballs, the boy with the wet face shaking a menacing finger at Amelia.

"What was that all about?" Shelby asked. She could tell her face was red, and her breath came in gasps.

Lorraine looked as if she was going to cry. Amelia went over to her and put a hand on her shoulder.

"Just some boys," Lorraine said, looking down at her feet.

"They were bothering you," Shelby said.

"That's okay. I'm used to it," Lorraine said, still looking at her feet.

"You shouldn't have to be used to it," Shelby said. "It shouldn't be happening."

"See what I mean, Mom?" Amelia said. "Those boys are always bullying Lorraine. There are others, too. They bully a lot of the kids at school."

"I'm proud of you for wanting to do something about it." Shelby put an arm around each of the girls. "And I'm proud of you for standing up to them." She put a finger under Amelia's chin and tilted her head up.

Amelia ducked her head. "Thanks, Mom." She turned to stare at the backs of the departing boys. "I hope they don't have it in for us in school tomorrow."

<hr />

A police car was in the driveway when Shelby and the girls arrived back home. A patrolman was walking toward it with a wad of black-and-yellow crime-scene tape bundled in his arms. He stopped by the side of Shelby's car when she pulled in.

"Afternoon, ma'am." He touched his free hand to his hat.

"Are you finished with the barn?" Shelby asked as she opened her door and got out.

The girls scampered toward the house. Shelby could hear Jenkins and Bitsy barking a greeting inside.

"Yes, ma'am. The detective said it was okay to take the tape down."

"Thanks. That's good news."

The black-and-yellow crime-scene tape fluttering around the perimeter of the barn had been a constant reminder of the tragedy that had taken place there. She was glad to see it go.

Now she could call Brian at the motel and let him know that they could have their practice space back again. No doubt he would be pleased.

18

Dear Reader,

Making your own pizza is a lot of fun and is a great project to do with children. You can make the dough in advance yourself if the prospect of flour all over your kitchen is too daunting. Children love picking out their own toppings. Amelia has always loved pepperoni and is a stickler for putting the slices on her pie in neat circles.

You can make the pizzas as gourmet or as simple as you like. Who doesn't love pizza, right?

Amelia had asked Lorraine to stay for dinner. The girl seemed exceptionally pleased with the invitation. Shelby really felt proud of Amelia for reaching out to her classmate.

Shelby had decided it would be fun to make pizzas for

dinner. With rapid-rise yeast, the dough wouldn't take that long. She had had fresh mozzarella in the refrigerator and there was plenty of basil to be picked in the garden. She could caramelize some onions and they could add the goat cheese she'd bought from the Frisches' farm. A drizzle of honey would add a lovely touch.

Shelby was kneading the dough when the telephone rang. She quickly wiped the flour off on her jeans—a bad habit she kept meaning to break herself of—and grabbed the receiver.

Bert was at the emergency room—her gallbladder had kicked up again and although she had surgery scheduled in the coming week, the surgeon wanted to remove it right away.

For a second, Shelby stood stock-still, staring at the pizza dough spread out on the counter without really seeing it. She couldn't let Bert go through this alone. Shelby wiped her hands again—this time using a paper towel—and grabbed her cell phone.

Kelly answered on the third ring. She sounded tired, and Shelby hesitated, but she didn't want to leave the children alone.

Kelly insisted she was more than happy to watch the kids when Shelby asked her. She assured Shelby she would be right over—it wouldn't take her more than ten minutes.

Shelby had to knock on Amelia's door twice—the girls had the door to Amelia's room closed and music playing.

Shelby explained that she was racing to the hospital to be with Bert. Amelia assured her that she and Lorraine could make the pizzas themselves and would be sure that Billy got his dinner and took a bath.

Dear Reader, that would be a bit like leaving the fox to guard the chickens.

"Kelly's coming over while I'm gone, so you don't have to worry about dealing with Billy."

Amelia's face lit up—she adored Kelly as much as Shelby did.

Shelby spared a minute for a quick glance in the mirror. She splashed some water on her face, brushed the flour off her T-shirt, and ran a hand through her hair. She would have to do.

The inside of Shelby's car was steamy and still smelled like the dog food she'd brought home the other day from the Lovett Feed Store. She put the key in the ignition and turned it. Nothing. She waited a second and tried again. Still nothing.

Shelby wanted to stamp her foot in frustration. Her pickup truck was almost out of gas—she'd never make it to the hospital—and the only gas station nearby closed early.

She clenched the steering wheel with both hands until her knuckles turned white. She couldn't let Bert down. She'd have to call someone. She grabbed her purse and fished out her cell phone, then stopped with her fingers poised above the keys.

Whom should she call?

Kelly was going to be watching the children. Coralynne or Mrs. Willoughby would insist on sitting with Shelby the whole time she was at the hospital, and she didn't think she could bear that. Besides, they would be scandalized by her appearance—neither of them ever seemed to leave the house in anything but a perfectly pressed dress appropriately accessorized and with every hair sprayed into place.

Suddenly Shelby thought of Matt. Matt! Her shoulders relaxed and she felt the tension that had been cramping her neck flow away. She brought up his number on the phone and tapped the button.

Matt answered on the second ring. He sounded pleased to hear Shelby's voice. She found herself smiling as well. Luckily he was more than happy to be her ride to the hospital and said he would be by in the length of time it took to drive from the general store to Love Blossom Farm.

Kelly arrived as Shelby was sitting on the porch waiting for Matt. She joined Shelby in one of the rocking chairs that had been on the porch since Shelby's grandparents' time. It was pleasant in the shade and Shelby rocked herself back and forth in one of the rocking chairs. Normally the motion soothed her, but tonight she was too agitated to settle down and she jumped up immediately when she heard Matt's car rumbling down the drive.

Unlike most of the inhabitants of Lovett, who bought American cars, Matt drove a Mitsubishi Montero SUV, which he affectionately called Monty. It was nearly twenty years old and had its fair share of aches and pains, as he put it. But he didn't want to part with it to get something newer—he would miss his old friend too much.

Matt parked and stood by the passenger door and watched as Shelby came down the porch steps, yelling goodbye over her shoulder to Kelly. He opened the door and gave her a boost inside.

"I can't tell you how much I appreciate you giving me a ride," Shelby said once they were under way.

"On the contrary, I can't tell you how glad I am that I could be of service." Matt glanced sideways at her and smiled.

Shelby felt a warm sense of contentment that had nothing to do with her sun-warmed seat.

The hospital was thirty minutes out of town, a short distance from the highway exit. It served a fairly large area and the medical helicopter was frequently seen landing and departing from its roof.

Matt deftly pulled the Montero into an empty space in the emergency parking lot and trotted around the car to open Shelby's door.

"I hope Bert is going to be okay," Shelby fretted.

Matt held the hospital door aside for Shelby to enter. "I'm sure she will be. She did the right thing coming to the emergency room."

"Can you believe she drove herself?" Shelby said, half-amazed and half-appalled.

"That's Bert for you. There isn't anything she can't do."

A woman was standing at the reception desk with a towel wrapped around her hand. Shelby noticed a thin line of blood trickling down her arm, which was being absorbed by the hem of her long-sleeved T-shirt.

Kitchen mishap? Shelby wondered.

A nurse whisked the woman into the bowels of the emergency room and looked up at Shelby expectantly.

"I'm looking for a Bert . . . I mean, Roberta—"

Before Shelby could finish, a voice called out from behind the reception desk. "I'm in here."

The nurse smiled at Shelby and Matt and handed them each a badge. "Room twelve B," she said before pressing a buzzer that let them into the inner sanctum.

They found cubicle 12B, and Shelby cautiously parted the curtain and peered inside.

"Come on in. I'm decent," Bert said.

She was lying on a gurney under a thin blanket, wearing a blue-and-white-print hospital gown.

"Seth has been by to see me, bless his heart," Bert said, straining to sit up.

"Don't," Shelby said. "Let me help you."

She poked all around the gurney, looking for the lever that would raise the head of the bed.

"I think this is it." Matt bent down and pressed something on the side of the gurney. There was a grinding sound and the head of the bed slowly rose.

"Whoa," Bert said, "don't send me flying through the curtain into the cubicle across the way. I don't know what he's got, but it sounds contagious. He's been making a huge fuss over there ever since I got here."

"Don't worry." Matt smiled and the skin around his eyes crinkled. "It's all under control."

He sat in one of the molded orange plastic chairs and Shelby sat in the other.

"You two are just wasting your time, you know," Bert said, fussing at the hem of the blanket. "Why don't you go get yourselves something to eat at a nice quiet and cozy place? I'm going to be fine."

"Not on your life," Shelby said with as much firmness as she could muster. "We're staying right here, and we'll be here when they wheel you out of surgery again."

"Suit yourselves," Bert sniffed. "I heard the cafeteria food isn't half-bad. Not much atmosphere, though."

Shelby laughed. "Don't worry about us. We'll manage." She had a sudden horrifying thought. She whirled around toward Matt. "I'm being awfully presumptuous. You must have things to do."

Matt gave a lazy smile and took Shelby's hand in his. "Nothing at all except sit here with you and keep you company."

An orderly came to wheel Bert down to the operating room. She left with a very satisfied smile on her face.

|||||||||||||||||||||||||||||

Bert came through the surgery with flying colors. Shelby and Matt waited until she was settled in her room before saying good night and heading out.

"I can't thank you enough," Shelby said when Matt pulled into her driveway.

"Like I told you—it was my pleasure."

Shelby noticed that only one lamp was burning in the living room and that Billy's bedroom light was out. He must have gotten tired and put himself to bed. Shelby would tiptoe in later and kiss him good night.

"Are you hungry?" Shelby said, suddenly realizing she was.

"Now that you mention it . . ."

"Come on in, and I'll see what I can put together."

The television was on in the living room and Kelly was watching a documentary on marine life in the Virgin Islands.

She got up, stifling a yawn, when Matt and Shelby walked in.

"How's Bert?" she asked, rubbing her eyes.

"Bert's doing fine. They took her gallbladder out and Seth said that will solve her problems."

"Good." Kelly stifled another yawn. "I'd better get going."

"Thanks so much, Kelly," Shelby said as she walked Kelly to the door.

"Don't mention it," Kelly said, giving Shelby a quick hug.

Shelby didn't want to know what she was going to find when they walked into the kitchen, but she was pleasantly surprised. Amelia had put all the dishes in the dishwasher and wiped down the kitchen table. Half a delectable-looking pizza was on a serving dish on the counter covered with plastic wrap.

Matt pointed to it. "That sure looks good. Or are you saving it for something?"

"No, I think Amelia saved it for us."

Shelby turned on the oven and slid her pizza stone onto the bottom rack.

"It won't take long to heat this up. In the meantime, I have some cold beer or a glass of wine?"

"Beer sounds good."

Shelby retrieved a bottle from the refrigerator and handed it to Matt along with a glass, then checked the oven temperature. She slid the remains of the pizza onto the now hot stone and set the timer.

"That should be ready in a few minutes."

"No rush." Matt twisted the cap off his beer. "Any news from your brother-in-law on the murder investigation?"

"No." Shelby perched on a chair and put the glass of wine she'd poured herself on the table. "Frank isn't sharing much with me." She thought for a moment. "He never does, but I suppose he can't."

"Have you learned anything new?" Matt poured his beer into the glass, the foam rising almost to the top. He took a sip and tilted his chair back on two legs.

"Quite a bit. I think Cody was killed because he knew something. Maybe he noticed that the killer's clothes were wet."

"Whoa." Matt let his chair drop back to the floor. "You didn't tell me about that. You mean there was a second murder?"

"Yes. Paislee found Cody in the barn. Strangled."

Matt frowned, his brows lowering over his eyes. "I don't like this at all. Are you sure you and the children are safe?"

Should she tell him about the threatening comment on her blog? Shelby wondered. No, she decided. It would only worry him more.

"I'm sure we'll be fine."

Matt didn't look convinced. "I wish they would nail whoever did this." He put his glass down. "I'd sleep a whole lot better at night."

His comment brought Shelby up short—he really *was* worried about her.

"Me, too." Shelby sighed. "There are almost too many suspects. Jax had several reasons for hating his brother. But then so did Paislee."

"Oh?"

The timer on the oven dinged, and Shelby got up to retrieve the pizza. The scent of basil combined with a warm yeasty smell filled the air when she opened the oven door.

"Travis and Paislee were having an affair. But when the band arrived here, Travis took up again with Jessie, his former fiancée." Shelby carried the pizza to the counter. "Let's just say that Paislee was less than pleased about that."

"That's easy to understand." Matt leaned back in his chair and stretched out his legs. "I suppose that gives her a motive." Matt took the plate of pizza Shelby handed him. "That smells delicious," he said, inhaling sharply. "But could a woman have killed Travis? It must have taken some strength to hold his head underwater."

Shelby shuddered at the thought. "According to the autopsy, he'd been hit over the head first. He might not have been knocked out completely, but he was definitely stunned enough to make killing him easier."

They talked of other things while they finished their pizza. Matt drained the rest of his beer and pushed back his chair.

"I'd better get going. It's late, and I know you have to be up with the chickens in the morning." He shook his head. "I don't think I could do it. I guess you can take the boy out of the city, but you can't take the city out of the boy."

"Do you miss it? New York City, I mean."

Matt tilted his head. "Sometimes. Sometimes when I read about a new exhibit that's been mounted or a new restaurant that's opened . . . but then I remind myself of everything I have here, and the longing passes."

"You can always go back for a visit." Shelby walked with him toward the front door.

"That's true. But I hate to go alone. I'd rather wait until I have someone to go with me." He stared pointedly at Shelby.

She felt her face becoming suffused with warmth. They were standing by the front door now, mere inches apart.

Matt leaned forward until his lips met Shelby's. His arms went around her and pulled her close.

Shelby was overwhelmed with sensations—warmth and contentment and the feeling of everything being right in the world.

||||||||||||||||||||||||||

Another storm kicked up during the night, and Shelby reached down and pulled up the comforter she'd folded at the foot of the bed. The thought crossed her mind that it would be nice to have someone to snuggle up to and of course she thought of Matt.

Bitsy and Jenkins were on either side of the bed, and one of them—Shelby thought it was Jenkins—was snoring softly. She punched her pillow a few times to bunch it up into her preferred shape, pulled the comforter up under her chin, and closed her eyes again. She could get up and close the open window—the lace curtains were being blown into the room by the wind—but the thought of her bare feet on the wood floor made her shiver.

She was about to drift off again when both dogs suddenly startled and jumped to their feet. They began barking furiously. Shelby felt the hairs on the back of her neck prickle. The dogs were used to all the nighttime noises at Love Blossom Farm. The only thing that would cause them to wake up and begin making such a racket was something out of the ordinary. Way out of the ordinary. Both Jenkins and Bitsy were deep sleepers.

Shelby threw back the covers and winced as her bare feet hit the floor. She tried to listen but could hear nothing but the dogs barking. She nearly ran into Amelia, who was standing in the hall looking like some sort of ghostly angel, her blond curls in a tangle around her face.

"Why are the dogs barking?" she said, her voice thick with sleep.

"I don't know. There's probably an animal outside that set them off." Shelby turned Amelia around so that she was facing her bedroom. "You go back to sleep. It's nothing to be worried about."

Amelia looked like a sleepwalker as she drifted back toward the open door to her room.

Shelby tiptoed down the stairs. The dogs were already by the front door. Their barking had yet to slow down, let alone cease. It was a miracle they hadn't woken Billy, but that boy was so active all day that at night he didn't so much sleep as fall into a coma.

Shelby realized she was shivering as she peered through the sidelights alongside the front door. She should have grabbed her robe before heading downstairs.

She couldn't see anything outside and was about to turn

away when a shadow momentarily blotted out the porch light she'd switched on. Her breath caught in her throat and she felt her heart hammering hard against her chest.

It was probably nothing. The dogs barked at everything.

Yes, but they don't usually rouse from a sound sleep, part of her brain argued.

Suddenly Shelby didn't feel so brave. She retrieved her cell phone from the table in the living room where she'd left it charging and dialed a familiar number almost without thinking.

Shelby stood in front of the living room window, wrapped in one of the throws she kept on the sofa, scanning the dark for the first pricks of light from a car's headlights. Finally she thought she saw something in the distance, and the light got brighter and brighter as the car came down the drive.

Shelby had thrown open the door almost before the car came to a halt. She ran toward it, a sob of relief catching in her throat.

The dogs, finally freed from the confines of the house, bolted outside, their noses to the ground as if they were bloodhounds and not a mastiff and a West Highland terrier.

A figure emerged from the darkness and put his arms around Shelby. She rested her head against his chest and slowly her heart and her breath slowed.

"Did you see anyone?" Matt said as he led Shelby back inside.

He looked around the porch. The floor was covered by a thin layer of fine dirt that had been blown onto it by the evening's wind. Matt pointed at something.

"Footprints," he said succinctly.

"Where?" The hair on the back of Shelby's neck prickled again.

Matt waved a hand toward the right side of the porch.

"Those are new," Shelby said, shivering. "I swept the porch earlier. The wind must have churned all this dirt up again."

Matt frowned. "Someone was standing on your porch." He shook his head. "I don't like it." He turned to Shelby. "I think you should call the police."

"It's the middle of the night."

Matt smiled. "That's what they signed on for, isn't it?"

"Whoever it was—if there *was* someone on the porch—has probably been scared off by now. I'll call them in the morning."

"Then I'll stay here and keep guard. I can sleep on your couch."

Matt was already reaching for the front doorknob.

Shelby wanted to argue, but she was shaken enough that the thought of being alone in the house with the kids spooked her.

She arranged the throw she'd been wrapped up in earlier on the sofa.

"I'm afraid it smells a bit of dog," she said, catching a whiff as she shook it out.

"My favorite smell."

"I can get you a pillow."

Matt put a hand on Shelby's arm. "Don't worry about it. I'll be fine. And I'll be sure to leave before the kids are up. No need to start tongues wagging."

Suddenly Shelby was very tired. Her eyes wanted to close and her limbs felt as heavy as tree trunks.

"I can't thank you enough."

"Don't worry about it," Matt said, putting his hands on Shelby's shoulders and turning her toward the stairs. "You look exhausted. Go get some sleep. It will be morning all too soon."

Shelby didn't argue. She dragged herself up the stairs and into bed but not before slamming the bedroom window shut. The room was still cold and she wrapped up in the comforter, tucking it securely around her feet. She couldn't help but think of Matt downstairs on the sofa.

She would be so much warmer if he would come upstairs and join her.

19

Dear Reader,

Chickens come in different sizes and you want to be sure you have the right one for the job. Broilers, fryers, and roasters are relatively interchangeable—it depends on what size chicken you need to feed your brood. They range from around two and a half pounds to five pounds. Want to roast, poach, or broil them? They'll all work. They're young chickens and will yield tender, succulent meat—just don't overcook them!

If you're making stew or soup, you can get away with an older bird—in this case, a stewing chicken. The meat is tougher and needs long, slow cooking to break down and become edible.

True to his word, Matt was gone when Shelby woke up in the morning, the throw neatly folded and draped over the arm of the sofa.

Shelby yawned, pulled on the fleece she kept by the back door, slipped on her clogs, and went out to feed the chickens. The sun was barely peeking over the horizon and it was quiet except for the sound of a car backfiring out on the main road.

Shelby scattered the chicken feed and watched in amusement as her Rhode Island Reds scurried around, picking it up. Her bucket empty and hanging at her side, she stood for a moment watching the sky lighten and the objects around her take shape, then returned the bucket to the barn and headed back toward the farmhouse.

Amelia and Billy would be up soon. Shelby retrieved several eggs from the refrigerator, cracked them into a bowl, added a splash of milk, and mixed them up with a whisk until the clear whites and the deep yellow yolks had blended to a light lemon color.

She had a frying pan on the stove with a nub of butter in it. Shelby lit the burner under the pan and swirled the butter around as it began to melt. She had her hand on the bowl and was about to pour in the eggs when she heard a car come down the drive. Moments later there was the sound of a car door slamming and then a timid knock on her back door.

Her first thought was that it was Matt—a thought that brought a smile to her face. She was mentally calculating how many more eggs to make as she pulled open the back door.

She was surprised, and—she had to admit it—disappointed, when she found Brian Ross standing on her back step.

He ducked his head apologetically. "I'm terribly sorry to bother you so early."

"Don't worry," Shelby said. "I've already been up for quite a while." She heard a sizzling noise coming from the kitchen. "Please come in. I have something on the stove."

"Now I really am sorry for disturbing you," Brian said.

Shelby saw the way his eyes lit up when he spotted the eggs in the bowl.

"Are you hungry? I have plenty of eggs."

"I couldn't have you go to so much trouble. You've done so much for us already."

"Don't be silly. I'm making another batch for myself anyway."

Billy walked into the kitchen. He was wearing his Cub Scout uniform and had even slicked down his hair with water. Shelby couldn't help but smile. Billy had an all-day Cub Scout jamboree being held at the school that day, and that had obviously motivated him to look his best. He stared at Brian for a moment, but his interest faded when Shelby slid his plate of eggs in front of him. He put his head down and began to shovel them in as efficiently as a machine.

Amelia walked into the kitchen with her phone in hand, pulling out her kitchen chair without looking up from the text message she was sending. When she finally did surface, she was so startled to see Brian sitting at the table that she jumped.

Shelby and Brian couldn't help laughing, although Amelia got that stormy look on her face that meant she was about to either slam out of the room or burst into tears.

Shelby grabbed three plates from the cupboard and portioned out eggs for Amelia, Brian, and herself.

Amelia picked up her fork but didn't make a move to eat her eggs and instead sat staring at Brian in a way that would have made most people nervous, but he seemed to take it in stride.

"Amelia and her friends are planning an antibullying campaign at her school," Shelby said, reaching for the butter. "Isn't that right, Amelia?"

A strange look passed between Amelia and Brian, but it was so fleeting that Shelby couldn't be sure she hadn't imagined it.

Brian tilted his chair back on two legs. "I remember being bullied myself. He was a big kid—a lot bigger than me. He used to intimidate me into handing over the chocolate chip cookie my mother always put in my lunch."

"What did you do?" Shelby reached for the saltshaker.

Brian shrugged. "Nothing. Before I could decide what to do, he moved away."

"Lucky for you."

"No kidding."

Amelia jumped up from her seat. "I'm going to Kaylee's house, Mom. Is that okay? Her mother is picking me up."

"That's fine. Have a good time."

If Shelby thought Amelia was going to kiss her goodbye, she was disappointed.

"Can I be excused?" Billy said, pushing back his chair.

Shelby smiled. "Sure."

Moments later they heard Billy's footsteps on the stairs leading to the second floor.

Finally Brian pushed his plate away and patted his stomach. "I haven't had that good a meal since we got here. Thanks." He smiled at Shelby.

Brian shifted in his seat. "I'm afraid I came to ask you another favor."

"Oh?"

He cleared his throat. "I wondered if I could use your garden hose and some of your water. I really need to give my car a wash. It's so dirty that I had to scrape the mud off the license plate before coming here for fear one of the cops patrolling the main road would pull me over."

"Of course. That's no problem at all."

Brian grinned. "Thanks. I know she's an old heap and not worth very much, but I hate seeing her so dirty. I don't know where Jax went out riding last night, but he sure got her muddy."

Shelby was about to get up but instead froze in her seat. Jax had been out last night?

Shelby laughed, trying to keep it light. "There aren't too many places to go in Lovett at night. Was it very late?"

"Must have been. I woke up when he came into my room to get the keys. I rolled over and glanced at the alarm clock and it was already after three in the morning. I would have asked him where he was going, but frankly, I fell back to sleep before he'd even fished the keys out of my pants pocket."

Where *had* Jax been going at that time of night? Shelby wondered. There was nothing open in Lovett and even the diner was closed. Had he been heading to Love Blossom Farm? And had he been the one standing on Shelby's porch in the middle of the night?

She shuddered to think what might have happened if the dogs hadn't woken up and scared him off. Who knew what he'd been planning to do?

|||||||||||||||||||||||||||

Bert was still in the hospital. They hadn't been able to remove her gallbladder laparoscopically but had had to operate the old-fashioned way. Given her age, it would be another day or two before she would be released back home.

Shelby planned to take her some food. The stuff they served in the hospital would definitely not be to Bert's liking. She filled a container with some of her homemade yogurt and got out her large soup pot. She'd make some chicken soup to take to Bert and they could have it for their dinner. Although it was warm—and sometimes even steamy—during the day, at night it was still cool enough for a hot meal.

She retrieved the last of the parsnips, turnips, and carrots she'd been storing in the root cellar. They needed to be used up right away and chicken soup was the perfect way to do it.

And of course she needed a chicken. And while she had a yard full of them back by the barn, she could never bring herself to kill any of them and eat them for dinner. She'd go to the Comstocks' chicken farm and pick one out. The birds were antibiotic and hormone free and a far cry from the meat found in chain supermarkets.

Shelby took off her apron, tossed it over one of the kitchen chairs, and grabbed her purse. The Comstocks' farm was only about five miles away.

Shelby heard the band's van coming down the drive. She peeked out the kitchen window. Brian's Taurus was no longer in the driveway, and the hose was neatly coiled back on its stand.

Shelby hesitated. Brian had told her he'd have some cash for her today. She put her purse on the table, retrieved her wallet, and poked around inside. She had a few limp dollar bills and not much else. If Brian did have the money for her, that would save a trip to the bank.

Shelby dashed out the mudroom door. Bitsy and Jenkins scampered out in back of her, quickly overtook her, and bounded toward the barn. The field was muddy and Shelby had to pick her way around the puddles that dotted the path.

Brian's car was parked in front of the barn. A few drops of water were sprinkled across the hood, and the dust and the dirt were gone except for a few new splotches of mud on the tires. The barn doors were open, and as Shelby approached, she heard voices. The female one had to be Paislee and the male one sounded like Jax. Someone was tinkering with a guitar in the background—Peter most likely—and Shelby thought it sounded like some of the chords from that haunting song she'd heard Jax and Paislee sing when they were practicing a couple of days ago.

Paislee and Jax were still conversing in urgent-sounding undertones, and Shelby was loath to interrupt them. She hovered a short distance from the open barn door, curious to know what they were talking about.

Paislee's voice surged louder and Shelby could easily hear what she was saying.

"That was my song, and Travis knew it," Paislee said.

"But it's all over now," he said. "We're going to sing it together."

"It still makes me mad." Paislee sounded petulant, and Shelby could imagine her sticking her lower lip out like a child. "He said he wrote that song for me."

Jax's sigh was audible. "By now you should know that Travis said whatever was necessary to get him what he wanted."

"That's not true." Shelby could hear the tears in Paislee's voice. "He wrote that song for me and the two of us were going to record it together. I know it would have been a hit. But instead he said he was going to record it with *her*."

Dear Reader, I don't know who her *is, but judging by Paislee's tone of voice, it's obvious she's not a fan.*

"Like I said, Paislee." Jax was beginning to sound frustrated. "It's over. You and I will record it together." His voice turned soothing. "And it will be even better than if you'd sung it with Travis. I promise."

There was a rustling sound, and Shelby moved away from the door. She made a point of clearing her throat loudly and shuffling her feet through the handful of dried leaves that had collected outside the barn door before she walked in.

Paislee and Jax were now standing with the others—gathered together in a knot by the equipment. Brian seemed to be holding some sort of meeting. Shelby hated to interrupt them and was about to turn and leave when Brian caught sight of her.

He walked over to where Shelby was standing.

"It's great to be back here again," he said, clapping Shelby on the shoulder. "We appreciate you continuing to let us use your barn." He chuckled. "I hope we haven't put your chickens off laying eggs."

"Not at all. I harvested a couple dozen just this morning."

"Good." Brian scratched at the stubble on his chin, making a raspy sound. "I hope we'll be out of your hair soon." He sighed. "As soon as the police let us go. It's been a week since Travis was killed—you'd think they'd be further along by now."

"But then there's Cody—"

"You're right. That's certainly put a wrinkle in things." Brian frowned and leaned closer to Shelby. "Between you and me, I wondered if it wasn't Cody who had done it. Murdered Travis, I mean."

Shelby didn't know what to say. She didn't want to admit that she'd suspected Cody herself. It occurred to her again that one of the killers could be here in the barn right now. She thought about the threatening comment on her blog and the person who had been standing on her porch and had to suppress a shiver.

She wished she could send the children somewhere—somewhere safe. But where could they go? Bert was in the hospital and her parents were somewhere on the West Coast touring in their RV. Kelly had to work, and Shelby couldn't imagine Mrs. Willoughby or Coralynne dealing with Billy and Amelia.

"Is there something I can do for you?" Brian said, interrupting Shelby's thoughts. He smiled. "Or did you just want to hear us play?"

"I'd love to hear you play, but you're right. You said you would be able to pay me today and that would save me a trip to the bank."

Brian slapped himself on the forehead. "Of course I did. I thought of it while we were having breakfast, but then it flew right out of my mind again." He stuck a hand in his pocket and pulled out a wad of cash. "Good thing I came prepared." He peeled off a number of bills and handed them to Shelby.

Shelby hated taking the money from them—it didn't cost her anything to let them use her barn—but she knew she was taking a risk allowing them to be on the farm in the first place. If it weren't for the money, she wouldn't be doing it.

"Say, you still writing that blog?" Brian said as Shelby turned to go. "What's it called? 'The Farmer's Daughter'?"

"Yes."

"My wife—she's back home in Iowa—reads it all the time. She loves it. She couldn't believe we were actually going to be playing here and that I'd get to meet you."

"Tell her I'm glad she enjoys it."

Brian looked down at his feet momentarily. "This is embarrassing, but would you mind if we took a selfie? I promised the wife I'd try."

Shelby laughed as Brian pulled his phone from his pocket.

"I probably look a mess."

"Not at all." Brian held the phone in front of them and clicked the shutter.

"Thanks."

That was a first, Shelby thought as she walked toward the house. Wait till she told Bert about it. No doubt Bert would quickly bring Shelby back down to earth again.

Billy was ready to go when Shelby got back to the house. She would drop him off at school on her way to the Comstocks' farm.

They went out to the car, which Shelby had finally gotten started, and Shelby buzzed down the windows. Billy fidgeted all the way to school and bolted from the car the moment they pulled into the driveway, throwing a *Bye, Mom* over his shoulder without looking back.

Shelby watched him as he went through the front door. He was growing up—there was no denying it. She felt tears pressing against her eyelids and dashed them away quickly.

Fresh air poured into the car as Shelby drove along. As soon as she neared the Comstocks' farm, however, the faint odor of chickens, their feed, and their waste drifted through the open windows.

Shelby pulled into a gravel drive that ran alongside a shallow culvert, which Arlene Comstock said was a menace in the winter when the ground was covered in snow and you couldn't see where the driveway ended and it began.

Shelby pulled into the small parking lot in front of the farm store. It wasn't a big building and it had rough metal siding and a corrugated roof.

Shelby walked inside, pausing for a moment by the door as her eyes adjusted to the change from broad sunlight to the dimmer interior of the shop.

A long piece of particleboard suspended between two sawhorses served as a counter. Behind it was a refrigerated space lined with shelves for the chickens that were processed and packaged daily.

Arlene's daughter, Danielle Comstock, was behind the counter, her blond hair hanging in long braids over each shoulder. She was wearing denim overalls that had been cut off at the knees and a T-shirt with writing on it that was obscured by the bib of the overalls.

Shelby knew Danielle from high school—not well; they'd always seemed to end up in the same gym class together—and Danielle had become a friend of Kelly's, too. She and her husband, Carter, had been invited to Kelly and Seth's wedding.

Danielle smiled and leaned her elbows on the counter as Shelby approached.

"That was a lovely wedding," Danielle said. "Except for that singer being killed. What a tragedy. I felt so bad for Kelly and Seth." Danielle tossed one of her braids over her shoulder. "I imagine they'll think of it every time they think of their wedding."

"I hope not. Hopefully they will have other, better memories of their day."

"Have they found who did it yet? I haven't heard."

"Neither have I." Shelby was beginning to wonder when

she'd be able to order her chicken and leave before Danielle asked too many more questions.

"I wonder if it was that man I saw arguing with the singer. They were going at it something fierce. That singer— Travis, right?"

Shelby nodded her head.

"He looked mad and embarrassed at the same time, if that's possible."

"Who was he arguing with?" Shelby tried to put the question as casually as possible, although her heart had begun to hammer hard against her chest.

Danielle pulled one of her braids over her shoulder again and began to fiddle with the end of it. "I don't know. I couldn't see his face on account of his back was turned toward me."

"Do you remember anything about him? What he was wearing maybe?"

Danielle shook her head. "Not really." She frowned, then suddenly smiled and snapped her fingers. "I know. Now I remember. He was wearing a hat." She put a hand on top of her own head. "A floppy sort of thing. Silly looking, if you ask me."

Shelby's mouth had gone so dry she could barely speak. That was Seth's hat Danielle had described. Had it actually been Seth whom the woman from Grilling Gals had seen arguing with Travis? And not someone who had picked up Seth's hat and worn it?

Shelby didn't believe it. Seth would never murder someone. But if the police heard about this, it would still look bad for him.

Danielle looked at Shelby, her eyebrows raised.

"I . . . I need a chicken, please."

Danielle laughed and cracked her gum. "I kinda figured that. What size?"

"Around three pounds. I'm making soup."

"You'll want a fryer, then. It'll cook up real nice and tender."

Danielle disappeared into the refrigerated storage area and came out with a neatly wrapped bundle. She slipped it into a plastic bag, handed it to Shelby, and rang up some numbers on the cash register.

Shelby dug her wallet out of her purse, put some bills down on the counter, and waited while her receipt spooled out of the cash register.

"Nice seeing you again," Danielle said as Shelby turned to go. "Sorry I didn't get to talk to you at the wedding."

Shelby gave a wan smile. "I'm afraid I was running around like a chicken with its head cut off most of the time."

Danielle threw back her head and laughed. "That's a good one." She waved. "You take care."

"Thanks."

Shelby walked out to her car and sat there for a moment. She put the key in the ignition but didn't turn it. Whoever killed Travis was wearing Seth's hat. When Seth first stormed out of the wedding reception after realizing Travis was going to be playing, he wasn't wearing his hat.

If that was the case, then Danielle must have seen them arguing later. Seth must have picked up his hat, put it on, and gone to find Travis to continue their fight.

Shelby shook herself. That made no sense. Surely if it had been Seth arguing with Travis, Danielle would have noticed something else about his clothes—his navy blazer, his linen pants . . . something . . . anything . . . besides just the hat.

And now that she thought about it, Valerie from Grilling Gals hadn't noticed anything particular about the man's clothes either. Had she been worrying needlessly?

Because it couldn't have been Seth. Shelby let out her breath in a whoosh. It had to have been someone else. And as she'd suspected before, the murderer had picked up Seth's hat from wherever Seth had abandoned it and put it on. And had then gone out and had that argument with Travis. Shelby shuddered.

And then he—whoever he was—had stunned Travis with a blow to the head before holding his face in the rainwater in Shelby's old trough.

20

Dear Reader,

Chicken soup is considered a remedy for what ails you in almost every culture around the world and has been considered a cure for the common cold since at least the twelfth century. Scientists believe that the steam from a hot bowl of soup helps nasal congestion and some even think that chicken soup might have anti-inflammatory properties.

I don't know about you, but I find a bowl of chicken soup comforting at any time. And although it's hard to find the time, making your own is much better than opening up a can and isn't very hard at all.

Travis certainly seemed to have told an awful lot of lies, Shelby thought—lies to get what he wanted and lies to avoid the things he didn't want. It was hard to know what had been the truth and what had been fiction.

Shelby was about to head out to the herb garden to do some weeding when she had a thought. Bert had said Travis's mother still lived in Lovett. Shelby racked her brain for several minutes before she came up with her name—Debbie Coster. Surely she should be easy enough to find in a town as small as theirs.

Shelby pulled out a battered and dog-eared copy of the Lovett telephone directory—so many longtime residents had resisted the trend toward digital and still wanted a copy they could hold in their hands.

Shelby thumbed through it until she came to the correct page. She ran her finger down the entries. There was a large stain in one corner—ketchup?—but fortunately it wasn't obscuring the listing for Debbie Coster, which she found near the middle of the page.

Her house wasn't far away—Shelby knew the street, which wound up the hill past St. Andrews Church.

On an impulse, Shelby jotted the address down and grabbed her purse. Weeding could wait. There were some questions she hoped Debbie Coster would be able to answer for her.

She found the address easily enough—a small but tidy brick ranch in a neighborhood of similar houses. The yard was narrow but deep, and Shelby noticed neat staked rows of overturned earth in a vegetable garden out back.

Debbie Coster opened the door almost as soon as Shelby had rung the front bell. She looked to be in her late forties with a thin stripe of gray along the part in her short brown hair.

Her voice was wary when she greeted Shelby.

"Can I help you? Because if you're selling something, you're wasting your time."

Shelby shook her head and held up a hand. "No, nothing like that. Mrs. Coster?"

"You're looking at her."

"I wanted to talk to you about your son Travis."

"You might as well come in, then. My name's Debbie," she called over her shoulder as she led Shelby into a small living room with worn but clean furniture.

"Have a seat." She waved Shelby toward a sagging sofa the color of pea soup, while she perched on the edge of an armchair.

"What about my son?" she said when they were seated.

"I'm terribly sorry for your loss," Shelby said. "I realize it must be difficult for you to talk about it."

Debbie grunted and looked at her hands.

Shelby leaned forward in her seat and clasped her hands between her knees. "I've met your other son, Jax, and his wife, Jessie, helps me out around my farm."

"Your farm?" Debbie looked up. "Is that where it . . . it happened?"

Shelby nodded.

"I always knew Travis—that's what he decided to call himself—would come to a bad end. Even as a boy—" She stopped and looked down at her hands again.

"As a boy . . . ," Shelby prompted.

"He was always running into trouble. And then he'd lie to get himself out of it. It got so you never knew if he was telling the truth or not."

"That's what I wanted to ask you about." Shelby held her hands out in front of her. "I heard that Travis left his girl-friend Jessie standing at the altar. That he was upset be-cause she'd been having an affair with his brother."

Debbie looked up sharply. "Who told you that?"

"One of the members of the band."

"That's probably what Travis told them, then. With Travis it was always what he wanted you to believe."

"So . . . it's not true?" Shelby raised her eyebrows.

Debbie shook her head. "No. At least not all of it. Travis did leave Jessie at the altar, but it wasn't because of Jax. He had nothing to do with it. Travis changed his mind, pure and simple, and didn't have the guts to break it off."

"I see." Shelby leaned forward and propped her chin on her hands. "And that accident that Travis and Jax had? I thought Jax was responsible, but then I read in the newspaper—"

"That was Travis again. Telling people what he wanted them to believe." Debbie closed her eyes momentarily, as if trying to blot out disturbing images. "Jax got a raw deal in that accident. Spent months in rehab. We didn't know if he'd ever get better or not. Meanwhile, Travis was gallivanting all over with that program *America Can Sing.*"

"So Jax wasn't driving when it happened."

"No. Travis was."

So the newspaper article had been correct, Shelby thought as Debbie led her back to the front door. Travis had caused the accident that had so badly injured his brother, and Travis had lied about Jax and Jessie having an affair. Debbie was right—Travis told people what he wanted them to believe, and it was always a version of the story that put him in the best light.

░░░░░░░░░░░░░░░░░░

When Shelby got home, she put the soup on to simmer over a low flame. In the meantime, she would get some work done outside. The rain had ensured that her plants were well watered but had also caused a crop of opportunistic weeds to sprout in all her gardens.

Then after the weeding, there were lettuce and herbs to pick—both were coming up beautifully. She would soon have a bumper crop to take to Matt at the general store.

Shelby was slipping into her gardening clogs when the telephone rang. She debated letting it ring—she really had a lot to do—but then what if the Cub Scout leader was calling to say Billy was sick or hurt and needed to be picked up?

She kicked off her clogs and ran into the kitchen, catching the call right before it would have gone to voice mail.

"Hello?"

"Shelby? This is Olivia Willoughby."

Shelby groaned inwardly. Was Mrs. Willoughby going to pester her for even more information about Isabel Stone?

"I don't know if you've heard, but Isabel Stone has had an accident."

"How awful! What happened?" Shelby asked, picturing all sorts of gruesome scenarios in her head.

"She caught her heel on a bit of loose flagstone on the walk leading up to her house. You know those shoes she wears—an accident waiting to happen. And she's broken her ankle, the poor dear."

Mrs. Willoughby's voice dripped with insincerity.

Shelby was wondering what this had to do with her.

"With her foot in that plaster cast, poor Isabel can hardly do a thing, so a number of us have banded together to bring her something for dinner until she's back on her feet again."

"That's a lovely idea."

"We're hoping you'll agree to join us."

Shelby glanced at the pot of chicken soup simmering on the burner.

"I'd be glad to. I have a pot of soup on the stove this very minute. How about if I take some of that to Isabel?"

"How wonderful!" Mrs. Willoughby cleared her throat. "Is there any chance you could take her some for tonight? We have the first few weeks covered, but on such short notice we couldn't find anyone to volunteer for today. I would do it myself, but I have my bunco group coming, I'm afraid. You're sure it's no trouble?"

"Not at all. I'm taking soup to Bert in the hospital. I'll drop some off for Isabel, too."

"You are a lifesaver, dear. I hated to ask—knowing how busy you always are." There was a note of censure in Mrs. Willoughby's voice. "Isabel is expecting someone and will be leaving the door open, so don't knock—go right on in."

"I'll do that," Shelby promised, and hung up.

iiiiiiiiiiiiiiiiiiiiiii

Shelby knelt in the herb patch amidst the oregano, thyme, and rosemary, enjoying the lush scent as well as the sight of all the greenery. After two hours her back was beginning to protest, her hands cramp, and her knees ache. She sat back on her heels and looked around.

Jessie was supposed to be helping her today. Normally Bert would have joined Shelby in the garden, but that wouldn't be possible for a long time. Shelby sighed and was about to bend to the task at hand again when she caught movement out of the corner of her eye.

Jessie?

Shelby looked up to see Jessie making her way toward the herb garden.

She couldn't walk any slower if she tried, Shelby thought. She really had to consider looking around for more reliable and energetic help.

"Hi," Jessie said as she dropped to her knees beside a row of basil. "Sorry I'm late. I've been having trouble getting going in the mornings." She pointed vaguely toward the barn. "It's the stress, I guess."

Shelby sighed. "Yes, I can imagine." She reached for a clump of weeds and pulled. "Hopefully the police will soon arrest the culprit, and we can all go back to normal."

"I don't know," Jessie mumbled. "With Travis gone, I don't know if things will ever be normal again."

Shelby shook the clump of weeds to get the dirt off. "Hopefully you and Jax can work things out. This doesn't have to mean the end of your marriage, you know."

"He's pretty mad," Jessie said, swiping at a tear shimmering at the corner of her eye.

"Maybe counseling?" Shelby suggested. "I've heard people say it can be very helpful."

But Jessie was already shaking her head.

"Or maybe talk to Reverend Mather. He's had experience with these sorts of things."

Shelby glanced at Jessie, but she was looking in the other direction, across the field toward the barn. And she had a look of horror on her face.

Shelby turned her head, but all she could see was Paislee trooping across the grass toward them.

"I've got to go," Jessie blurted out. "I'll be right back." She jumped to her feet and began to run toward the farmhouse.

"What's wrong with her?" Paislee said when she finally reached the herb garden, where Shelby was still kneeling. "Not that I care or anything."

She was puffing on a cigarette again, and Shelby wrinkled her nose against the smell. Shelby looked back toward the house. She couldn't imagine what had gotten into Jessie. Maybe she should go check on her?

"Excuse me," she said, getting to her feet almost as quickly as Jessie had. "I've got to see to something."

Paislee shrugged. "Fine. I just thought I'd say hello. I'd better get back anyway." She dropped her cigarette on the ground and rubbed out the remaining spark with the toe of her shoe. "Jax is quite the slave driver. He's still not satisfied with the new song. Even Brian told him to chill out, but he won't listen."

"Good luck," Shelby called over her shoulder as she set off toward the house at a brisk pace.

She found Jessie in the kitchen, sitting at the table, her head resting on her crossed arms. She jumped when Shelby walked in, her chair squeaking in protest as it scraped against the floor.

"You look like you could use a cold drink," Shelby said, opening the refrigerator and retrieving a pitcher of lemonade.

She didn't say anything else as she got two glasses out, filled them, and carried them to the table.

"It's rather stuffy in here, don't you think? Why don't we take our drinks out to the porch and get some fresh air."

Shelby knew from experience that rocking in the rocking chairs could be very calming and practically therapeutic. She hoped it would have that effect on Jessie.

Jessie still didn't say anything but heaved a deep sigh as she settled in the chair. A slight breeze was blowing and the faintest smell of manure hung in the air.

Jessie rocked back and forth rhythmically, pushing off with first one foot and then the other. The rocking seemed to be soothing her, Shelby noticed. Her breathing was quieter and the stiff set to her shoulders was easing.

Suddenly the rocking stopped. "She hates me, you know," Jessie said.

"Who hates you?"

"Paislee."

"Why do you think that?" Shelby asked, although she could guess the answer easily enough.

"Because of Travis. But doesn't she understand? He was mine long before he ever met her."

Dear Reader, talk about flawed logic! Jessie seems to have forgotten she'd married Jax in the interim.

"But you're married to Jax now, right? Isn't it worth trying to work things out?"

Jessie grunted. Shelby couldn't tell if the noise was meant to be affirmative or negative.

"It's not just that," Jessie said, starting to rock again.

"It's not just what?" Shelby was beginning to find this conversation confusing.

"It's not just about my affair with Travis."

"Oh?"

"You know that song Travis wrote? That Jax is now singing with Paislee?"

"The new one?"

"Yes." Jessie stopped rocking again. "Travis wrote that song for me. For us to sing together. He'd already talked to his record label about it, and they'd agreed. That was to be our song."

Shelby didn't know what to say. After talking to Travis's mother, she knew Travis wouldn't hesitate to lie when it suited him. Had he lied to Jessie? Or was it Paislee he'd lied to?

"That's really why Paislee hates me. When she found out she wasn't going to record that song with Travis, they had a huge fight. She said she'd never forgive him."

Never forgive him, Shelby thought. Had Paislee decided to murder Travis as well?

|||||||||||||||||||||||||||||

Shelby sat for a moment after Jessie left. She'd sent her inside to splash some cold water on her face—her eyes were puffy from crying. Jessie had insisted she was fine and had gone back to weeding the herb garden.

The scent of chicken soup cooking drifted out from the kitchen, and Shelby knew she should go check on it, but she didn't want to get up. The breeze felt good and the rocking was so soothing. She felt her eyelids getting heavy—the interrupted sleep she'd had the night before had hardly been refreshing.

A noise startled her, and her eyes flew open. Bitsy and Jenkins came bounding onto the porch just as Paislee turned the corner and came into view.

Shelby groaned inwardly. Dealing with Jessie had worn her out—the last thing she wanted was a run-in with Paislee.

"You look comfortable," Paislee said as she mounted the steps to the porch.

Dear Reader, Paislee apparently does not see the irony in pointing out how comfortable I am while she proceeds to disturb that very comfort.

"Do you mind if I sit down?" And before Shelby could say anything, she plopped into the rocker Jessie had recently vacated.

"I know Jessie hates me," Paislee said. "She thinks I stole Travis from her, which is ridiculous, since Travis left her a long time ago."

Shelby felt as if she were hearing an echo. Jessie had so recently said much the same thing about Paislee. "I don't think she hates you," Shelby protested.

Paislee stopped rocking and turned to stare at Shelby. "Please. I know she does. And I don't mind. Believe me."

"But as you said, you didn't steal Travis from her, did you?"

"No." Paislee began rocking again. "It was already long over." She picked at the threads surrounding a small rip in the knee of her jeans.

"I don't think Jessie hates you," Shelby said again. "I think it's you who hates Jessie."

"What?" Paislee froze. "Why would I hate Jessie? I hardly know her."

"That song Travis wrote—you think Jessie stole that from you."

Paislee gave a humorless laugh. "Jessie didn't steal it from me. What are you talking about?"

Shelby began to wonder if she'd got hold of the wrong end of the stick, as her grandmother used to say.

"Jessie said Travis wrote that song for her. And that he planned to record it with her."

Paislee's pale cheeks turned red. "No, he didn't. He only said that to string her along. And she fell for it." She began playing with the loose threads on her jeans again. "Travis wrote that song for me. And we were going to record it together." Paislee lifted her chin. "And now I'm going to sing it with Jax." She gave a not very nice smile. "I wonder what Jessie will think of that."

▪▪▪▪▪▪▪▪▪▪▪▪▪▪▪▪▪▪▪▪▪▪

Somebody was lying, Shelby thought as she walked into the house. Either it was Jessie or it was Paislee. She remembered that conversation she'd overheard Paislee having with Jax. Paislee had been upset that Travis had been planning on singing that new song with someone else, and now Shelby knew who that was.

If Jessie was telling the truth, she was the one Travis had

decided would replace Paislee. Was Paislee mad—not just at Jessie, but at Travis, too?

The delicious aroma of chicken soup now filled the kitchen. Shelby checked the pot—not much longer now. Long enough for her to get cleaned up and change her clothes. She peeked at the gas flame under the pot and turned the knob slightly to lower it.

By the time Shelby was finished making herself present-able, the soup was done. She decided she would take Bert a small container now—Bert claimed the hospital food was nasty, although Shelby suspected it was the low-fat diet the doctor had put her on that Bert didn't like. She would save the rest of the soup to take to Bert when Bert went home, which would hopefully be very soon.

Shelby was pouring the soup into containers when there was a knock on her front door. She frowned, wiped her hands on a kitchen towel, and headed toward the foyer.

"Shelby," Frank said as soon as Shelby opened the door. "Why didn't you call me?"

"Call you?"

Frank snorted with impatience. His tall, muscular frame was dominating Shelby's small foyer, making her feel crowded.

"Yes. When you found those footprints on your porch. You should have called me."

Shelby put her hand on Frank's arm. "Let's go into the living room.

"I didn't want to bother you," Shelby said when she was perched on the arm of the sofa and Frank was pacing the room.

Frank turned and looked at her, his eyes unreadable . . . sad, maybe?

"But that's my job, Shelby. I'm a policeman. Never mind that I'd promised Bill I'd look after you and Billy and Amelia."

"How did you know about the footprints anyway?" Shelby asked, suddenly suspicious.

"Matt told me."

"Matt told you?" Shelby repeated. "Why on earth—"

"Because he was worried." Frank began pacing again. "To think of you and the kids alone here at night and someone lurking around the farmhouse after two people have already been murdered—it would drive anyone mad."

Shelby opened her mouth, then decided not to tell Frank that Matt had spent the remainder of the night on her sofa.

"You know you can count on me, Shelby."

"Yes, of course, Frank. I do. And I can't tell you how much I appreciate it."

Frank gave her a strange look.

"What does this really mean, Shelby?"

"I . . . I don't understand."

"About you and me." Frank stopped pacing and stood in front of Shelby. "I thought you and I . . ." He ran a hand across his face.

Shelby felt trapped. She could no longer put it off. She'd made up her mind—she had to be honest with Frank.

"Frank, you know I care about you," she began.

Frank gave a bitter laugh. "You care about me. Why do I think I know where this is going?"

He shoved his hands in his pockets and leaned against the arm of the chair opposite Shelby. He stretched his long legs out, and they nearly reached all the way across the rug to where Shelby was sitting. She drew in her own feet self-consciously.

Shelby was riddled with doubt. Seeing the look on Frank's face—so like his brother's—she wanted to smooth away all the lines and the stress with her own hands.

But she took a deep breath instead. "I know we both thought—"

"That we loved each other? I still do."

Shelby looked down at her hands.

Frank exhaled loudly. "Are you . . ." His voice broke as if he'd felt a sharp pain. "Are you in love with Matt?"

"Yes," Shelby said, suddenly realizing that she meant it.

Frank stood up. "Okay." He paused with his arms dangling loosely at his sides. "I'll still look after you and the kids like I promised. You can't take that away from me."

Shelby nodded.

Frank walked to the front door, opened it, and left.

Shelby burst into tears.

ıllıllıllıllıllıllıllıllı

Shelby dried her tears, dabbed some powder on her nose, and carried the soup out to the car. She'd put Bert's portion in a thermos so it would be warm when she got to the hospital.

She'd decided not to think about her conversation with Frank right now.

Dear Reader, does that make me sound like Scarlett O'Hara?

There would be plenty of time to think about it later.

She had the radio on as she drove. The only time she ever sang was in the car. Alone. Once she forgot and started to belt out a song in front of the kids, and Amelia had laughed so hard she'd nearly peed herself.

A new song came on—the disc jockey called it a golden

oldie. Shelby was slightly miffed; she remembered the tune from high school, which wasn't that long ago—at least not in her mind. She remembered slow dancing to this song with Bill at the Winter Ball. She'd worn a shimmery silver dress that she and her mother had driven two hours to find, and she'd had her hair done by a neighbor who knew her way around a blow-dryer and a can of hair spray.

Bill's cheek had felt so soft against hers—years later he'd admitted he'd shaved twice just to be sure. Shelby couldn't help smiling at the memory.

The song ended and Shelby let out a sigh. The melody, although not the words, reminded her of another song— something recent—but she couldn't put her finger on what it was. Maybe she'd heard it playing in the background somewhere but had forgotten.

Thinking about Bill had made her think about Frank, and she pushed the thought firmly from her mind. Later, she told herself.

It was a short drive to Isabel's small house. It was obvious from the exterior that Isabel was quite the gardener. Flowers lined the flagstone walkway to the front door, and under the windows on either side were deep beds filled with annuals and perennials artfully planted according to height and color, creating a pleasing design.

Shelby did as she had been told by Mrs. Willoughby and didn't knock but opened the door and walked into the tiny foyer, where there was a tiny table topped with a vase full of flowers.

"Hello?" Shelby called out. "It's Shelby McDonald. I've brought you some dinner."

"In here." Isabel's husky voice came from the room on the right.

Shelby walked into a parlor that was small but attractive with bookshelves lining one wall, a comfortable-looking sofa and armchair, and a worn but colorful Oriental rug.

Isabel was on the sofa, her foot, which was encased in plaster, propped on a tufted velvet ottoman. She was wearing a floral-patterned silk dressing gown.

"I've brought you something for dinner," Shelby said, holding out the container. "Homemade chicken soup."

"It probably won't cure my ankle," Isabel said dryly, "but I'm sure it will taste delicious." She waved a hand toward the hall. "Would you mind putting it on the kitchen counter for me?"

Shelby took the container into the kitchen, which, although small, was spic-and-span and very comfortable looking with a round table, covered in a white cloth, with another vase of garden flowers in the center.

Isabel's laptop was sitting on the table with a thick stack of papers next to it. Curious, Shelby glanced at the top sheet, but there were only a few words printed on it. Shelby wondered if this was a manuscript. Dotty at Glide had said Isabel wanted to be a writer. It looked as if she might have kept at it.

"Your house is lovely," Shelby said when she returned to the parlor.

"Thank you." Isabel smiled.

Shelby gestured toward the bookshelves. "I take it you like to read."

Isabel gave a small smile. "I have to fill my evenings."

Shelby nodded and scanned the titles lined up on the shelves. It was an eclectic collection, but right at eye level was a row of ten Damian Devine novels, their dust jackets shiny and crisp.

"You're a fan?" Shelby said, pointing to them.

Isabel looked slightly flustered. "A fan?"

"Of Damian Devine. I see you have a number of his books."

"Oh." Isabel gave a dismissive wave. "I've read them. Have you?"

Shelby shook her head. "Matt from the general store was reading one the other day. He said he couldn't put it down. Do you mind if I borrow one?"

"Please, go right ahead."

"Which one do you suggest?"

Isabel pursed her lips. "Start with the first one—*The Decoy.*"

Shelby ran a finger along the spines of the books until she came to the one Isabel had recommended. She pulled it from the shelf and tucked it under her arm.

"Thank you."

"No," Isabel said, "*thank you*. I'm sure I'll enjoy the soup."

<hr />

Shelby pulled into the parking garage at the hospital twenty minutes later. She hated parking garages—either she forgot what level her car was on, or she went the wrong way when she was ready to leave and ended up having to go all the way to the top level in order to circle back down again to reach the exit.

She made a mental note that she was on level five as she walked toward the hospital. Hopefully she would remember. She tried to think of something to peg the number to but failed.

Hospitals had certainly changed since she'd visited her grandmother in one when she was a little girl. She'd been frightened of what horrors she might see and had been relieved when they had finally reached her grandmother's room.

Now there was none of that sickly antiseptic smell and instead of drab industrial beige paint, bright paintings lined the walls. Bert had a single room complete with a flat-screen television, wallpaper in a soothing blue-and-green pattern, and blue curtains.

The requisite hospital equipment was still there, though—the oxygen, the IV stand, the box of disposable gloves for the doctors and nurses.

Bert was propped up in bed, the remote control in her hand and *Days of Our Lives* on the television.

"I've brought you some soup," Shelby called out as she walked into the room.

Bert pressed a button and the television dimmed and went off. "Aren't you a sight for sore eyes?" She smiled.

"It's chicken soup," Shelby said, putting the thermos down on Bert's bedside table. She fished in her purse. "I've even brought you a spoon and a plastic bowl." Shelby retrieved them from her purse and handed them to Bert. "The soup should still be warm, too."

Bert grabbed the bedside table and pulled until the top swung over the bed. She fumbled with the lid of the thermos.

"Let me." Shelby twisted it off and placed it to one side.

Bert poured some soup into the bowl, dipped in her spoon, and scooped up a mouthful.

"Delicious," she declared with a sigh. "I've so missed having something decent to eat."

Shelby pointed at the bowl. "Hopefully I won't get in trouble with your doctor for bringing you that."

"Bringing you what?" said Seth as he strode into the room.

He had a stethoscope draped around his neck and three different pens sticking out of the breast pocket of his starched white coat.

"Nothing," Bert said, pushing the bowl of soup to one side.

"How's my favorite girl today?" Seth said as he unwound the stethoscope from his neck.

Bert chuckled. "You can't fool me. I know who your favorite girl really is." She peered at Seth. "How is she doing, by the way?"

Seth sighed and perched on the edge of Bert's bed.

"She's so worried about this murder. I've told her that the police interviewing me doesn't necessarily mean anything. They have to question everyone." He shook his head. "I'm afraid this might affect the baby."

Bert snorted. "You should know better than that after all those years in medical school." She wagged her finger at him. "Babies have been born amidst all sorts of turmoil and have come out just fine. Make sure she gets plenty of rest and has plenty of good food to eat."

"Yes, Doctor," Seth said meekly. "Now, let's see how you're doing."

Seth checked Bert's heart and pulse and her incision, which was healing nicely. He folded up his stethoscope and wound it around his neck.

"Everything looks good. I'll get the discharge papers drawn up. No reason you can't go home if you promise to take it easy for a few more days."

"That's good news," Shelby said.

"You can say that again," Bert said as she began to swing her feet over the edge of the bed.

"Whoa." Seth put up a hand. "Take it easy. It can take a few hours to get the discharge instructions ready. You might as well lean back and get as much rest as you can in the meantime."

Bert frowned, but she pulled the covers back up to her chest.

Seth leaned over and squeezed Bert's shoulder. "Take care of yourself. I'll have my office manager call you to arrange a follow-up appointment in a week."

Seth had no sooner left the room than Bert began to question Shelby. "What news is there about the murder?" Her eyes glowed eagerly. "I feel like I've been cooped up here forever."

"Let's see." Shelby went through what she knew in her mind. "It turns out Travis was cheating on Paislee in more ways than one."

"Oh?"

"Not only did he take up with Jessie again, but he'd apparently been planning on recording a new song he wrote with Jessie instead of with Paislee."

"That must have made Paislee mad."

"I certainly think it did. The whole thing can't have made Jax too happy either." Shelby walked over to the window and glanced out. Bert had a marvelous view of the parking garage, which loomed like a giant concrete monster in the distance.

"We can't forget about Cody," Bert said, moving her legs back and forth under the covers. Shelby could tell they weren't going to be able to keep her in bed much longer. "What motive would any of them have had for killing him?"

"My best guess is that Cody knew something. Maybe he saw the killer after they'd murdered Travis and noticed that the person was wet—although at the time they probably didn't realize the relevance of it."

"What about some of those others in the band? The older guy—I think he's the drummer."

"Brian?" Shelby shrugged. "I don't know. So far I haven't uncovered any reason he might have had for killing Travis. Although Paislee did admit that Travis wasn't easy to work with. Maybe Brian thought the same thing."

"Can you find out more about this Brian? Where he comes from—what he's like?"

"I suppose. Paislee seems willing enough to talk about her colleagues."

Bert was squinting in the sun coming in the window, and Shelby adjusted the blinds.

"You've sure got yourself quite a puzzle there," Bert said, leaning back against the pillows.

Her face was pale and Shelby thought she was beginning to look tired. She picked up her purse.

"Not me. It's up to the Lovett police to find the culprit. For all I know, they're about to arrest someone this very minute."

Dear Reader,

You never know where information is going to come from in a murder inquiry. The police interview people, of course, but many times they reveal more in ordinary conversations with friends or neighbors—things they didn't think were important or things they didn't think of at the time. I know I should leave the investigating to Frank and his team, but sometimes I'm able to pick up nuggets of information that can be valuable in solving a case.

The phone was ringing as Shelby walked into the house. She threw her purse on a chair and managed to grab the receiver right before the answering machine picked up.

Shelby listened to the caller in alarm—it was Billy's Cub Scout leader and it seemed Billy had developed a fever and had broken out in a red rash on his back and abdomen. Shelby would have to pick him up.

She sighed, grabbed her purse, and fished out her keys again. She glanced out the kitchen window—the rest of her chores would have to wait.

Shelby pulled up to Lovett Elementary School—a long, low building with children's colorful artwork hanging in all the windows. The middle school was up a slight hill and the high school just beyond that—creating a large compound where the students moved from one building to the next as they progressed.

Shelby pulled into the circular drive and parked at the curb. She was trying to control her anxiety—the leader hadn't sounded as if Billy was deathly ill. Nonetheless, Shelby's heart was beating hard as she walked at a fast trot down the long corridor to the main office. The leader had said that the school secretary was on duty during the jamboree, and she would be keeping an eye on Billy until Shelby got there.

Billy was slumped in a chair in the corner, his face red from the fever.

"Can I help you?" The secretary swiveled her chair away from her computer screen and toward Shelby. "Oh, Ms. McDonald, it's you." She leaned her elbows on the desk. "I loved your blog the other day about making herb tinctures. I remember my grandmother doing that."

"Thank you." Shelby gave her a weak smile and gestured toward Billy. "I've come to collect my son. I understand he has a fever—"

"And a rash. You might want to get him in to see a doctor as soon as possible in case it's something contagious."

"I'm taking him right away." Shelby turned to Billy. "Come on, sweetie. Let's go see Dr. Gregson."

Shelby wasn't sure if the look on his face was indicative of his embarrassment at her using a term of endearment in front of someone else or his dislike of visiting the doctor.

Billy had dozed off in his seat, his head lolling over his right shoulder, by the time they pulled into the parking lot of the building where Seth's practice was located. Shelby hated to wake him, but he was too big to carry. That thought gave her a pang—where had the time gone? Before she knew it, he would be a teenager and would no longer need her for certain things—like tucking him in at night and checking to make sure he'd washed behind his ears.

She shook him gently and his eyes fluttered open, closed, and then finally open again.

"Come on, bud. We're at Dr. Gregson's."

"I won't have to get a shot, will I?"

Shelby took a deep breath. She tried not to lie to her children, but occasionally a half-truth was called for.

"Probably not. You'll probably only have to swallow some icky medicine."

Shelby put her arms around his shoulders. She could feel the heat of his body through his shirt and panic clutched her.

"Here we go." She held the door open.

The waiting room was empty except for a well-dressed woman sitting in the corner, reading a magazine. She lowered it and peered over the top at Shelby.

"Nancy," Shelby blurted.

"Shelby," Nancy said at the same time.

Nancy was wearing navy-and-white-print pants with a navy blouse, a navy-and-white scarf, and white shoes trimmed with navy. As usual, she made Shelby feel sloppy, ill put together, and slightly grubby.

Shelby got Billy situated in a seat. He shook his head

when she asked if he wanted to look at any of the issues of *Highlights* strewn across the table in front of the sofa. Shelby watched as his eyes slowly closed, and his head dropped to his chest.

"I hope everything is okay," Nancy said.

Shelby took a deep breath. "I hope so. Billy has a high fever and a strange rash. It can't be measles—he's been vaccinated."

Nancy raised one perfectly plucked eyebrow. "It could be roseola. It's a virus you don't hear much about, but I remember Seth getting it when he was around Billy's age."

Shelby looked at Nancy in alarm. "It's not serious, is it?"

Nancy shook her head. "Give him something for the fever and let him rest, and I'm sure he'll be fine."

"Are you here to see Seth?"

Nancy put her magazine down in her lap. She looked around the waiting room, but they were still alone.

"I came to talk to him," Nancy said in a low voice. "Kelly told me that the police have questioned him about that dreadful incident at their wedding."

"I think they've spoken with everyone," Shelby said.

Nancy stuck her nose in the air. "I told him not to say anything unless Glen Crawford was there."

Shelby raised her eyebrows.

"He's our attorney. Very clever man. I don't know what we'd do without him."

"I don't think Seth needs an attorney, do you? The police can't possibly believe he had anything to do with Travis's death."

"One can't be too careful, you know." She lowered her voice further. "Kelly told me the police were asking about an argument between that singer and someone who looked like Seth. Or at least someone told the police it looked like Seth. All because of that silly hat of his. I can't tell you how many times I've begged him to get rid of it."

"But anyone could have picked up Seth's hat and put it on—he said he left it on a table somewhere and forgot about it."

"That's what I want to talk to Seth about. I saw the man who was arguing with that fellow who was killed."

"Really?"

Nancy nodded slowly and her ash brown hair brushed across her cheek.

"Who was it?"

She shrugged. "I've never seen the man before. All I know is it wasn't Seth."

"Did you see what he looked like? Can you describe him?"

"You're certainly taking an interest in this, aren't you?" Nancy smoothed the front of her blouse. "But I suppose that's natural since all of this took place on your property."

"Yes, that's it exactly."

Dear Reader, do you think she can see my fingers crossed behind my back?

Nancy pursed her lips. "I only saw the fellow from the side, but I knew it wasn't Seth. He wasn't wearing linen pants like Seth, and he wasn't wearing blue jeans like the others in that dreadful rock group. Besides, I should think I would know my own son." Nancy cocked an eyebrow at Shelby.

"What was he wearing? Do you remember?"

Shelby glanced over at Billy, but he was still asleep, his head resting against the back of the chair.

"Of course I do. He had on a pair of khaki trousers that were desperately in need of a good pressing and a striped shirt with the sleeves rolled up. I don't understand why men insist on putting on a perfectly good button-down shirt, then ruining the whole effect by messing about with the sleeves."

Shelby was picturing Kelly and Seth's wedding in her mind. As Nancy had said, Travis and the group were in blue jeans and Seth was in linen pants. For a moment Shelby was stumped. Then she remembered Brian—the first time she met him, he was in khakis and he was still wearing khakis when the group performed at the wedding.

He must have been the one arguing with Travis. What had they argued about? Shelby wondered. And had the argument been serious enough to lead to murder?

iiiiiiiiiiiiiiiiiiiiiiiii

Amelia was up early on Sunday morning—almost early enough to feed the chickens. Shelby had just come back from the barn when Amelia appeared in the kitchen, sleepy-eyed, with her hair in a tumble of curls around her face.

She slid into a seat at the table and propped her chin in her hands.

"I hope everything goes okay with the campaign kickoff today."

"You still haven't told me what the big surprise is," Shelby said as she broke two more eggs into the sizzling fat in her frying pan.

"It's going to be epic, like I told you." Amelia smiled, a fleeting look of doubt crossing her face. She poked at the fried eggs Shelby put in front of her. "I have to text Katelyn to see what she's wearing," Amelia said suddenly, pulling her cell phone from her pajama pocket.

Dear Reader, I know I'm always joking about it, but it looks like she really does sleep with her phone!

Amelia poked at her eggs some more, eating a few bites that would barely keep a sparrow alive, before bolting to her room to get ready.

Shelby scraped the rest of the eggs into Jenkins's and Bitsy's bowls and put the dish in the dishwasher.

Billy stumbled sleepily into the kitchen.

"How are you feeling?" Shelby asked, touching Billy's forehead with the back of her hand. It was cool—his fever had broken.

"I'm hungry."

"Eggs?"

Billy grunted.

Shelby scrambled an egg for him, which he downed in practically one gulp. Children certainly recuperated quickly, Shelby thought. Yesterday he had fallen asleep before dinner and he hadn't woken up until this morning.

Shelby supposed she ought to get ready, too. She didn't want to embarrass Amelia in front of her classmates, although that was practically a given, considering her wardrobe. Amelia accused her of wearing "mom" jeans, which puzzled Shelby. She was a mom and they were jeans—she couldn't imagine any way to get around those two facts.

Neither Amelia nor Billy wanted to go to church, but Shelby insisted, although both of them fidgeted so much during the service that Shelby wondered if either of them had heard a word Reverend Mather had said. Shelby wished Billy could have stayed home in bed, but there was no one to stay with him, and besides, he insisted he felt fine and was completely better, although the dark circles under his eyes worried Shelby.

Finally, it was time to file out of church and head to the high school.

Katelyn was waiting outside the school by the main entrance when they arrived. She clapped her hands when she saw Shelby pull around the circular drive to let Amelia off.

"Hi, Mrs. McDonald," Katelyn said as Shelby zapped down her window.

"I hope your kickoff is a big success," Shelby said.

Katelyn rolled her eyes. "I hope so. I hope the band shows up. They promised Amelia they would."

Shelby felt her mouth go dry. "Band?" Maybe Katelyn was referring to a group of students who'd formed a rock group?

Shelby caught a glimpse of Amelia's face out of the corner of her eye. Amelia had gone white and was fiddling with the door handle, accidentally locking the door in her haste to get out of the car.

"What band?" Shelby said.

A look passed between Amelia and Katelyn, and Katelyn began to stammer.

"The band that's been practicing in your barn. You know—Travis Cooper's backup musicians." She glanced at Amelia in confusion. "I thought you knew."

"Amelia!"

"We've got to go, Mom. We have a lot to do."

Shelby gripped the steering wheel, heat flooding her face and roaring in her ears.

"Does the principal know about this, Amelia? Does he know it's the same band that might be involved in two murders?"

"Mr. Danbury doesn't care," Amelia said as she slammed the car door in back of her and took off at a trot.

Doesn't care? Shelby thought to herself. *Or doesn't know?*

⸿⸿⸿⸿⸿⸿⸿⸿⸿⸿⸿⸿⸿⸿⸿⸿⸿⸿⸿⸿

Shelby was pulling into a parking space in the rapidly filling lot when she noticed the Lovett General Store truck maneuvering into a spot at the entrance of the lot. She got out of the car and stood by the door, squinting into the distance. That was definitely Matt opening the back doors of the truck.

"Can I go into the gym, Mom?" Billy said, hanging back.

"Sure. You go help your sister."

Shelby had barely finished speaking before Billy dashed off.

She walked over toward where Matt was continuing to off-load cartons. As Shelby got closer, she could see the boxes were filled with bottles of pop and individual bags of chips.

Shelby's stomach was in knots, and she regretted the scrambled eggs and bacon she'd made herself for breakfast. She didn't know what to do. Should she hunt Mr. Danbury down and warn him about the band? The parking lot was filling rapidly with a line of cars waiting to get in. It would be a huge embarrassment to Amelia if the show didn't go on as planned. She doubted Mr. Danbury would want to cancel the event now.

"What's wrong?" Matt said when Shelby reached him.

Shelby explained the situation.

Matt furrowed his brow. "I think you're worrying for no reason," he said, placing a hand on Shelby's arm. His palm was warm against her skin, which had suddenly gone cold. "You don't know for sure that the band members were involved in the murders. And besides, it seems likely that Travis and Cody were targeted specifically. It's not like there's a serial killer on the loose."

"True."

"I'm sure everyone will be perfectly safe."

Shelby sighed. "I'm furious with Amelia for not telling me. She said she wanted it to be a surprise."

Matt's eyebrows lifted. "A surprise?" He laughed. "It sounds more like she was afraid you'd say no to the idea."

"Darned right I would have." Shelby's fists clenched at her sides.

Matt rested his hand on Shelby's shoulder. "I wouldn't worry. I'm sure everything is going to be fine."

"I hope you're right," Shelby said. She gestured toward the cartons Matt was pulling from the truck. "I didn't know you were going to be here."

"I agreed to donate some snacks to the effort. Amelia said they're hoping to raise some money from the sales for their campaign."

Matt pulled a red handcart from the back of the truck and began stacking the cartons on it.

"Can I help with anything?" Shelby asked.

"Thanks, but I think I've got it."

They began walking toward the front of the school. Shelby held the door open as Matt wheeled the boxes inside and down the hall.

The auditorium was already half-filled, and excited high-pitched chatter echoed from the rafters. Amelia had a clipboard clutched to her chest and was talking to a young man. She appeared to be giving him instructions. In spite of her anger, Shelby couldn't help but be impressed with how Amelia was handling herself and with all the work she had done to pull off this event.

The band had straggled in, pulling their instruments on a large cart with *Lovett High School* written in black marker on the side. They began setting up on the stage. Shelby wandered into the hallway. Matt was busy organizing his wares outside the doors to the auditorium, and more and more students were filing in, clutching cans of pop and bags of chips. Matt gave Shelby an encouraging smile and she gave a shaky one in return.

Shelby went back inside the auditorium. The band had their instruments set up on the stage. Peter, the guitarist, was perched on an amplifier, tuning his instrument. He strummed his fingers across the strings a few times, made an adjustment, and began picking out a tune. Jax, who was fiddling with the microphone stand, began to hum along. The mic was live, and his humming, albeit muted, carried out across the auditorium.

Shelby thought she recognized the tune as one the band had played at the wedding. She didn't think they'd recorded it, because she'd never heard it on the radio, although she had heard one or two other songs that Travis had recorded.

The tune also reminded Shelby of the song she'd heard on the radio the other day—the oldie that had brought back such clear, bittersweet memories of her husband and their courtship. She stopped and listened more carefully to the music.

The melody *was* the same as the song she'd heard in her car the other day. Without the different lyrics, the similarity was more obvious. She glanced toward the band again. Brian was mounting the steps to the stage, his hands clenched at his sides. Shelby noticed that unlike the rest of the group, he was wearing khakis again and a button-down shirt with the sleeves rolled up his thick forearms.

He strode toward Jax and Peter, waving his arms frantically. As soon as they saw him, Peter's strumming and Jax's humming stopped abruptly.

What was that all about? Shelby wondered.

Paislee wasn't onstage yet, but Shelby found her in front of the mirror in the girls' bathroom down the hall from the auditorium. Shelby noticed that nothing much had changed there since her day. The metal stalls were slightly skewed after years of students banging the doors shut. Some of the tile was chipped and the industrial beige paint was grubby around the light switch.

Paislee was leaning toward the mirror, lining her eyes in bright aquamarine eyeliner that contrasted with the mascaraed black fringe of her eyelashes. Her cosmetic bag was open on the counter in front of her.

Shelby went to the sink next to Paislee and turned on the tap.

"It looks like you've got a good crowd out there." Shelby gestured toward the door of the washroom with her shoulder.

Paislee gave her a shy smile. "I'm glad. This will give me and Jax a chance to iron out any kinks in the new song we've been practicing."

Shelby pumped some soap onto her hands from the dispenser on the wall.

"Can I ask you a question?" Shelby said, turning toward Paislee.

"Sure."

"Peter and Jax were playing a song just now—maybe not playing—Peter was strumming on his guitar and Jax was humming along. Travis sang the same song at the wedding. For some reason, it seemed to have made Brian angry. It reminds me of an old song I heard on the radio the other day, but the words are different and the melody is a bit slower."

Paislee made a face. "No kidding it sounds familiar. Travis and Brian had such an argument over it."

"Why?" Shelby reached for one of the folded brown paper towels stacked in the dispenser attached to the wall with a rusted screw.

"It's pretty obvious, don't you think? Travis stole the melody from that old song, dashed off some new lyrics, and tried to pass it all off as his own. Brian was furious when he found out."

Paislee retrieved a tube of mascara from her cosmetic bag. She pulled out the wand and began adding a second coat to her already heavily made-up eyelashes.

"And it's not like Travis couldn't write his own music." Paislee turned toward Shelby and pointed the mascara wand at her. "Take that song he wrote for me." She put a slight emphasis on the word *me*. "It's pure Travis's and it's brilliant. He had no need to steal someone else's melody. Not when he could write music like that."

"How did Brian find out that Travis had plagiarized that song?"

"The woman who wrote the original got herself a lawyer, and the lawyer called Brian and told him that the band had better stop playing the song or else."

"Or else what?"

Paislee shrugged. "I don't know. Or else they would sue, I suppose."

"So Brian and Travis fought about it."

"Yeah." Paislee dropped her tube of mascara into her open cosmetic bag. "Travis kept insisting that he hadn't stolen the melody—that he'd written it himself." She pulled a pot of eye shadow and a cosmetic brush from her bag and began swiping the dark blue color across her lids. "Brian didn't believe him—that's exactly the sort of thing Travis would do. Besides, it wasn't worth the expense and legal hassle if that woman did get her lawyer to sue."

"But the band played the song at Kelly's wedding."

"And Brian was furious with Travis for pulling that stunt."

"Why didn't Brian stop him?"

"It would have made more of a scene than letting the band finish the song. Besides, it wasn't very likely that anyone in the audience would have recognized the similarity to that older song. People don't much listen to the music at weddings—they're too busy chatting and getting drunk."

"I wonder why Travis did that. I mean, if he knew it would make Brian mad."

Paislee fished around in her cosmetic bag and pulled out a tube of pale pink lipstick. "I think he wanted to thumb his nose at Brian. Travis considered himself the star of the band—which he was—but Brian was the manager. He put everything together, and without him, Travis would have been nothing but a pretty face and voice."

"Do you know if Brian said something to Travis afterward about playing that song?"

"I'm pretty sure he did. He followed Travis outside of the barn as soon as the set ended."

Was this the answer? Shelby wondered. Had Brian been so furious that he'd caught up with Travis, they'd argued, and Brian had hit him over the head before drowning him in the trough?

Shelby had found Brian to be very polite and pleasant, but plenty of murderers had charmed their victims into complacency. She shivered when she thought of Brian sitting down to breakfast with her and her kids. Had she served up scrambled eggs to a killer?

|||||||||||||||||||||||||

The group performed at least ten songs and gave a performance that had the audience on their feet, dancing in the aisles. Shelby even noticed a few teachers moving to the music.

When Jax and Paislee put their heads together for the romantic ballad Shelby had heard them practicing in the barn, the girls all looked as if they were about to swoon. Paislee was right—Travis had no need to steal music when he could write songs like this.

Shelby searched the audience for Amelia and Katelyn and found them in the front row, leaning forward, their faces glowing. It certainly looked as if their antibullying campaign kickoff was a huge success.

The concert ended and the audience burst into applause. The band members hopped off the stage as the principal walked out. It took him a while to get the audience's attention—they were still so pumped up from the excitement of the concert.

Shelby left the auditorium through the double doors at the back. Matt was busy packing up the few cans of pop and bags of chips that hadn't sold.

"It looks like you did a brisk business," Shelby said.

Matt leaned over and dropped some bags of chips into a crate.

"I did. I think the girls have raised a tidy sum for the campaign." He paused and looked at Shelby. "What are they going to do with the money?"

"They're hoping to bring in some well-known speakers to talk at assemblies and have even discussed creating an antibullying public service announcement."

"I'm impressed." Matt smiled. "Sounds like they've got some excellent plans."

"Something occurred to me while I was listening to the band," Shelby said. "Actually right before the concert—when they were warming up and tuning their instruments."

"Oh?"

Shelby explained about the song Peter had started to pick out on his guitar with Jax humming along.

"Brian went charging up to them. He seemed frantic to get them to stop."

Matt raised his eyebrows. "That's odd. I wonder why."

"Paislee told me that a woman was threatening to sue the band because the melody of that particular song was taken from one she'd written quite a while ago. One Trick Pony recorded it. I heard it on the radio just the other day."

"So someone plagiarized the music?"

Shelby nodded. "Apparently Travis did. He claimed he didn't, but I don't think Brian believed him. In any case, Brian felt it wasn't worth the hassle of a lawsuit if that woman did decide to go ahead and sue. But Travis had the band play the song at Kelly's wedding. Afterward, Brian followed Travis out of the barn. Paislee said he looked furious."

"That doesn't necessarily make him the killer, does it?"

"No, but Seth's mother saw Brian arguing with Travis shortly before Travis was killed."

Matt retrieved the handcart from where it had been leaning against the wall.

"I'm not sure what to do," Shelby said as she helped Matt load the crates onto the cart.

"I think the best thing to do is to call your brother-in-law and give him that information. Let him take it from there. He'll know what to do."

"You're right." Shelby gave a sigh of relief and dug her cell phone out of her purse. She glanced at it. "I'm not getting any reception in here—I'd better go stand outside."

As Shelby headed toward the doors exiting the school, she thought she saw a movement in the shadows, but when she looked again, nothing was there.

22

Dear Reader,

Cell phones can be so finicky, can't they? Usually when you need them the most—when you're stuck beside the highway with a flat tire and need to call a tow truck, or you're running late for an important appointment and want to give the person a heads-up.

But I can assure you that incidents like that are mere blips on the radar compared to having your cell phone malfunction when you're trying to call the police because a killer is after you.

Shelby stepped outside and was momentarily blinded by the sunlight. She blinked rapidly and put up a hand to shield her eyes.

She walked a short distance away from the school and

squinted at her phone. Three bars—her call would go through.

She quickly dialed Frank's number and prayed he would answer.

Frank picked up on the third ring. Shelby explained the information she'd put together and how she was convinced it all pointed to Brian.

"Where are you?" Frank asked, a sense of urgency in his voice.

"At Lovett High."

"Stay out of sight until I get there. I'm on my way."

The call clicked off and Shelby stuffed the phone into her pocket.

"Shelby!"

She heard someone call her name and spun around to see who it was. The person's outline was fuzzy in the bright sun, but she recognized him anyway.

It was Brian.

He was smiling at Shelby, but she felt a chill snake its way down her spine. She started to walk away. Brian began to follow her, and she picked up her pace, glancing over her shoulder occasionally to see how close he was.

Shelby made her way around the side of the building, keeping to the shadows, alert for the clatter of footsteps in back of her. Her heart was beating so loud she was afraid it would drown out the sounds. She should have turned tail and run back into the school building, but it was too late now.

At one point, she thought she heard Brian right behind her but was too afraid to turn around and look.

By now she was running, her feet slapping against the ground with every step. She rounded the south corner of the building and found herself behind the school.

She had a stitch in her side and finally had to stop for a

moment until the cramp eased, leaning over with her hands on her thighs. Brian was nowhere to be seen. Had he given up? Shelby wondered. Perhaps he really had only wanted to talk to her, and she'd blown things out of proportion? He might even now be wondering what on earth had gotten into her.

But Shelby doubted it. She had the feeling Brian knew that she had figured out he was the one who'd hit Travis over the head and drowned him in that old trough. And he must have been the one who'd strangled Cody, too.

She leaned against the building, the brick warm from the sun, the texture rough against her bare arms. If she could get back into the school building, she could blend into the crowd or even hide somewhere. By the time Brian found her, Frank would be there.

Shelby made her way along the perimeter of the building until she found a pair of double doors. She grabbed the handle of the first one and pulled, but it was locked. She checked the second one, and it swung open easily.

Warm, moist air wafted toward Shelby. She was in a section of the gym where an indoor pool dominated the room. A ceiling skylight cast a beam of light on the rippling water, where a lone red ball bobbed up and down. The volleyball net had come undone on one side and trailed across the width of the pool just under the surface of the water.

Shelby was making her way around the edge of the pool when a dark shadow was suddenly cast across the shimmering expanse of blue water. She whirled around to find Brian within arm's reach behind her.

She gave a little cry and quickly took a step back. She hovered for a second at the edge of the pool, but the wet concrete was slippery and she lost her footing, falling backward into the water.

Shelby sank below the surface, her wet clothes dragging her down. Her foot touched the rough bottom of the pool and she kicked off, gasping as she finally broke the surface. At first, in a panic, she thrashed about in the water, but as she caught her breath, she was able to settle into the rhythm of treading water.

She'd barely gotten her breath back when there was a splash behind her as Brian jumped into the pool to join her. Shelby tried to scramble away from him, but he reached her quickly with two powerful strokes.

"What do you want with me?" Shelby cried.

"You know," Brian said, swiping away the water streaming down his face.

"No. No, I don't know. I don't know anything," Shelby said, attempting to maneuver away from him.

Fear and stress were making Shelby tired and her head dipped below the surface. Water went up her nose and stung her eyes, and she coughed and sputtered, trying to get air into her lungs.

Brian reached out and shoved her back under the water, holding her head down as she scrabbled frantically at his hands, trying to free herself.

Shelby felt pressure building painfully in her chest. She didn't know how much longer she could hold her breath. She kicked out furiously, but none of her blows connected with Brian, and he didn't loosen his grip.

Then Shelby had an idea. She would dive down even deeper—to the bottom of the pool—and away from Brian's grasp.

It wasn't easy—every fiber of her being was urging her to fight, but instead she resisted and let herself go limp instead. The pressure on her head eased, and Shelby was able to tuck in her chin and dive down and away from Brian.

She pulled herself along the bottom of the pool, away from Brian, until she could hold her breath no longer. She shot to the surface like a comet, gasping and inhaling huge lungfuls of precious air.

She had a moment of respite before Brian was on her again, forcing her head underwater once more, only this time he'd grabbed ahold of her shirt, making it impossible for Shelby to squirm away from him.

She felt panic overtake her and she flailed about wildly. Her frantic, grasping hands touched something floating in the water. At first, she wasn't sure what it was, but then she realized it was the volleyball net. She reached out again and grabbed it firmly, using it as leverage to pull herself away from Brian. She felt her blouse give way and suddenly she was free of him.

Finally Shelby was above the surface of the water, breathing in great gulps of air. She felt dizzy from lack of oxygen but forced herself to concentrate. Brian was reaching for her again and Shelby had barely enough energy left to aim weak and futile kicks at him while attempting to move beyond his reach.

One of Brian's hands closed around Shelby's ankle. She tried to shake free but had no strength left.

Thoughts of Billy and Amelia crossed her mind. She couldn't leave them all alone—she couldn't. The thought gave her a burst of energy that coursed through her like electricity. She gritted her teeth and steeled herself to continue fighting.

She realized she was still grasping the volleyball net. With a surge of strength she lifted it out of the water and tossed it over Brian.

Shelby thought she would always remember the look of incredulity on his face. The more he struggled to free himself from the net, the more tangled he became. Shelby immediately struck out for the side of the pool. She had to pause a moment to gather her remaining strength to grasp the ladder and pull herself up the first step.

She heard a splash behind her and didn't have to turn around to know that Brian had untangled himself from the net and was once again after her. She managed to haul herself up another step on the ladder before collapsing half on the concrete pool deck and half in the water. She dragged herself forward, barely conscious of the rough surface scraping her bare arms.

She could hardly move and suddenly her arms gave way, leaving her sprawled, panting, on the ground.

She felt a hand grab her foot and at the same time the doors to the pool room burst open and Frank, along with two patrolmen, barreled in. The patrolmen had their guns drawn and pointed at Brian.

"Let go of her, Brian," Frank said.

23

Dear Reader,

I love happy endings. Don't you?

The day channel WXYZ planned to shoot their cooking show at Love Blossom Farm with famed chef Michelle Martini dawned clear and bright with enough of a breeze to keep the day from becoming sweltering. And luck was with them and the breeze was blowing away from the farm, so the odor of manure from Jake's pasture was being wafted away from them instead of toward them.

Shelby was up early and out in the garden with her wicker basket. The television producer had sent her a list of the vegetables and herbs they would need for Chef Martini's segment.

As Shelby knelt on the damp ground to pick lettuce, she was struck by how thankful she was to be alive and safely back home. The ordeal with Brian had left her shaken, but she had resolved to put it behind her.

Brian had confessed to murdering Travis in a fit of anger when Travis refused to own up to having plagiarized the music to that song. If the original composer had gone ahead with her suit, it would have ruined not only Travis but all of them. Their names would be forever associated with the scandal.

Then Cody had tried to blackmail Brian. He had noticed the damp patches on Brian's clothes the day Travis was killed, but it had taken him time to put two and two together. Brian had admitted that he'd planned to fire Cody—he'd had his fill of Cody and Paislee's on-and-off-again romance and the fact that it was affecting their work.

Shelby had talked to Jessie, and Jessie had confirmed that Travis had indeed left her standing at the altar. But it hadn't been because she and Jax were having an affair—that was a lie. Travis had just received word that he'd won a spot on *America Can Sing*, and he didn't want to be hampered by a wife—it didn't jibe with the image he wanted to project to the fans he was positive would soon be worshipping at his feet.

Shelby filled her basket with lettuce, a variety of herbs, and other produce that would be used during the show. Chef Martini would be shown on camera picking a few things herself, but there wouldn't be time for her to harvest everything she needed.

Travis had certainly caused enough trouble for three people, Shelby thought·as she carried her basket into the kitchen. It didn't justify his murder, though. Nothing did.

‖‖‖‖‖‖‖‖‖‖‖‖‖‖‖‖‖‖

A crew from the station arrived early to set up the tables and other equipment that would be needed for the demonstration. Felicity was there, too, standing with her arms crossed over her chest in the middle of all the action, ordering everyone around.

They'd decided to place the table in a grassy area with the tidy rows of Shelby's lettuce showing in the background. The location would also give viewers a glimpse of the barn where one of the murders had occurred. Felicity had assured Shelby that that alone would boost ratings of the show sky-high.

Shelby was to be introduced at the beginning of the segment as the owner of Love Blossom Farm and also as the blogger the Farmer's Daughter. She and Kelly had spent several hours in front of her closet putting together the outfit she would wear on television.

"No stripes," Kelly said. "They go all wavy on the screen. Oh, and no white or black or red either."

"What's left?" Shelby asked, standing by the bed with a discarded shirt in her hand.

"Blue. Blue is the safest color."

"How do you know all this?"

"I looked it up on the Internet."

"I want to look approachable," Shelby said, eyeing the outfits laid out on the bed. "And maybe a little homey."

"Not too homey. But not too sophisticated either," Kelly said, squinting at Shelby's pile of clothing. "How about your nice blue shirt tucked into a pair of dark jeans with a sharp crease? And your navy blue espadrilles," Kelly said, pointing to a pair of shoes in the corner.

"Those are ancient," Shelby protested.

"No one will know. They're perfect for the outfit."

Shelby's hands shook a little as she donned the clothes Kelly had picked out for her. She'd never been in front of the camera before, although Felicity had assured her she would be a natural. A natural what, Felicity hadn't specified.

The farm was buzzing with activity by the time Shelby got downstairs, dressed in her carefully chosen outfit, with her hair combed into submission and a dab of makeup on her face. She was surprised to see Mrs. Willoughby coming down the driveway carrying armloads of colorful flowers. Isabel Stone followed behind her, gliding along on one of those knee scooters for people who had broken ankles or who had had foot surgery. A large straw tote was slung over one of the handlebars.

"Mrs. Willoughby! I didn't expect to see you here," Shelby said.

Dear Reader, I can't begin to imagine what excuse Mrs. Willoughby has used to get herself involved in this television shoot.

"I'm here to help Isabel," Mrs. Willoughby said, clutching the dozens of flowers to her chest. "The *Hive at Five* producer approached Isabel about doing the flowers for the show—you know she has the most wonderful garden, and she's terribly talented when it comes to creating arrangements. As soon as I drop these off, I'll scurry back to my car for the vases we've picked out."

Well, that was something, Shelby thought—Mrs. Willoughby and her nemesis, Isabel, working on something together. Had Mrs. Willoughby called a truce to their hostilities?

Shelby was surprised when she saw the Lovett General Store truck pull into the driveway with Matt at the wheel. He came to a stop in back of Mrs. Willoughby's car, opened the door, and jumped out.

"I didn't know you were coming," Shelby said when she reached him.

"I'm providing some of the staples for Chef Martini's dishes—olive oil, salt and pepper, wine—things like that." He laughed. "They promised to mention the store on the air—not that I need the publicity. There's no place else to shop within spitting distance of Lovett."

Matt pulled a red plastic crate from the back of the truck.

"Where do you suppose they want this?"

"There's a table all set up for the filming. I'll show you."

Matt followed Shelby around to the back of the house, where Felicity rushed forward to greet him.

"If you'll put that over here," she trilled in her throaty voice, leading Matt over to the table where assistants were busy arranging pots and pans and cooking utensils under the direction of a short man with a mustache wearing a polo shirt with *WXYZ* embroidered on the front.

Felicity ran past Shelby with her arms outstretched.

"Michelle, darling, so happy to see you."

Shelby turned and watched as Felicity greeted Chef Martini—a tall, big-boned woman with dyed blond hair gelled into spikes all over her head.

"Shelby, dear." Mrs. Willoughby tapped Shelby on the shoulder. "Can you possibly lend a hand? Isabel needs a table to work on and a chair, if you don't mind. Do you have something she can use?"

Isabel had managed to maneuver her scooter down the dirt path leading to the backyard and was waiting patiently with the flowers and their vases piled next to her.

Shelby caught Matt's eye and together they carried the small table Shelby kept in the foyer to pile mail on out to where Isabel was waiting. Matt took off at a trot and quickly returned with a folding chair.

Isabel sank into it gratefully. She smiled at Matt.

"Thank you." She pointed at the scooter. "Getting around with that thing is terribly tiresome, but hopefully it won't be much longer. Dr. Gregson says I'll soon be ready for a walking boot."

A woman wielding a makeup brush came looking for Shelby, and although Shelby protested she was fine the way she was, she soon found herself sitting in the makeup chair, having various creams and powders applied to her face and eyelids.

Finally the man with the mustache called for everyone to take their place and Shelby found herself in front of the camera. Afterward she thought of a million things she should have said, as well as better ways to have said what she did say, but she was proud simply to have gotten through the ordeal.

When the cameras stopped rolling, she realized how damp her underarms were and how her hair was sticking to the back of her neck.

Then it was Chef Martini's turn to take the stage. Isabel had done a beautiful job with the flowers, massing them in two containers on either side of the table, and one of the assistants had dragged out two of Shelby's pots of boxwood to flank both ends of the table.

Chef Martini made several dishes—a chicken dish with pesto made with Shelby's basil, focaccia sprinkled with rosemary from Love Blossom Farm, and a colorful salad of mixed lettuce Shelby had picked that morning, bathed in a dressing that included more fresh herbs.

Isabel continued to sit at the table Shelby and Matt had set up for her, even though she had finished with the flowers. She had a stack of papers in front of her and was making notes on them with a red pen. It looked like the same stack of papers Shelby had noticed on Isabel's kitchen table next to her laptop the day she'd brought Isabel the chicken soup.

Shelby ducked into the kitchen, grabbed a glass from the cupboard, and filled it with iced tea.

"You must be getting hot," Shelby said, offering Isabel the iced tea.

In fact Isabel looked as cool as the proverbial cucumber in a light silk dress in a pastel floral print with a large straw hat shading her face.

She looked up from the pages she was marking up and smiled.

"I don't mind the heat, to be honest with you. It's the cold that gets to me. But thank you for the iced tea." Isabel raised the glass to her lips and took a sip.

Suddenly a strong gust of wind came along, caught the papers stacked on the table in front of Isabel, and scattered more than a dozen of them across the lawn.

"Oh!" Isabel cried, slamming her hand down on what remained of the pile.

"Don't worry. I'll get them," Shelby said, stooping to pick up the sheets closest to her.

Each gust of the wind lifted the loose papers on the lawn and moved them farther away, sending Shelby chasing after them as if they were playing some sort of childish game. As Shelby bent to pick up the last page, several images rushed into her head—Matt engrossed in that Damian Devine book behind the counter at the general store, Isabel with her shelf of pristine volumes by Devine, the stack of papers by Isabel's laptop on her kitchen table. Dotty had said that Isabel wanted to be a writer—that she spent her lunch hours working on a manuscript instead of going out. Was it possible that the terribly demure Isabel Stone was actually Damian Devine? Shelby dismissed the thought almost as soon as it crossed her mind, but then as she added that last piece of paper to the ones she'd already collected, the heading caught her eye—*The Man Who Knew Too Much* by Damian Devine.

Shelby stood stock-still for a moment.

Dear Reader, Isabel, dear sweet Isabel, is Damian Devine?

Shelby looked over at Isabel—so feminine and ladylike in her flowing summer frock and strappy sandals. Was it really possible that Isabel was Damian Devine? It would certainly explain where Isabel's money was coming from—not a rich ex-husband and a generous alimony, as they'd all assumed. No, it appeared as if Isabel was actually a best-selling author.

Shelby carried the papers back to Isabel. Isabel glanced at them nervously, obviously noticing that the title page of her manuscript was on top, and that Shelby couldn't have failed to notice it.

She looked up at Shelby. "You won't tell, will you? Promise me you won't."

Shelby could easily imagine what Mrs. Willoughby and Coralynne and the other ladies at St. Andrews would make of this piece of news.

"I won't breathe a word," Shelby said.

Isabel gave a sigh of relief.

<hr/>

By the time everything was set up to Felicity's satisfaction and filming was complete, it was already late afternoon. Matt had hung around and made himself useful, helping the crew break down the set and load it into the truck.

Shelby convinced Matt to stay for dinner, and he proved himself to be quite adept at throwing around a baseball with Billy and Amelia, while Shelby grilled a steak and made a salad.

After dinner, while the children were up in their rooms getting ready for bed, Shelby and Matt adjourned to the front porch. The sun had finally dipped below the horizon, and the air was deliciously cool after the heat of the day.

Matt looked over at Shelby. "You know, you really had me scared yesterday," he said as he gently rocked his chair back and forth.

"I have to admit to having been quite scared myself."

"I can imagine. It makes me so mad to think . . ." Matt stood up, took Shelby's hands, pulled her from her seat, and held her close. "Promise me you'll be careful from now on."

"I will," Shelby said, barely able to concentrate with Matt holding her so close.

His lips hovered over hers. "I wish I didn't have to go." He sighed.

"Me, too," Shelby breathed. She motioned toward the house. "But the children . . ."

"I understand," Matt said, tightening his arms around Shelby. "But you have to promise that someday you'll consider letting me make an honest woman of you."

Shelby smiled as Matt brought his lips down on hers.

RECISES

LOVE BLOSSOM FARM
MACARONI SALAD

2 cups elbow macaroni, cooked
1 small green pepper, chopped
½ cup celery, diced
½ cup carrot, diced
1 small red onion, chopped

DRESSING
½ cup mayonnaise
¾ teaspoon dry mustard
1½ teaspoons sugar
1½ tablespoons cider vinegar
3 tablespoons sour cream
salt and pepper, to taste

Place cooked elbow macaroni in a serving bowl. In a separate bowl, mix dressing ingredients until well mixed. Add vegetables to elbow macaroni, stir in dressing, and taste for seasoning.

|||||||||||||||||||||||||||||||

COWBOY CAVIAR

½ cup olive oil
½ cup sugar
½ cup cider vinegar
dash of hot sauce (optional)
½ green pepper, diced
½ red pepper, diced
1 small red onion, chopped
3 plum tomatoes, diced
1 teaspoon chili powder
½ teaspoon cumin
1 bunch cilantro, chopped
1 14.5-ounce can black-eyed peas
1 14.5-ounce can black beans
1 14.5-ounce can pinto beans
1 11-ounce can shoepeg or white corn
½ tsp salt, or to taste

Place oil, sugar, and cider vinegar in a pan and bring to a boil. Boil for one minute. Add hot sauce if desired. Combine ingredients from green pepper through salt. Toss with oil, sugar, and vinegar dressing. Taste for seasoning.

CHICKEN WITH ORZO

1 tablespoon olive oil
4 to 6 chicken thighs—with bone or boneless/skinless
1 cup orzo pasta
1 medium onion, chopped
2 cloves garlic, minced
1 cup chicken broth
1 14.5-ounce can diced tomatoes
1 teaspoon Italian seasoning or a blend of oregano,
   thyme, and basil
several grinds of fresh black pepper
1 teaspoon salt, or to taste
½ cup Kalamata olives, pitted and cut in half

Heat olive oil in a sauté pan and add chicken thighs, skin side down (if using thighs with skin). Sauté until skin is nicely browned.

Remove chicken and place on a plate. Add orzo to pan and sauté until golden. Add onion and garlic to pan and sauté until onion softens.

Return chicken to pan and add broth, diced tomatoes, seasoning, and olives. Bring to a simmer and cook over low heat until chicken is done—approximately 20 minutes—and broth has been absorbed and orzo is al dente.

Ready to find
your next great read?

Let us help.

Visit prh.com/nextread